River Ghosts

River Ghosts

B. R. Robb

FIVE STAR
A part of Gale, Cengage Learning

Detroit • New York • San Francisco • New Haven, Conn • Waterville, Maine • London

Set in 11 pt. Plantin

Printed on permanent paper.

LIBRARY OF CONGRESS CATALOGING-IN-PUBLICATION DATA

Robb, B. R., 1958–
River ghosts / B. R. Robb. — 1st ed.
p. cm.
ISBN-13: 978-1-59414-654-1 (hardcover : alk. paper)
ISBN-10: 1-59414-654-3 (hardcover : alk. paper)
1. Racially mixed people—Fiction. 2. False imprisonment—Fiction. 3. Race relations—Fiction. I. Title.
PS3618.029R58 2008
813'.6—dc22 2007047644

First Edition. First Printing: May 2008.

Published in 2008 in conjunction with Tekno Books and Ed Gorman.

Printed in the United States of America
1 2 3 4 5 6 7 12 11 10 09 08

To P.E.S. and A.D.S.,
without whom nothing else would exist.

ACKNOWLEDGMENTS

I am indebted to Pastor Anne Kohutko for her dedication to faith and forgiveness, perhaps more so for her time and willingness to undertake challenges in our conversations, and her ability to give as good as she can take. Thank you also, Anne, for your gift of precious books, the gift of your friendship, and for your direction in study required to create this story.

A long-overdue thanks to Rachel Tecza, teacher and writer, for being the first to pluck me out of the masses and put me in print, as well as to D.C. Brod, respected author and friend, for her support over the years.

It's a big deal to ask of anyone the often-dreaded question, "Will you read my manuscript?" I am grateful to Hal and Cheryl Croasmun on many levels. Also to the St. Charles Writers Group in general, and to Don Bingle, Kitty Jarman, Fran Fredricks, Alice McGee, and Rick Holinger in particular. To Shari Bertane and Patrick Dixon, David and Kellie Stern, Anne Kohutko (once again), and the incredibly good-natured NancyLee Browne and Halle Mikyska, thank you only scratches the surface.

A special thank you to John Helfers, Tiffany Schofield, Amanda Fowle, and Alja Collar, as well as to the instructive and entertaining Gordon Aalborg, who patiently waits for me and my computer to arrive in the 21st century.

1

Henry Clayton was nineteen at the trial, eighteen when I watched him kill my parents. A white boy with small bones, skin paler than milk, and a black swastika imprinted below his right ear.

I was nine at the trial and couldn't imagine how to describe what I had seen. In his opening statement to the jury, the prosecutor used words like horrific, tragic, and sickening. He said I was a hero, a victim, a lost child, an orphan. Then the prosecutor aimed his finger at Henry Clayton and called him an animal.

The defense attorney hunched inside his wrinkled suit and appeared more interested in his crossword puzzle than his client. He remained seated for his opening statement, told the jury I was eight at the time of the murders, an emotionally lost boy, and referred to my parents' murders as the incident, the event, the crime charged. He said I was mistaken. I took the witness stand and, imitating the prosecutor, pointed at Henry Clayton. The turtleneck he wore in the steaming courtroom couldn't hide the swastika on his neck from the jury, or from my memory.

"He's the one I saw," I said, and trembled at the way Henry Clayton looked back at me. Not in the threatening way I had expected and was warned about by the prosecutor. And not with hatred contorting his face, as I had witnessed from under the table. In his defendant's chair, he presented a tranquility I could not fathom, his eyes wet, showing pity not for himself, but for me. My testimony tripped over his display.

"Richard, I'm sorry," the prosecutor said. He smiled as if he enjoyed the moment and didn't sound sorry at all. "You have to tell the jury precisely what you saw."

I cried so hard my mouth could barely form the words, and the court reporter asked me over and over to slow down, to repeat myself so she could make her record. While the jury deliberated, I overheard the prosecutor tell his assistants how wonderful a show it was, for me to fall apart the way I did in open court.

Henry Clayton never testified. Neither family nor friend appeared on his behalf. A defense psychologist had little to report other than to say that what goes on in Clayton's mind, and the society he keeps, he keeps to himself. My observations differed somewhat from the psychologist's. It was as though Henry Clayton didn't care to be present in any form, that the trial itself was irrelevant, a place to exhibit his pity for me, and mull over other plans.

Sixteen years after the murders, I think about what happened that night, how I hid beneath the dining room table, the tablecloth draped low to the floor. Momma put me there when the trouble began at the front door, before Henry Clayton could notice me. Clayton forced Poppa inside and tied his wrists behind his back to a radiator, put a rag in his mouth and secured it with rope. Then he went after Momma, tore her dress off and whipped her face twice with a gun. Standing over Momma's white body, he said, "Now, missy. Why'd you have to go on and marry a colored boy?"

Henry Clayton undressed. He did things to Momma so Poppa could see, to humiliate her and emasculate him at the same time. I saw the swastika on Henry Clayton's neck, below his right ear, another between his shoulder blades, and a third on the narrow curve of his long back at his hips. If Poppa had dared to open his eyes at them, and I don't know whether he did, he would have seen the swastikas on the back of the man who entered Momma.

Poppa kept his face turned toward me, his eyes red and tearing. He shook his head when I began to lift the tablecloth and lean out. So I sat there, quiet as dust inside my make-believe fortress, and listened to the sounds of rape and murder, my muscles squeezing in on themselves and my bones to make my body disappear. Then the stillness but for Clayton's breathing while he lingered to absorb what he had done. He clapped his hands once, emitted a muted howl of euphoria, and was gone.

The moment I crawled from under the table, I found parts of them separated from their bodies, their blood spilled like paint, staining my hands and knees while I reached for the phone to dial 911. Two policemen caught Henry Clayton running through the streets in my neighborhood with his shirt off and the swastikas showing on his body. A gun without bullets stuffed in his back pocket.

The police questioning, six weeks in a foster home away from school, the trial continuances, the testimony making my parents into an anatomy lesson. Nobody asked me about Momma's and Poppa's kisses, their touch, their laughter. Momma's love of classic books; Poppa's love of black and white movies, especially Hitchcock movies, and for Momma. Their adoration of me, their only child, showered on me with their time. Then came the guilty verdicts: rape and multiple homicide in the first degree. Two months later, the jury decided on death by lethal injection.

At the sentencing hearing, the prosecutor must have thought I was a prop, hardly caring I was around. His reaction to his assistants, with me in his office, was like a cheer after winning a ball game. "Didn't think the jury would give death without Clayton's fingerprints found in the house, especially with my victims being a mixed family and a mulatto boy."

As for Henry Clayton, though heavily shackled and escorted by guards, he moved through the courtroom with his feet quiet over the floor. His eyes searched for no one; he didn't seem to breathe or know his need to take a breath. He convinced me he had already fled to his future, and what he left behind in the courtroom was no more than his molted shell.

All those days and months, stretching into a year, ended in the verdict I knew was true, and the revenge I had hoped for. But that year has never gone away. It's one big yesterday, and never a moment away before I'm thinking about all of it again. I remember no matter what else I do, no matter what else I dream, yesterday is with me.

The mail arrives this afternoon. In the stack, an envelope bears the seal of our county court's prosecutor's office. I tear it open, thinking of Henry Clayton and his swastikas and his eyes looking at me with tears in them the moment I pointed him out in court as the one. What I see next couldn't be expected, but it's clear enough on the paper.

Two years ago, the initial letter arrived. More came every few months afterwards. In each letter, below the official state seal, the typed words expressed full assurance. Although there had been no official news yet, I shouldn't worry about the last gasps of a doomed man.

The initial letter marked the first time I sensed Momma and Poppa's presence. A chill through my skin, their image staring back at me from my own face in the bathroom and bedroom mirrors. I took the sensation as a show of their confidence, to let me know there was nothing to worry about; yet the frequency of the chill, its increased intensity throughout the day, frightened me. Although my nightmare of being under the table comes nearly every night, and has since the first night, the prosecutor's letter and my parents' presence not only heightened the pace, but also brought the nightmare to my days.

I wrote back to the prosecutor's office, insisted I didn't want to receive these letters, and went to the Victim Assistance Division after the next one showed up anyway. The assigned assistant prosecutor claimed she understood, and agreed it was hard enough for me without reminders of the past. Her promise to tell the Chief Prosecutor's Office, and put an end to the letters, came true. They stopped coming for over a year. And my fantasy about sensing the presence of Momma and Poppa came to an abrupt end too. Until this letter.

Four months ago, DNA testing exonerated Henry Clayton. His governor's pardon unopposed because of my own demands to be left alone and uninformed.

The chill through my bones again, Momma's and Poppa's voices more clear, and profoundly sad. They realize how unusual their initial presence must have felt to me, how unaccustomed I would be to their language. What I had interpreted as confidence was meant as a warning.

Now Henry Clayton is free, a completely free man. I remain imprisoned in yesterday.

2

There's no mention of Henry Clayton's release on the local five-thirty news. Same with the national news at six and ten. Nothing on the radio. My telephone doesn't ring. It's the way things go in a town like mine.

Red River Falls is a place where people feel caught inside one of those water globes, but without the colorful confetti or snow to pretty things up. Turn it upside down and shake it all you want, the streets and buildings appear the same as they did decades ago. A town surrounded by Midwest prairie, large enough to hold forty-seven thousand people, three McDonald's, two hospitals, eleven churches, a synagogue, a mosque, and three grocery stores. Visitors often ask if there is in fact a waterfall in Red River Falls, and show surprise when the situation is explained to them.

There is a waterfall, and the water flows reddish brown from the iron in the earth. People laugh or shake their heads when they first learn it's located inside Leaper Street Cemetery. Visitor or resident, most say a town naming itself after a waterfall splashing inside a cemetery must have its problems. As a boy, I disagreed with this conclusion. After Henry Clayton murdered my parents, I couldn't agree with it enough.

Charlie Watts lived across the street from me, my best friend until third grade. We often rode our bikes together to the Falls to sit and watch. A fifty-foot drop frothing at the bottom, with a hundred foot expanse. Its steep banks cut by centuries of current held enormous trees growing from sheets of rock as thin as our boyhood legs, leaving unexplained why the trees didn't topple over. Like trees rooted in almost nothing, the Falls held a mystery for us. Being in an old, overgrown cemetery only heightened the mystery.

"Where do you suppose the water goes to after it falls?"

Charlie's voice still had a much smaller child's sound, although we were seven then. Skin darker than mine, ears cupped like ice cream scoopers sticking out from his head, Charlie was named after the Rolling Stones' drummer, his mother being the only black woman on the block who listened religiously to the Rolling Stones. Adored them, she said. She insisted, "The fortuitousness of our last name made the fulfillment of Charlie's first name inevitable."

Charlie hated the Rolling Stones. All I cared about was how much he devoted himself to me, how he was the only black boy who completely ignored the light brown I inherited from the mix of Momma and Poppa.

"I don't know where the water goes," I told Charlie. "Most of it goes down the river, I guess."

"Seems there's more water falling over the cliff than there's water floating away." His ears tended to wiggle some when he was nervous, and they wiggled a lot at the moment. "Bet some of it goes down to the coffins. Bet a lot of it goes down to the coffins."

"Then what do you suppose happens?"

"I dunno." Charlie hugged his legs so tight, and it sure seemed as though he had an idea. "Maybe they leak inside the coffins and water the bodies. Maybe that's really why the water's kind of red. Or maybe," he hushed, "the red water makes the bodies come alive!"

"Cut it out, Charlie Watts," I said, and punched him in the shoulder.

"Got you going. Got you going."

I scrunched my face up as serious-looking as I could manage. "Maybe the bodies flow through the ground into the Red River."

"Like ghosts?" Charlie asked. "River ghosts?"

I lay on the bank, my hands a pillow under my head. "Now who's got who going, Charlie Watts?"

Charlie lay beside me, our legs dangling over the bank's edge, and we both thought about it some more. I thought about it, and I knew Charlie thought about it because he was so quiet, elbowed up every minute or two to look behind him at the gravestones. "River ghosts," he said with an anxious sigh, and his ears wiggled nearly like wings.

Of course things do change in Red River Falls. For most, it's hard to notice until years later. For me, though, everything changed the night Henry Clayton showed up. Until then, I was the son of Nathan Hill, a black man living in a black neighborhood who owned every black-and-white movie Alfred Hitchcock ever made. He routinely invited neighborhood boys and girls over to watch his movies. Children filled our living room time after time, spilled over to the attached dining room, stares fixed on our small TV screen. Some wanted to know where the color was. Poppa mistook this and said, "No black men or women in Hitchcock movies, not really. Those were those times."

We watched, caught in mystery, stopping the VCR only for bathroom breaks and nerves. I suppose Poppa was responsible for most of the childhood nightmares on our block. Still, his Hitchcock movies brought children into my home. They became comfortable enough with Momma and her whiteness made whiter among so many black and brown faces. She asked the children to call her by her first name, Diane, and proved her whiteness didn't despise them, nor wish to bite. She looked into their eyes, like no other white person ever had done before, and gently held their hands.

Poppa's scary movies, Momma's color blindness brought children to me, gave me my friends. Made me believe the mix of me could not only turn out to be all right, but wonderful.

Becoming a witness to murder, though, changed everything. Even now I cannot fully explain the emotions only such a witness possesses. There's no word, no phrase I've found for them yet. Then consider a witness who also sees the rape, the double homicide, and the aftermath. And the breadth of it all compacted into the head of an eight-year-old boy. A boy who did nothing but hide. A coward, especially since it was Momma and Poppa destroyed, even if all I did was obey their last wish so I wouldn't die with them.

How could I explain to people, to children, even to Charlie Watts who I loved and trusted most of all, emotions I still can't explain to myself? The closest I've come was during the trial, but my testimony was a mere chronology, fact after fact through my chorus of tears. Children watched me from the courtroom pews, clutched by parents, all there to show their support. How horrified they looked. About my testimony, yes. But also in response to my eyes, my clenched jaw, the spasms attacking my face, the ugliness of my voice. The emotions I held, though I couldn't describe them, transformed me into a boy my friends could neither recognize nor tolerate.

My last contact with Charlie Watts in any meaningful way was also my last contact with friendship. I withdrew back under the table after the trial, waiting for the nightmare to arrive as it always did and still does, and for the cold touches of Momma and Poppa, whispering to me in the odd language of ghosts. Not trusting them and, therefore, no longer listening to what they had to say.

It's no surprise to me the outside world ignores what happened sixteen years ago, and the release of the only man the police ever suspected. Henry Clayton, who I pointed out in court. The man I forever see in my nightmare, hovering over Momma.

3

People in Red River Falls say I became a police officer when I turned twenty-one because of what happened when I was eight. They say I bought my parents' old house because it helps keep Momma and Poppa with me in some fashion. And I'm not married or seeing anyone because all of it makes me too odd for any woman to consider. The words are not spoken to me directly, but at a distance, when my presence causes a quiet conversation to start across the room, and people think I'm out of earshot.

I stay in Red River Falls because it's what I'm used to. I became a police officer so I wouldn't be hassled by police officers, as black men often are in Red River Falls, and mixed blood men even more. Our force has sixty-seven officers rotating over three shifts. All men. Sixty-four white, two black, and me. Green eyes staring through light brown skin doesn't seem to satisfy either side. As for women, I can't answer. I hardly have the nerve to ask myself about women. There are times when I glance at my image in windows and mirrors and I see the blend: Momma's beauty cast in Poppa's tall, high-cheeked stature, ruined by a memory of sixteen years ago that shapes my expression into barely restrained anger.

When I bought the old house, I tore out the carpet and sanded away the shadows of blood stained into the oak floor. I removed everything other owners left behind which had belonged to my parents: fishing pole racks, ceiling fixtures, closet organizers, a height chart of me etched into a door frame; even the seashell doorknobs Momma chose to Poppa's dismay. All removed.

Except for Momma's books. New shelving fills with them everywhere in the rectangle formed by the living room and dining room. Every book Momma ever read and encouraged me to read. Books with bindings frayed at the edges, smelling like the centuries they describe. Her favorites by Twain, Austen, Whitman, Emerson, Dickens; poems by Billy Collins, novels by John Irving, Alice Walker, Joyce Carol Oates, gather alongside Douglas Adams's *The Hitchhiker's Guide to the Galaxy,* and everything ever written by Joan Collins and Danielle Steele; her required reading, Shakespeare, Alexander Pope, Byron; writings by Dr. Martin Luther King Jr., Harold Washington, Malcolm X, and Carver.

The walls of Momma and Poppa's house now wallpapered with the books Momma once stored in closets and in the attic to allow space for Poppa's videotapes, VCR, TV, and Hitchcock posters. Among these books, *Mein Kampf.* The only real argument I remember between Momma and Poppa was over Hitler's book. "You have to draw from all walks of life when you read books," Momma insisted. She played with strands of her light brown hair, nervous fingers, her creamy face flushed crimson. "Especially with enemies of peace, it's necessary to know the enemy to understand how to defeat the enemy." Poppa's opposition withered beneath the persuasion of Momma's logic, perhaps influenced more by her beauty, but he said he wouldn't read it, and told Momma never to ask him to try.

Since the news about Henry Clayton arrived this afternoon, a ghost hushes at my ear, *Know the enemy to defeat the enemy.* This only affirms I will never read *Mein Kampf,* even if it's Poppa's voice I hear insisting I should.

Sitting in my recliner, hitting the remote so the television screen turns black, I think about Henry Clayton. I find my service revolver in the upstairs bedroom's bureau drawer and lie on my back in bed with the gun resting on my chest beneath the cover. In sleep, my nightmare will find me. It always does. This time I'll try not to look at Poppa's face, so twisted in anger and fear, or the resignation on Momma's and her wishfulness for her torment to end. Instead I'll try, I swear I'll try, to look for the markings on the white man's back and neck, and the narrow curve of his body, and the shape of his face. To see for myself, and know I was not wrong about Henry Clayton.

My fingers dig into the mattress, tensing. I hold on to Momma and Poppa's house so no one else can have it.

4

I tell my squad partner Henry Clayton's out of prison. He reacts before I can tell him why.

"Shee-it."

Jack Harter is a white boy in his early forties who goes out of his way to talk about injustices rendered against the black man. When he talks to me, he floats his eyebrows up his forehead, nearly to his hairline. "Shit" comes out of his mouth the way black men said it in those movies white boys made in the 1970s. "Shee -it."

Again he tells me, "The Constitution of the United States of America . . ." so I know which constitution he's talking about. How it allowed for slavery and separate but equal for 170 years, and how white boys who don't get into the college of their choice because of affirmative action should be glad they weren't whipped and torn from their parents and wives and children for over three hundred years. He wants to be my friend, and works hard at it. Jack reminds me his great grandfather on his mother's side was Jewish; last year it was his great grandmother. Either way, he says he has an idea of my suffering. Although he's got five inches on me, and bricks for fists, sometimes I think I should have decked him long ago.

While he drives our routine patrol, Jack habitually starts the squad's turn signal a block before he turns. It confuses drivers behind us approaching parking lot entrances and residential driveways. Jack explains, as he always does without being asked,

"It keeps Theresa from reminding me where to turn when I already know, and she knows I already know, but she'll remind me anyway." I remind him I'm not his wife. This conversation is our routine too. He considers my news some more, driving our squad car toward the cemetery. Bungalows edge the streets behind pocket lawns, two-story homes built of dark brick and thick plaster walls. Squat and impenetrable like military pillboxes in a row. Though solid as they are, they seem to lean toward us while we drive down Leaper Street. "It's Greg Kostner's fault," Jack says. "I wouldn't let him defend a hangnail let alone a death penalty case like Clayton's."

"Kostner wasn't the problem."

Jack ignores what I have to say, as he usually does when he's talking about my life. "Greg Kostner. Shee-it. You know what the department chief used to say about him? When a defendant's got no defense to a case, hire Kostner. On appeal, the court will throw it out 'cause the lawyer was so damn bad."

"Kostner died long ago. He's not the reason anyway. They don't release a prisoner because his attorney was a wreck at trial."

"Oh? Then why's Clayton out?"

"DNA."

"What?"

"DNA tests got him out."

For the moment, Jack has nothing to say.

It's our routine every Tuesday to go to Leaper Street Cemetery, to visit Poppa and Momma. Jack insisted on it the day I arrived on the force three years ago and he took me as his squad partner. Before then, I hadn't visited their graves since the funeral. Never thought there would be anything to see. By agreeing to stop by every Tuesday morning at the start of our shift, I got Jack to shut up about it. I suspect he's lazy and wants to do it to pass a half hour.

Leaper Street Cemetery looks the same whether in rain or in sunshine. Its burr oaks long ago matured to the point where their canopies touch one to the other, blanketing the ground, walking paths, and headstones in twilight. Respectful, mournful, the way a cemetery should be.

Jack parks half into the grass, as he always does, where he lets me out at the brick walk leading to the headstones. He stands at his door with his arms resting on top of the squad car, and sends his eyebrows floating with concern.

I carry two red roses, one in each hand. This time I'm not here to appease Jack. I want to see their graves. Perhaps I need inspiration. In my three years as a Red River Falls police officer, I have witnessed my share of people seeking solace at graves. To concede that something here might be of value to me now comes from no small effort on my part. Clayton's release, despite what I see in my nightmare, forces possibilities.

The path curves slightly left, beyond a sapling struggling to find sunlight beneath taller trees. Crowded headstones in misaligned rows, like chess pieces laid out in strategic battle, wait eternally for the next move. Poppa's and Momma's headstones rise at the end of the path. "I'm here now," I whisper to myself. I focus on their headstones' rectangular peaks, waist-high, their names, Nathan Xavier Hill, Diane Elizabeth Hill, etched into the gray mass, streaked haphazardly in black. Finally, the numbers: their birth dates apart by three years, dead at the same moment.

I'm filled with the rush of the waterfall, its heavy scent of iron-filled moisture, its sound of distant applause. Although hidden from view beyond headstones, a berm in the earth, and an untamed stand of trees and undergrowth, the Red River engulfs me. I'm held by the way it takes my thoughts to a time when this place was a simple, boyhood adventure, Charlie Watts and me counting numbers on headstones over buried strangers, figuring how old they all were, who had lived the longest life, who had lived the shortest life. One time Charlie Watts stood so sadly at a lone grave beneath a dying honey locust. His playfulness evaporated away, and he dried into a gravestone himself. "This girl was only two," he said. "Her name's April." He started to cry. "There aren't any graves by it. No momma or poppa with her. She's all alone."

"She's just waiting," I said, and put my hand on his back. His bones felt sharp, as if his flesh withered.

"Waiting for what?"

"Her momma and poppa. I'm sure she's waiting for them in heaven."

Charlie thought about it, doubt downturning his mouth. By his eighth birthday, he had already turned suspicious about God. I was the one back then who tried, in earnest, to convince him about the happy truth of heaven.

Coming here over the last three years, standing before Momma's and Poppa's graves, has brought me more to my memories of Charlie Watts than to anything else. He's alive somewhere, a man, perhaps married, with children who suffer ears like his, but who hold him and love him just the same. The boy I remember left the neighborhood soon after the trial, and I'm convinced I was the one who chased him and his family away. The Charlie Watts I know is buried here within the mist of the Red River Falls. With him lies buried my boyhood, the rush of water emulating tears shed over the heaven I once believed in.

If he stood with me now, I would say to Charlie I still believe in river ghosts. They are real. But they are far different from what we had imagined.

This morning, for the first time since these visits began three years ago, I feel their presence at the graves. A touch of chill at my back penetrates my memories of Charlie Watts. Without words, the ghosts work to soothe me; movement of hands over my back the way Momma and Poppa used to soothe me in a time of more innocent nightmares. I'm drawn to wonder why I'm in need of soothing beyond what I already know. Perhaps I shouldn't again mistake their touch for something else.

My strength drains through my feet into the earth, to be with Poppa and Momma and my boyhood that died with them and my loss of Charlie Watts. I bend low to feel the moist crabgrass overtaking their plots. Between the headstones, a bouquet of daffodils, faded yellow and wilting, leans against Momma's, their stems tied together within dirty string. I assume it's from my auntie, from the flower shop she owns. My Auntie Doria. My father's sister. She eventually won court approval to take me in after she spent a month convincing Children Services her small house was big enough, considering the size of her heart.

My roses look newborn beside the daffodils, and I lift the bouquet from the ground. There, stuck among the stems, is a small note inside a plastic bag. I feel heat enter my fingertips, like embers wishing to ignite my flesh, the soft hands of ghosts suddenly frantic over my back. I tear the plastic from the stems and the note from the plastic. It's my inherent perception of things concerning my parents, anything at all dealing with them. The sharpening of my senses and more. Premonitions and warnings that allow me to experience ghosts yet leave me short of full understanding.

I know about this note. I expected this note.

On my knees, arms collapsed to my lap, tears come unabated. I'm cowering beneath the table again, shrouded in cloth, losing my mind to madness; and on the witness stand, struggling to talk in court, forcing myself to describe to strangers what I had seen, and what is stuck in my memory forever.

Jack's hands brace me. He thankfully says nothing, and I reach across my chest to touch his fingers and their grip on my shoulder. The note floats to the ground over Poppa and

Momma, landing with its message facing me, appearing more like a vision than words. I read it one more time before tears drown my vision.

> Praise Jesus, Officer Richard Hill.
> I need to talk to you. Urgently!
>
> Henry Clayton

5

"Praise Jesus," Jack says, spitting on the floor. He's been this way all shift. Back at the station, he continues deriding Henry Clayton in the officers' locker room. He's at his locker in the next row over, talking with three other officers about Clayton's freedom, and his note. I sit alone on the narrow bench in my street clothes, facing my open locker, empty as usual. My uniform and service revolver stuffed in a duffel bag I'll carry to Momma and Poppa's house. Everything personal and work-related stays at home. Never use the station's showers after shift. As other men talk, I'm spying on my own life.

"Shee-it. I've met Jesus a thousand times," Jack says. "Sure I have. When I was at the Chicago Police Academy, I found Jesus rides the subway and wears a green leisure suit and carries a bottle in a brown paper bag."

Phillip Dranowski's voice rises over Jack's laughter. "Half the men I arrest find Jesus in jail. Always the worst half, the meanest half. They claim they find Jesus in their cells and become new men."

Jack cuts in. "Until they make bail. Jesus stays behind bars. Nobody posts His bail."

"What's Rich gonna do?" Drano says.

My fingertips grip at my knees and muscles strain in my forearms. If I were to look in a mirror, I'd see my face tensing the same way. It's as though a beast I've made an uncomfortable truce with has escaped and paces inside me.

"I'm still here," I say.

"Oh!" Drano says. A locker slams shut and footsteps hurry to the end of the row. Dranowski frowns at me, flushed. His shape resembles a bowling pin. After twenty-three years on the force, he's still a patrol officer, at peace with his workplace nickname. "Didn't mean anything by it. Just making a joke." Perhaps he expects something from me beyond my stare. He begins to whither, says finally, "Never mind," and pivots away.

Jack comes around the corner and sits beside me. "If you think I'm gonna apologize," he says, "you can forget it." He calls me an ass.

"I know," I say.

Larry Grimes stands at his locker on the other end of the row, one of two black officers arriving for second shift. He swears at something, gives me a quick glance and shakes his head. Like the white cops here, he barely speaks to me unless he has to, shows his disdain with a glance that doesn't focus on my eyes. The whites here consider me a novelty, a mixture of chemicals whose interaction remains in doubt though likely volatile. With Grimes, his repulsion makes it clear he's made up his mind. I'm an aberration, an experiment already proven to be a failure.

Jack waits for Grimes to leave before he speaks his observation. "You freak people out."

"I know."

"You need to get laid. I've got a sister."

"I've seen her. She looks like you."

"Right," Jack says. "Gorgeous."

"I wish you hadn't told Drano."

Other officers return from first shift and the air fills with their rush of steps, the dull peal of boots, holsters, and guns tossed inside metal lockers. Their talk blends together, shattered echoes within the hardness of this room.

"Looked like a Red River Falls phone number at the bottom of the note," Jack says. I lift my hands from my knees. Henry Clayton's note, nearly dissolved into threads, sticks to the sweat on my right palm. "You should call the prosecutor's office."

"What for?"

Jack scratches at his chin. "Closure."

"Closure's for talk show psychologists," I say. "It's an imaginary line, and you don't realize this until after you think you've crossed over it."

There are two light bruises, one on each side of my ribs, maintained by Jack's three-year history of elbow-nudges to prove his camaraderie. This time, his arm reaches over my shoulder, and the weight of his hand bears down on my back. I remember his touch at the cemetery.

Standing, Jack seems to rise miles over my head. He needs a shave, and his dark eyes move slowly behind his lashes. "You can call me," he says. "Anytime."

He leaves me for his locker, his steps soon lost in the noise of other officers. I think of Jack Harter. A giant man, intrusive, opinionated, a professor of the world without a college degree. He has a way of confusing my thoughts on occasion. Maybe it's guilt. But guilt implies I care what he thinks about me. I need to talk to somebody. Might as well be Jack.

I wipe the ruined paper away from my palm. Its numbers stay permanent in my memory. As much as Henry Clayton himself.

6

Auntie Doria makes my dinner tonight. She does almost every night. "It's one of those facts of nature," she says, standing large at her stove. "Most men can't cook, or pretend they can't cook. Can't clean much either. So they get married."

She looks back over her shoulder at me, the skin under her eyes nearly black, shining like worn leather through her glasses. Black-framed, thick-lensed, her glasses became relics long ago. She engages in casual battle with them, swiping one hand then the other to the bridge, lifting. Gravity takes a few seconds to return her glasses to the tip of her nose. Her deep brown face reminds me of my father's. Except on her, the familiar features appear exaggerated and blown out at the cheeks and chin, and all of it sits on her neck quivering from the edge of her jaw into a pedestal of gelatin squeezed below the top button of her shirt. My father's features weren't meant to live prettily on a fat woman's face.

Never married, Auntie Doria quickly became one of those women who long ago stopped caring whether she looked like a woman. She cares for her devotion to her religious faith, and for me. Always has. When she flashes her big teeth at me, I tell myself I love her. How sweet she is. Her look is the way she is, a fact of her existence. To me, she's beautiful. When she swipes at her glasses again, keeps her smile aimed my way, I know, sometime soon, I should say I love her out loud.

She pats her big hands over the front of her skirt. "Except for my Richie," she says, and laughs. "You can't cook or you don't want to, and you're not going to get married. So you come to your Auntie Doria's home for good food."

I look away from her face to the cabinets, then to the floor. Everything looks worn; wood veneers scraped away by Auntie Doria's hands, a path eroded into the linoleum around the table and stove by her heavy, dragging feet. The doors to this house as well as the sliding door to the patio in back are guarded by empty soda bottles, lined like military men at the threshold. It's something she's been doing since I first came here after Momma's and Poppa's murders, and continues on as her own habit. Several more bottles, these filled with layers of colored salt, sit on windowsills, projects I made as a boy which Auntie put to good use. Entering and leaving Auntie Doria's house takes some time for glass soldiers to retreat then retake the perimeter.

"I'm getting married someday."

Auntie Doria smiles at me. "Soon? Any lady I know?"

I tell her what I've told her before. "There's no woman right now."

"A man? I could learn to understand if it was a man." Auntie Doria turns back to her stove, flipping chicken breasts in a pan, letting smoke billow into her face. "But having no one at all isn't natural."

"No."

She glances at one of her dozen or so photographs of Denzel Washington taped all over her home. It's a contest between Denzel and the Holy Crucifix in terms of number and attention. This particular photo she cut out from *People Magazine's 50 Most Beautiful People* edition, and keeps posted on the refrigerator with two cross-shaped magnets; the paper curls as though Denzel struggles to pull himself off the refrigerator and escape from Auntie Doria. Lifting her glasses again, she smiles at Denzel's picture in a girlish way that embarrasses me. "If you know you're not acting natural," she says with a sigh, "then I guess there's some hope for you."

"You should let me buy you new glasses."

"There's nothing wrong with these glasses." She sweeps her hand up and raises her chin to keep her glasses from sliding back down. A silly pose, as if frozen in the instant before letting loose a momentous sneeze. I can't bring myself to tell her about her habit with her glasses. I never have.

"Maybe you should have laser eye surgery."

"Who's gonna pay for it?"

"I might."

Auntie Doria frowns at the chicken frying in the pan on her stove. I believe I hear her glasses thump to the tip of her nose. "My momma, rest her soul, bought me these frames and they don't need replacing, just the lenses now and then."

"Wouldn't you like to see twenty-twenty the moment you open your eyes in the morning?"

"Honey, it's hard enough seeing my kisser in the evening, do you have any idea what I look like in the morning these days?"

"Auntie Doria," I start to say, but she faces me quickly and lets her glasses hang below her eyes.

"You get me laser eye surgery under one condition, honey. Talk to the doctor and tell him I don't care about seeing twenty-twenty when I open my eyes in the morning. Get it so that laser makes me wake up in the morning and see the Lord Jesus out one eye and Denzel in my bed out the other, um hmm." She breathes as though in expectation, and repeats *Denzel.* "You get the eye doctor to make it so I see like that and I'll be the happiest woman on earth. I'll sing the doctor's praise to Jesus. I'd never get out of my bed. I'll give the eye doctor every last damn penny I own."

This time the lift of her glasses looks as though she's punched herself in the face. "You arrange it for me, and I'll throw away my glasses forever." She places a chicken breast on a plate, with steamed carrots and a baked potato, and slides it to me on the kitchen table. "This whole thing's about you anyway, child," she says, sitting beside me with her own plate. "I can see Denzel in my mind's eye whenever I want to. What I want to know is, who are you looking at these days?"

I start to eat and it takes a long time before I talk. When I do, Auntie Doria knows I'm answering her question. "Nobody."

"Um hmm."

"There's no woman yet."

"But it would be a woman if it were anybody?"

"Yes."

Auntie Doria takes a bite of chicken and sighs. "It's not like I wouldn't accept things if you came home with a man."

We eat together in silence, staring at our food, catching glimpses of each other. Her hand, holding a fork, swipes at her glasses, and I wonder what habit of mine she sees, something she won't tell me about. I suppose it's what I already know; it's what crawls beneath my skin. It's what should frighten her, like it does most people, except for Jack Harter. Somewhere along the line, making an ass of himself trying to prove he's for the black man's cause, Jack became a friend. As much of a friend as I will allow. Auntie Doria accepts my habits in silence out of love. I suppose, then, when she swipes at her glasses twice more while chewing her last bite of chicken, and I say nothing about it, she understands my devotion to her.

We sit with the coffee and sweet cake she's made. I ask her, "Have my grandma and grandpa ever talked to you?"

"Honey, you know my parents died a while back. What foolish thing are you asking me?"

"Momma's parents."

"Oh." The flesh over Auntie Doria's face seems to disconnect, hangs loose from her bones. "Why are you asking me this now?"

"Something I thought about at the cemetery this morning."

She studies me, doubts my motivation. "You certain you want to know? Doesn't seem to be any reason to discuss it after all these years." She sighs at my stillness, punches her glasses up. "I never met them. Never talked to them. Your momma said she preferred it this way if they weren't going to accept your poppa."

Over Auntie Doria's shoulder, on a mantle above a small fireplace, a photo stands nearly lost among figurines of Jesus and Mother Mary. Momma and Poppa at their flower shop, standing before the storefront with a bouquet of red roses their first morning in business. He left his job as a chemical engineer, she her job as an English teacher, to open their shop together. They bought the shop where a white neighborhood and our black neighborhood come together; separated is more accurate, by a divide of traffic moving down a four-lane road. They figured to draw from both sides, only the best, most thoughtful people, who would most likely buy lots of flowers, and named their shop *Naiveté*. It's odd to think now that a shop named *Naiveté* sustained Momma and Poppa, filled their modest home with books and old movies. In the picture, Poppa wraps his left arm around Momma's waist, his hand strong below Momma's left breast. And Momma smiles like she doesn't mind, her hand under his, perhaps guiding his hand to hold her there.

Auntie Doria knows what I'm looking at and glances over her shoulder a bit to look at the photograph too. It's her shop now, has been since she quit her job as a secretary and took over soon after their murders. *Naiveté* sustains her, though less so than it did Momma and Poppa because of the flowers she gives away to her church. "Your momma's parents never came to the wedding. As far as I know, they're dead or might as well be."

"How did Momma and Poppa meet?"

"How many questions like this are you asking me tonight?"

"Auntie," I say, and I fall into her at the table, my eyes shut. Words I need to speak pour from my mouth like something vile. "They let Henry Clayton out of prison. They say he didn't murder Momma and Poppa." Now I know, after telling Auntie Doria, monsters inside me have found their way out through my pores, with my sweat and tears. Their smoke orbits about this kitchen like comets, and they dive their fiery heads at me, brush their whiplike tails against my body with their whispered laughter, low and angry.

They first came to me the night after my parents' murders when I was supposed to go to sleep. How does a boy find sleep after witnessing his parents' murders? While other children lived their days seeing the world in front of them, I remained swallowed inside a moment. The images of Henry Clayton and what he did to Momma and Poppa. Then at night, these images melted into distortions and swirled about my bedroom.

On my sixteenth birthday, Auntie Doria ran her fingers over a small mustache on my upper lip, emphasized how she had to look up a bit to look me in the eye, and declared I had grown into a man. In the evening, I wrapped a piece of birthday cake in a paper towel. As a present to myself, I figured out how to shut the images down by convincing myself monsters weren't real. By forcing my memories of my parents' lives into an artificial past. By pretending to forget the unforgettable. Rather than drive the monsters away, they took refuge inside me, and reminded me of their presence with their hot touches beneath the surface of my skin. I threw the cake wrapped in paper in the trash, an offering to the truce I had made with my memories, at a time in my life when I believed closure was possible.

Tonight, Auntie Doria holds me the way she did when I was a child screaming at my nightmare in her home. This time, though, she doesn't coo at me and doesn't recite nursery rhymes. When I explain why Henry Clayton was let go, she doesn't tell me everything will be all right. Her body feels like a blanket wrapped around mine, and she lets my tears fall over her.

Weariness overtakes me. Swirls of smoke begin to fade. With her soft tone, Auntie Doria makes it clear how much she loves me. She doesn't say the words. She doesn't say the things she once did when I was a boy unable to sleep at night because of monsters. "You need to find things out," Auntie Doria says. "It's what you need to do."

Hearing such advice from Jack Harter is one thing, from my auntie quite another. If such different people agree, then my purpose should be clear.

Auntie Doria invites me to stay overnight in my old room, and when she turns from the door, I ask her, "When I was born, did Momma's parents call then?"

"You're suffering enough, child. Why are you doing this?"

"So I know, Auntie. Things I should've asked before they died. Still, I'd like to know now."

"No, Richie child. When you were born, it was the same as before. They never called."

"Thank you, Auntie."

She smiles weakly, overtaken by sadness. Before she closes the door, she says, "Your momma saw your poppa in a park and fell in love with him right then and there. One back scratch from your momma and your poppa did the same. That's how they met, simple as can be."

When I lie in bed, rather than search for things I kept here as a boy, I search for peace in the darkness. I find it in the thought of the holes in my life. Answers to questions every child should have without a second thought. Instead, fundamental pieces are missing, substantial gaps, as if I've been built like a house on an incomplete foundation. Such thoughts should disturb me and would keep any other man awake through the night. They work to distract me, causing my nightmare and monsters to exist outside of me rather than within. Tonight, in Auntie Doria's home, I feel as though I'm in her embrace, an embrace that embodies everything I am, or at least everything of me that remains. She provides the peace I need to fall asleep.

7

There's a perception in Red River Falls, and I suppose in most towns, that police officers and prosecutors get along with each other. Bullshit.

Prosecutors pass judgment over the arrests we make, often refusing to authorize felony charges, or charges at all, for reasons having more to do with politics than with facts. They display their diplomas on their office walls, and never come to the police station to see if we have walls.

The friction between police officers and prosecutors is both natural and obvious. Prosecutors either patronize or condescend, depending on their mood, and they glance at the service revolvers on our hips as if uncertain of our sanity. For me, their uncertainty seems heightened. Whether it's a white, or one of the two blacks in the office, Red River Falls' prosecutors stare at my dark blue uniform over my biracial skin as if someone in charge of hiring has made a mistake.

Jack waits beside me in the lobby outside the chief prosecutor's office on the second floor of the courthouse. All the chairs in the lobby force him to crouch low with his knees high in the air. He tells me he's certain the prosecutors planned it this way, to make him look like he's taking a dump wherever he sits. "So I'm changing Tyler's diaper last night," he says. "Quite a load. The wife's happy I'm doing it, and the kid's gurgling one of his nursery rhyme songs. A nice moment for a father in spite of the stink. Real nice."

"It's all right if you let me do this by myself."

Jack nudges his elbow into my side. "So I think to ask my son, I mean I'm just playing, but I ask him, 'What do you want to be when you grow up?' All of a sudden, the boy stops singing, and his face gets this real stubborn look. He tells me."

"Good."

"A sock puppet."

"What?"

Jack lowers his head and pinches the bridge of his nose. "Tyler, my only child, told me he wants to be a sock puppet when he grows up."

"Your son's two."

"Almost three."

The door beside Jack's chair opens and Marla leans her head forward. "Mr. Schumacher will see you now."

Marla Weist has been around a while. Prehistoric, Jack likes to say. Her iron-gray hair piles up thick, a tree trunk adding a new growth ring every few months. It's been rumored the courthouse was built around her a hundred years ago, and each morning she sneaks bottles of peach schnapps past courthouse security, stashed inside her mass of hair. Jack starts these rumors; Marla's aware of it. After they exchange scowls, she looks at me with the same pity she displayed when she held my hand during Henry Clayton's trial.

I walk past Marla's plastic cubicle, then pause at the entrance to the chief prosecutor's office. Jack asks the top of Marla's head, "What do you have on tap?"

She thuds into her chair and hisses at him, "All men grow up to be sock puppets."

This space hasn't changed. Its ancient walls, so impenetrable, hold words inside echoes only I can hear. As a boy, I studied these walls, noticed how the texture of the paint puckered like pores in human skin. Old white men in dark suits, weathered prosecutors, gathered together and sipped from coffee cups and soda cans. They discussed their courtroom battles from the past. Always victories, never a word about their losses. Marla had interrupted them, poked her head in, and said in the flat tone she uses today, "The jury's in with a verdict."

Marla's face didn't have the deep creases it has now, around her eyes and mouth in particular, and her hair, brown then with only a few strands of gray, flowed over her shoulders. She took me gently by the hand to the courtroom, to stand between me and Auntie Doria while the jury foreman stood and pronounced the verdict.

After the foreman sat, the judge asked the defense attorney if he would like to have the jury polled. Greg Kostner nodded and the judge turned to the jurors, one by one. "Was this then, and is this now, your verdict?" As each white face took its turn to pronounce a guilty verdict, Marla Weist squeezed my hands tighter, until the twelfth juror, when Marla kissed me on the cheek and assured me this was the last day I'd ever have to worry about Henry Clayton.

The cold metal desk, chairs, and cabinets from those days are gone. Fred Schumacher brought in his own furniture. Oak and plush. He's placed them the same way, as if this office permits one arrangement. He hasn't bothered to hang pictures on the walls, and the two frames on his desk are set so I can't see the photographs. No diplomas on display. Although he won re-election for the second time five months ago, his office gives the impression he's ready to move out.

Keeping his stare low over a police report on his desk, he asks me and Jack to sit. "Hey, Freddie," Jack says, dropping deep into a chair beside mine. "I voted for your opponent last time. Twice."

"I didn't have an opponent last time."

"Then I voted for the blank space below your name. Like I

said. Twice."

Schumacher pushes the report away and raises his head. Because of his voice, he's known in the courthouse as The Foghorn. The length of his body, narrow even in his suit, and his vertical face create the impression he's being squeezed. When he speaks, there's an inconsistency between his sound and shape, and it appears as though someone else is doing the talking. He wears a headache across his face this morning, and he blinks as though a pain throbs inside him to the beat of his heart. Jack leans over the police report on Schumacher's desk.

"One of Drano's," Jack observes. "I can tell by the typos he put in his name."

Schumacher nods and glances at an aspirin bottle on his desk, then to one of the photographs. He doesn't look my way when he talks to me. "You do pretty good work, Officer Hill. Clean police reports. You could stand to use a little more factual detail. Otherwise, I've got no complaints." He slides Drano's police report to the side of his desk, then at last manages to look at my face. "I'm sorry about Clayton."

Before this appointment, I had thought of so many things to say to Fred Schumacher; now I'm undecided about the right words to choose.

"Why would you say you're sorry," Jack says, "if DNA proved Clayton was an innocent man?"

Schumacher ignores him, keeps his stare on me. "You didn't want my office to notify you. You said our letters brought up bad memories. Marla insisted on your behalf, so we left you alone."

"The first letter, the ones after," I start to say, and freeze at the sensation of trembling inside my chest. Schumacher wasn't here when a past generation of prosecutors exchanged courtroom war stories. Those white men were oblivious to a brown boy sitting on the floor in a corner of this office, a boy fighting to forget a nightmare by studying paint on walls.

A hairline crack sloped up one of the walls, like an outline of a mountainside. Someone had drawn a stick figure near the top, legs extended as if climbing up the slope, about to reach the summit. The drawing caught my attention, made me wonder which one of the old men in suits may have stood on top of a chair to create it. However brief a moment, concentrating on the drawing more than anything else, I had managed to forget about myself long enough to smile. The sloping crack in the wall remains, but the climber has been painted over.

"The initial letters sounded so certain," I say to the men in this room, and to the men here fifteen years ago. "I was certain."

Schumacher's voice rumbles into my bones. "What are you certain of now?"

Jack tells him to piss off.

I close my eyes and the familiar image appears. A thin, white boy tattooed in swastikas, empowered by a gun. The dimensions of the white boy's face, the locations of the markings. All of it matched what I saw in the courtroom when I pointed at Henry Clayton and told the jurors what he had done.

"You didn't have to agree to Clayton's release," I say. "You still had the right to prosecute him. You didn't have to go along with the pardon." There's a noise in this room, a thunder rolling in from nowhere. When it subsides, I see my fist firm on Schumacher's desk.

Schumacher leans back in his chair, taps his fingers against his lips while he talks. "A killer may still be out there. Maybe he's already dead. But it's not Clayton." He pulls a clipped stack of papers from his desk drawer and drops it beside my fist. "As far as DNA forensics is concerned, out of five potential categories, your parents' murders fall into a category one situation." He retreats once more to the back of his chair. "Category one, examples three and four specifically apply here."

"Don't treat this like a math test, Freddie," Jack says. "Don't be an asshole. Not about this."

Schumacher pushes at the papers, forces them against my fist until I open my hand and take them. "Go to pages four and five."

Someone took care in designing the cover page. *U.S. Department of Justice, Post-Conviction DNA Testing: Recommendations for Handling Requests.* An artist's rendition of DNA swirls, and the scale of justice tipped to the right. I turn to page four and begin to read. Schumacher keeps talking as if he were complaining to someone who's not here.

"A man with a long rap sheet gets paroled early," he says, "goes out a few days later, cokes up, and murders a mother and her three young children. The story becomes the lead for the ten o'clock news, and screams from the front page of every newspaper in the country. The public demands the death penalty, whines about the unholy delay in the march toward death by the appeals process, and accuses the defense lawyer of pandering to the media at the expense of dead babies and their mother. Our legislators react by announcing plans to streamline the appellate process and do away with time-served credits. Then a month later, a man convicted of murder, a minute away from lethal injection, is saved by college students who prove the man's innocence. Suddenly the same public ready to lynch last month's mass murderer does an about face. Now the death penalty is too dangerous, unfairly applied, an act of revenge rather than justice. Politicians call for its abolishment. They insist innocent people have been put to death by the court system, and wonder out loud about the souls of prosecutors and law enforcement."

"Freddie," Jack groans. "You going anywhere with this?"

Schumacher clasps his hands together and leans over his desk toward me. "We live in an anecdotal society, Officer Hill. The public mood turns schizophrenic depending on the direction of the latest horror story. But DNA forensics is different," he says, turning to Jack. "It's bipartisan. The Department of Justice expects prosecutors to understand the science, and respond quickly to the answers it provides."

Schumacher pauses as if he knows I've reached the part in the report he wants me to read. Category one, examples three and four. "In your parents' case, there was one set of perpetrator DNA left behind. From your mother's rape test kit. You testified one man committed the crimes. Just one man was there, Officer Hill. Those were your words I reviewed in the trial transcript. If A equals B," he says evenly, "but B does not equal C, then A cannot equal C. You understand, don't you? This is exactly like a math test."

Schumacher waits for me to finish reading. I drop the report to my lap and see discomfort in the way he runs his hands through his hair. We both realize what he has to say next. "Long ago, your sworn testimony produced the equation. Now DNA forensics has provided the numbers to plug in to your equation. It equals complete exoneration. I had to let Clayton go."

Jack grabs the report and flips through some of its pages. "This thing's from 1999. Janet Reno's name is all over it for chrissake. Don't you have anything from this century, Freddie? Shee-it. What if things changed?"

"DNA science only improves with time, and the public's demand on prosecutors to act grows louder."

Schumacher looks over my head as if staring into his own haze. This meeting was part of his job, something difficult he had to complete before going on to some other task. He says how sorry he is, perhaps he said deeply sorry, I can't be sure with the storm in my ears. It's the boom of the sworn testimony I gave as a child, unaware at the time that my own words had created an inevitable future. This meeting with Schumacher.

My complete failure. Henry Clayton's freedom.

"This is my fault."

Schumacher stands and steps to the side of his desk. "Not fault. An undoing of an injustice."

"But I saw him. I saw Henry Clayton."

"You were a small, traumatized boy."

"Now you sound like Clayton's attorney."

"You need to see someone about this, Officer Hill."

"That's why I'm here."

"Not about Clayton's trial." Schumacher widens his eyes and jabs a forefinger against the side of his head. "You really need to see someone."

I don't respond. I won't respond. Even when he warns me not to let this interfere with my work.

"What happens now?" Jack says.

"My office registered the DNA results in the nationwide database." He extends his right hand toward me. "Nothing's matched under the current list. What happens now is we wait."

I stand and look at Schumacher's right hand, so expectant to clasp mine. "I'm a lefty," I say, and turn to leave. Jack warns Schumacher he'll vote against him three times next election if he doesn't make things right. "You never vote at all," Schumacher replies, then asks Jack if they're still on for golf this Saturday.

Passing Marla at her cubicle, I hear her softly call my name. Like Schumacher, she tells me she's sorry, deeply sorry.

Jack coughs beside me in our squad car. Parked outside the courthouse, he glances at me several times but appears more comfortable looking at his hands on the steering wheel.

"You need to let me do the talking," I say.

"Then you need to speak up more."

"Why do you give a damn about me?"

"I give a damn about everybody. You happen to be around me more than most people. Besides, you're the most damned man I've ever met in my life." He looks at his watch and smiles. "Since when did you become a lefty?"

"Never."

Jack shakes his head then slumps a bit. "I put Schumacher's Department of Justice report in the back seat. Read it if you ever get bored with yourself."

"Does he know you took it?"

"I left a quarter on his desk."

There will be no sleep for me tonight, I'm already aware. I consider the report's small print, gray columns, footnotes and references to an index. A call comes in from dispatch directing us to a disorderly conduct a mile from our location. Small matters, really, to help me get through the day, and survive the night.

8

The dispatch takes us to a home converted into a dance studio on Volker Lane. It's in an unusual neighborhood for Red River Falls. The only one with broad, grass medians separating single lanes of traffic and with trees reaching eighty feet into the air, arching their branches together and creating tunnels speared by shafts of sunlight. Large homes, large lots, a gated community. It's a neighborhood Red River Falls police officers serve and protect but can't afford to live in regardless of rank or skin color.

2131 Volker Lane. A substantial brick-and-stone two-story, now with four cops standing on the lawn, looking into the front window. Jack and I, Drano and a blond-boy rookie I haven't been introduced to. Blond Boy appears ridiculous in his uniform. Although large, he still looks like a child trying on a costume, lost beneath a man-sized hat. He's even more ridiculous when he glances at Drano, as if Drano might be able to teach him something about being a good cop.

A woman in a business suit leans over the porch of the house next door. She shouts her demand: *My taxes pay your salaries! Do something or I'll call your supervisor!*

"You need backup for this?" Jack asks Drano.

"Always white men doing this sort of crap, it's embarrassing." Drano nods at me in particular. "Your average American black man has his hands all over every other crime, but it seems white men still have the market cornered on perversion." Shaping his hands into blinders at his eyes, Drano touches his nose to the windowpane, peers inside. "Guess it must be hard for you, Rich, getting bad habits from both sides."

Jack insists Drano's kidding. "Right, Drano? 'Cause if you're not kidding, I'll have to shove your head up your ass so you can see where you're coming from."

The laugh comes from Blond Boy. Drano eases back from the window and tells him to shut up. "I've got nothing to kid about," he says to me. "You act like I'm not here. I can say what I want and it's like I'm having a conversation with myself. You never look at me, not even now when I'm talking right at you. It's been like this from the moment I first said hello."

"We were introduced, you whistled and said goddamn."

"That's my hello. Ask anybody."

He stands there, face pitched toward mine, anticipating a reaction. But he's right to the extent I ignore him, and I shouldn't have said anything at all. Gives him more reason to talk, more reason to exist.

"We were inside," Drano says, "but Riddy would only speak to Officer Hill. I don't need backup for Howard Riddy."

Blond Boy touches a metal sign bolted to the brick. Rust flakes surround its red lettering. *We Teach All Ballroom, Salsa, Jazz, & Tap. Special Rates for Children Under Ten.* "Isn't salsa a ballroom dance?" he says, glancing at Drano.

Jack steps around me to Drano. "How do you know Riddy asked for Rich?"

"Because he asked for him specifically. He told me to go to hell."

A screech from the neighbor's porch. *I swear I'll call your supervisor. I swear it!*

"Nothing to arrest him for," Drano says. "There never is." Drano turns toward the woman on the porch, his face crimson.

"Stop peeking into people's windows, Mrs. Furmer. That's a crime."

"When will you learn?" Jack says. We're hit with more threats to have our jobs served up to our supervisor.

"I got the Riddy lecture yesterday morning," Blond Boy says. He stuffs his hands into his pockets. "What kind of parent would bring his kid to Riddy, even if the lesson's free?"

Every rookie cop in Red River Falls gets what seasoned cops call the Riddy-lecture before the first beat patrol. I remember how I heard it, from shift command and separately from Jack, the story was the same.

Howard Riddy turns seventy-nine next month. Never married, Howard lived with his mother most of his life. Marilyn Riddy was a dancer. She made her way to New York and succeeded for several years on Broadway as a performer, then another decade as a choreographer, before returning to Red River Falls to local fame, this house, this dance studio, and a son who couldn't make it on his own.

Red River Falls has its harmless lunatic in Howard Riddy, especially since Marilyn died twenty years ago. Eccentric, loud, believing he possesses his mother's talents, he advertises for students by dancing on street corners, in restaurants, and near middle school playgrounds, accessorized by many of his mother's Broadway costumes. The fact that he lives among the blue-blood addresses on Volker Lane, next door to the neighborhood association president, keeps us coming out for the latest complaint. Because he held his mother's hands for seven months while she withered away from breast cancer, we have standing orders from our department chief, orders in place since Marilyn's death: if a cop ever arrests Howard Riddy, he'll be looking for a new job in the morning.

Over the last year, Howard has been hawking trampolines when he isn't dancing on street corners. And for the last few months, a trampoline has filled the front half of the living room Marilyn Riddy long ago converted into a dance studio. It's been accepted by the town that this one trampoline, which Riddy sold to himself, is the only sale he has made so far.

I press my face against the plate glass. Today, Howard Riddy, almost seventy-nine, rises over his trampoline toward the peak of the vaulted ceiling, smiling his false teeth at me. Naked.

Jack whispers into my ear, "Here's how the old man gets it up, at least on the way down."

I pull away from the window, listen to muted, rhythmic thumps coming from the trampoline. "Why does he want to see me?"

"Are you asking?" Drano says. " 'Cause if you are, it doesn't exactly sound like you're asking me. Sounds like you're talking to yourself again."

"Answer the question," Jack says.

"I want Hill to look at me first. So I can tell him hello."

Jack groans. "Look at him, Rich. Get it over with."

With some effort, I'm able to look away from the glass toward Drano, averting my stare to focus on his hair rather than his eyes.

"Riddy asked for you specifically," Drano says, "because he wanted to let you know Henry Clayton was in his house this morning. Henry Clayton left a message for you with Riddy."

Blond Boy says, "When did he tell you that?"

"Pay attention," Drano snaps at Blond Boy. "It's what the old man said."

I lower my stare, see Drano's shoulders beneath Jack's hands. And Drano's eyes, narrowed at me. There's joy in the way they glisten. Matches the spite in his grin. He raises his right hand and gives me a wave. "Goddamn, Officer Hill. See? It's how I say hello."

My legs move as though I'm not in control, stepping over the lawn to the walk, down the walk to the entrance door at the side of the house. The swing of my arms with fists at the ends and the pounding of my feet on cement seem to satisfy the screech from the porch next door. It pierces into my brain. *Finally! It's about time one of you did something about this crazy man!*

Jack calls out my name, but he doesn't reach me until I'm already inside the house, my chest at the edge of the trampoline. "Shee-it, Rich," Jack says. He elbows my ribs. "What're you planning to do, tackle the old guy? Maybe you can undo the springs so he crashes to the floor."

Drano and Blond Boy remain standing on the front lawn, looking in, faces at the glass. Howard Riddy thumps on the trampoline, spins about in the air to face me, his hands resting beside his dick.

"Look," Jack says, and pulls at my shoulders to turn me around. "The walls."

Bolted to the paneling, layers of shelving fill the room floor to ceiling. Each shelf crowds with photographs of Marilyn Riddy. It's the same black and white picture inside each frame, and the frames are set at matching forty-five degree angles from the walls. Youthful in the photograph, stunning, Marilyn Riddy's hair flows thickly to her shoulders. Tender skin, lips parted in a subtle smile, eyes staring aloft toward a hopeful future.

Howard Riddy stands at the center of the trampoline, his stare aloft like hers, lips parted in a failing smile. He says toward the ceiling, "Mother Marilyn." His rectangular face doesn't resemble his mother's, and there's no picture of his father on these shelves.

"Howard," Jack says. "When did you put these up?"

The old man's smile widens. "She's so lovely. Thanks for noticing."

Jack runs his hands over the trampoline's frame. "Do you

think you could close your curtains?"

"I could, but I wanted Mrs. Furmer to call the cops." Howard scratches at his shoulders and moans. "She always calls the cops." The skin over his face appears more than pale, as if it has lost something since I last saw him; his beard looks plucked clean, his eyebrows thinned to pencil strokes.

"Henry Clayton was right about you," Riddy says. His stare moves over my face as if the sight of me makes him angry. "He told me you never smile. Even if you saw an old man jumping naked on a trampoline, you'd look like you were at a funeral. So here I am, a naked old man bouncing on a trampoline. And there you are, watching a naked old man bouncing on a trampoline, looking like you're at a funeral."

The mention of Clayton's name in this space numbs me. I could be walking where he recently walked, breathing air he exhaled. The thought shakes the flesh over my bones.

Riddy cocks his head as if irritated I don't believe him. "There's a picture. Mr. Clayton was here this morning and left it for you. I've got my own copy tucked away, you know, for the pleasure of fond memories."

I scan the pictures crowded on the shelves, hear Riddy tell me I'm warm, then cold, then warm again. Toward the left corner beside the front window, one of the frames doesn't match the uniform forty-five degree angle, but rests on a middle shelf, placed parallel to the wall.

"Very hot, Officer Hill," Riddy says, then laughs. "Be gentle with it or I'll call the cops."

Marilyn Riddy, so forever lovely in hundreds of pictures, keeps her stare aloft and away from me. This particular framed photograph, now in my hands, gives me a distant feeling. Her youth, this captured instant, faded away long before I was born. "She's beautiful," I say, handing the photograph to Jack. Riddy nods.

"Rich," Jack says. He points back at the shelf, to where I had removed this particular frame and photograph. Another photograph leans against the wall. I reach to take it in my hands and see the young men. Late teens. Perhaps some in their early twenties. Shaved heads, khaki gray pants tucked inside shin-high, black boots. No shirts. A dozen white boys, thin and muscular, each with a black mark at the side of his neck, below the right ear. They had angled themselves toward the camera, made sure their marks were clear for the shot. And I see. Swastikas tattooed below each white boy's right ear.

Drano calls through the plate window, "What's going on?"

Jack yells at him to shut up, and leans over my shoulder toward the picture. "Shee-it. Fucking supremacists. They all look like the same pointy-headed sperm."

"Henry's upset you haven't called him," Riddy says. "He wants you to make the first call, at least to thank him for the yellow daffodils. Especially since he bought them at your auntie's shop. Paid in cash too."

"Why would Clayton contact you?"

Sunlight through the window flares in his eyes. "Can't you see the paneling?" Even as I look to the photograph again, and the walls in this room, Riddy tells me. "Henry Clayton stands second from the left. I know 'cause I took the damn picture."

Outside the window, Drano has faded to black, white, and gray, an antagonist from one of Poppa's Hitchcock movies. He's animated by laughter I cannot hear, Blond Boy unmolded clay beside him.

Jack's face fires up red. Reaching for his handcuffs, he moves fast toward Howard Riddy.

9

"Are you fired?"

Jack sits beside me at my locker. He tells me he isn't fired.

"What did the chief say?"

"He said, 'Under these special circumstances.' " Jack peers into my locker, opened and empty. "He ordered me to enroll in a cultural sensitivity program. Shee-it. Seventeen years into my career and I've got to learn to be sensitive to an octogenarian neo-Nazi." Jack's whisper proves his exhaustion. "Why do you bother with a locker? It's like you sit in front of it just so you can stare into an abyss."

"It's my special circumstances."

"Do you know why I arrested Riddy?"

"I think I do."

He elbows my ribs. "I think you don't."

Jack presses his hands on his knees and stands from the bench. "I'm sure I've got a poopy diaper to change at home. Compared to your abyss, the thought of a poopy diaper cheers me up." He nods at me and smiles. "See you at morning roll call."

To the slow beat of Jack lumbering away, my hands squeeze Schumacher's DNA report, and I consider its thickness. I slip it inside my duffel bag with my uniform and the photograph. I should have thanked Jack for keeping his mouth shut about taking the picture from Riddy's house.

Shift change reminds me of a relay race, a half-hour time

period in which batons are passed from one squad team to the next. Except with cops, there's no end to the laps we have to run, not until retirement, whether voluntary or forced. I have enough information, I suppose, to be a successful criminal. Shift change, for example, means fewer cops on the streets and the best time to commit a crime. I think about this carrying my duffel bag over my shoulder, feeling the weight of the stolen report and photograph against my back.

First and second shift officers part for me. Larry Grimes, alone at his locker, looks away as I approach. "Don't say a thing to me," he drones, "if you're not talking to the white boys." I hesitate a step past him. Admire his skin, the depth of his brown complexion, how it gives his face the clarity I'm missing.

"I wasn't going to."

He throws a towel into his locker. "Don't."

"Guess I just did."

"Well stop it."

His eyes are nearly black; they encourage me to move along. Since my first day here, this place reminds me of my high school locker room, cement gray beneath a fluttering fluorescent glow. Eyes of white boys glared their anger at me for being alive among them, wishing to attack if only I'd give them the smallest excuse. Boys of color were far outnumbered. We knew to be cautious, to avoid standing together in one place for too long, conscious of avoiding the appearance of a black coalition.

Somewhere behind me, Drano wishes me goodnight. I don't respond. "Absolute silence," Drano laughs to somebody, who laughs back. "You owe me a buck for that."

At the metal door to our booking room, I press an intercom button. "Officer Hill," I say into the speaker grate. The return voice through the grate sounds confused, and I repeat myself. "Hill. Star number 471."

"Look into the camera."

I tilt my head back, aim my face toward the lens over the door. With the buzzer, I pull the door open.

Inside, the cement floor narrows into a hallway, and runs by five cages in a row. Each cage has a bench in the back to sit, a slit in the bars to pass food, a chrome toilet, and a basin to wash up and lap water. The officer at the observation desk calls himself Zookeeper. The lighting deepens his ancient scars from teenaged acne. He smiles at me, then brushes limp strands of hair off his forehead. "First time I've seen the old guy naked. Hopefully the last." He shows me the release form. "Five more minutes, I'll be done and he can go."

I move slowly by the first cage, past an unshaven white boy sitting inside with his elbows spiked into his knees, hands clasped over his head sagged toward the floor. Track marks swell over his forearms. With a subtle shift of his head, he appears to nod at me without seeing who I am, then droops closer to the floor.

The next three cages are empty, and the last holds Howard Riddy, standing on top of the bench, his gut rolling over a towel wrapped around his waist. "No bounce to this thing," he says. "Can't wait to get back to my trampoline."

"Keep your curtains closed."

"Fine."

"I mean it."

"I said fine."

"You're out in five minutes."

"Wearing what?"

"The department will give you something."

Riddy slides down the wall until he's sitting on the bench. "It'll probably be ugly, something irritating to my skin. You should know I have very sensitive skin."

"Officer Harter offered to give you clothes from your closet."

"Irritated skin is worth irritating that bastard."

"Tell me about Henry Clayton."

Standing, Riddy moves toward me with an odd shuffle. A dance of some sort, a hiss of his bare feet over smooth cement. "Henry said you'd ask me about him sooner or later. I didn't think it would be this much later. Why don't you call him and find out for yourself?"

"How much did he pay you?"

"Pretty well. You should call him. Ask him where he gets his money. You'd think a man in prison all those years would have trouble finding a job. Or maybe it's the cash settlement this state pays a man for losing his youth to a wrongful murder conviction." Riddy cocks his head, hissing his feet in place, his stare again moving over my face as if expecting a violent reaction from me. I disappoint him, and his odd little dance stops.

"Tell me about this," I say, removing the photograph from my duffel bag.

"Looks like you took something from my house, Officer Hill. Isn't theft a crime?" Riddy shrugs at the photograph. "It's in color, but it's so hard to tell 'cause those boys don't like color."

"What were you doing photographing skinheads?"

"If you think I'm gonna call you the 'N' word," he says, raising his hands, "you're absolutely wrong. Mother would kill me from her throne in heaven if I ever used the 'N' word. She'd stand right up and destroy me in her home with a lightning bolt if she had to." He lowers his hands, looks at the photograph more thoughtfully. "Twelve young men. Very young. In case you haven't noticed, I'll tell you. I've always preferred young men." He pinches at the towel draped around him. "The photo's from seventeen years ago. Tastes change after seventeen years."

"When was Clayton in your house?"

"Which time?"

"The last time."

"This morning."

"Why?"

Riddy's stare remains on the picture. "First I've got to tell you something. It's this funny thing I've learned about the law. Listen well now because it's important and it goes like this. If a girl is one day away from her seventeenth birthday and has voluntary sex with her seventeen-year-old boyfriend, it's a felony in this state. A serious felony. The boyfriend's branded a sex offender for life, same as a real pedophile rapist. Sex offender lists don't make the distinction. People so goddamn holy about who's living in their neighborhood can look him up on the Internet, track him down, and harass him until he kills himself. But once the same girl gets a day older, an old man like me can have her body any way he wants to, and if she's willing it's not even a traffic ticket." Riddy shakes his head. "Don't you think that's funny, Officer Hill?"

"You can stay here as long as it takes to answer my question."

"I'm answering your question, like singing a song. A few verses here and there before I get to the chorus." He reaches to the photograph and runs his fingers over the glass. "I learned the law, then I learned to adapt. Seventeen is as low as I'll go. Seventeen is like a minimum speed limit, only fatal if you go too young." He smiles his hopeless smile. "Seventeen's not young enough to fully scratch my itch. But it has to do."

Glancing over my shoulder at Zookeeper, Riddy reads my mind. "This whole town treats me like a mascot, squeezes my cheeks and pats my mischief lovingly on the head. But I bet you'd like to choke me. Maybe you'd yank my prick off, which is all right with me since prick is a good name for it these days. I'll tell you what, though, I don't like you either. You think you're so damn special, and you've got your mind made up about everybody else. You and those skinheads, you and Henry Clayton. You're more alike than different."

I step away from the cage and Riddy laughs at me. "Look

how you remove yourself from the situation, Officer Hill. Don't let yourself get caught doing anything rash to a lovable old man on a booking room video camera. Too bad. Me and my lawyer could use the extra cash."

"You know Clayton murdered my parents."

"Who the hell cares what you think I know, I wasn't there. Although it's clear the prosecutors and the governor disagree with you."

"You're a pathetic old man."

"Then the difference between us is limited to age."

I stuff the photograph into my duffel bag, walk away from his cage. He had his answers prepared and my questions triggered them for his amusement. Riddy shouts after me. "Call Henry Clayton!"

The earnest shift in his voice distracts me, causes me to suspect there's some concern in Riddy after all. I stop and look back at him. "If I decide to call, what should I say?"

Riddy drops his towel, rests his hands beside his prick. "I don't give a fuck," he says, and laughs. "But I get an extra two thousand if you do." Scratching himself, Riddy says lightly, "And now, my verse and chorus are at an end."

"Look at you," I say. "What would Mother Marilyn think of her baby boy now?"

As I pass the control desk, Zookeeper moans at me. "Wish you hadn't said that."

Howard Riddy's howl fills the booking room. "Don't you speak Mother's name again! Don't even think it!" The rage aggravates Zookeeper, but it soothes me. It calms the violence I was prepared to commit against an old man in a cage.

The motor within a surveillance camera comes to life. Mounted to the ceiling of the police station's underground parking garage, the camera groans, turns until its black lens aims at me, then falls silent.

I remove a note from beneath my car's wiper blade. Initialed "H.C.," the note lists a telephone number I've already memorized. A cell phone number, it emphasizes, so I can reach him anywhere, at any time. The note has less impact on me than the paper it's written on. Letterhead from the desk of Fred Schumacher.

10

I star-67, then dial the number.

Lying in bed, lights out, I listen to the start of the first ring and feel a connection develop through plastic, wires, and air. I hang up before the start of the second ring. This was something I had to do, to toy with my own tension.

My phone rings four times before the answering machine picks up. The flatness of my recorded voice makes me cringe. *I'm not available to answer. Leave a message.*

After twin beeps, words come over the answering machine as if spoken through a cloth covering the speaker. "You know who this is, Officer Hill. Daffodils. Why won't you call me about the daffodils?"

"Don't screw with me," I say to the machine, then pick up the phone. "Up yours, Jack. Don't joke with me. Not about this." I slam the phone back in its cradle. It's the sort of thing Jack does to me, always looking to make a joke without thinking things through. It makes me wonder why he bothers with me, all his sensitive talk, when he pulls this kind of shit.

A glow from the streetlamp flows over my bedroom ceiling. The effect resembles a movie screen the moment before the start of the picture. Poppa's favorite Hitchcock movie comes to mind. *Vertigo.* The image overhead makes me wonder if I'm afraid of looking up.

I consider the distance between my bed and the coffee table downstairs in the living room, where the Department of Justice report lies opened between the first two chapters. Unbearable, I had thought, and soon realized the small print and scientific language agitated me rather than put me to sleep. Tragedy fit into types and categories. Categories more like road maps to predetermined destinies. When winter arrives, I'll invite Jack over so he can watch me throw it into the fireplace.

The phone rings four times again and I expect Jack will offer his apologies through my answering machine, with an order for me to lighten up. Instead, Auntie Doria's desperation fills the room. "I know you're home, Richie child."

I'm breathless at the receiver. "Auntie?"

"He won't leave my kitchen."

"Who won't leave?"

Her voice cautious. "He's sitting here at my kitchen table, quoting Scripture. It's after midnight."

"Auntie—who?"

There's a sound like a rush of wind through the phone.

"When you call about the daffodils," Henry Clayton says, and his voice claws inside my head, "let my phone ring more than once."

11

Only the bulb over the stovetop glows in Auntie Doria's kitchen. The room flickers as if a draft toys with a candle's flame. Auntie Doria sits at the table, half lost in a shadow. Without her glasses, in shadow, her eyes appear retracted beneath folds of skin. Perhaps it's best, considering the man sitting beside her.

"Now," Henry Clayton asks me. "Do I have your attention?"

He pushes his chair back from the table and clutches a book to his chest, its dark cover embossed gold with the words *Living Bible.* Dressed in a black suit, coat buttoned over a white shirt and black tie. It's the uniform of the religion peddlers that police chase away from storefronts, most often on Mondays after Sundays' encouragement to proselytize. Over the blackness of Clayton's coat, and his shadows, the words of golden color, *Living Bible,* float blazing above his heart as if uncertain where to land. His eyes capture the weak light in this room, shine at me their pale blue.

"I see you put on your police uniform for me," he says. "No tie or hat, though. Bet you look good under your hat. Squares your jawline and all that." He nods his head toward the barrel of my gun. "Are you here to make an arrest, or kill me?"

I take a step closer to the table and extend my weapon. "Let me see your wallet."

"You could at least have called to thank me for the daffodils, Richard, considering the tip I gave to Doria here. A thank you would have been nice of you."

I gesture for the wallet.

"I've been ordained, Richard, can't you see?" He twists his head in an odd half circle toward his right shoulder, a small gesture he repeats, then blinks. "Is this how you treat men of faith, an exonerated man of faith in particular?

"Do it."

He pauses at the sight of my gun, smiles when I lean forward with the barrel, then reaches inside his suit coat. "Matthew 22:20," he says in a chant. He tosses his wallet on the table. "Do you know what I'm talking about, Richard? Matthew 22:20. Jesus said, 'Give to Caesar what belongs to him. But everything that belongs to God must be given to God.' "

Auntie Doria exhales and coughs twice. It's her sound of disapproval, an inherent reaction even now, whenever she believes a heathen has manipulated Scripture. She turns toward Clayton, her eyes remaining invisible. "You got the numbers wrong."

Clayton twists his head toward his right shoulder once more, a bit deeper, this time starting with a bit of a jolt. "I did?" He smiles broadly, as if trying to distract himself from his odd motion.

"Matthew 22:21. You said 22:20. It's 22:21. And what has Matthew got to do with you anyway?"

He raises his *Living Bible* to his chin. "It has everything to do with me, Doria. It's the Lord's prohibition against using His name to justify disobedience against civil society. In this case, Matthew 22:21, forgive my math, Jesus instructs even those who despised Caesar to pay their taxes to him." He taps his *Living Bible* on his lower lip, watches me fumble with his wallet in my left hand, my gun gripped in my right. "Jesus tells us to follow man's law. And under the law, a man doesn't rape or murder. Did you know I've always believed this way, Richard, Doria, even before I found the Lord? I'm a man of faith now, have been for a long time, an exonerated man of faith."

"Ordained by who?" Auntie Doria says.

"Does it really matter by who, or where, or by what? Jesus appears most often the strongest in the souls of the discarded and imprisoned. He detested tradition over substance, and He branded traditional religious leaders hypocrites for failing to recognize how simple this substance is. Jesus is Lord, and His is a Kingdom of Heaven, not of earth. This is the Good News, Doria. If you've truly read the substance of Matthew instead of memorizing its numbers, the substance over the tradition, you know I'm ordained as thoroughly as any other preacher."

Auntie Doria snorts. "You're not proving your religion quoting this and that from the Bible in my kitchen, passages a child would know to say like a parrot, and getting the numbers messed up. Getting the numbers messed up means you don't know where to look."

His driver's license appears authentic, but his picture looks as though it came from a prison-booking photo. Maybe it's the best he can do in front of a camera. It identifies him, Henry Clayton, matching date of birth, and an address in a part of Red River Falls that keeps the police force busy. A few dollars inside the billfold, a Dollar-Mart receipt, and the rest of the pockets are empty. I toss it on the table. For the sake of Auntie Doria, I shouldn't say a thing; because Clayton's here, there's no way I'm avoiding it. "Words in the Bible mean whatever people want them to mean."

Clayton reaches for his wallet, slips it back in his suit coat. "It sounds as though you spent your youth on death row instead of me. For crimes you didn't commit."

I'm more of a witness to my reaction than anything else, beside him watching the back of my right hand rise, attached to my gun, falling fast, striking sideways against his face. My hand again in the air, Clayton unmoving in his chair, face turned aside, ready to take it.

"Richie!" Auntie Doria's hand clasps around my wrist. She repeats my name softly, her grip as strong as any man's.

"It's all right, Doria," Clayton says. His eyes blink at the light over the stove. "Matthew 5:39, Richard. I am not to seek out personal revenge against you, but to turn the other cheek. I am here to love you, to help you, to take on your extraordinary burdens you do not ask or even want me to take on. Like Jesus, Matthew 5:40 and 41, you are the soldier, I am your subservient. I am here to willingly carry your burden an extra mile. I've got it right, Doria, don't I? You know I've got the numbers right this time."

Clayton's neck stretched below me, I notice the scar under his right ear. Thick and purple, etched in broad grooves, as though leeches lay crossed over his skin where his swastika had been. By her small gasp for breath, I know Auntie Doria notices the mark too, and I wonder whether it's a horror or a miracle she sees, a cross such as this rising from the blackness of a ruined swastika.

"Even on death row, I had the option to remove it by laser." Clayton straightens and brings his fingers to his scar. His twisting motion, this time, is more subtle. "They say there's a student ranked last in every medical school graduation class. Their last place finish lies masked beneath the title of doctor; they find work in prisons. Like Job, I needed to suffer for my sins. But my sins are not murder, they are not rape. I am here to walk that extra mile for you, Richard."

Auntie Doria releases my wrist, and I fall back in the chair opposite Clayton. "You're still wearing the skinhead's haircut."

Clayton brings his *Living Bible* to the welt rising on his cheek. He smiles. "Well, Richard. I take after my father. Bald as an eagle since twenty-four. I suppose I should have grown it while I had it. Try telling that to a punk, the way I was back then."

I stare at the length of my arm, to my right hand still gripped around my gun. The barrel shifts a bit, away from Clayton toward the kitchen window reflecting my darkness among dim light and gray shadows; the barrel's length seems to grow, its potential devastation magnified as if expecting a decision to be made.

"I didn't rape your mother," Clayton says. "I didn't murder your parents. I am here to help you find the truth, and this truth is not written within my heart, but within the evil heart of another man."

I close my eyes, hear the cocking of the hammer, pound the butt of the gun on the table. Auntie Doria reaches for my wrist once more and I order her to sit. "Please, Auntie," I say. My words tremble; sweat mixes with tears below my eyes. "Let me deal with this."

Clayton repeats his denials, forces me to listen with . . . forces me with what? I'm drawn to listen by his preacher's voice, something like a bellow, and words sounding as though forced through the shape of a stagecrafted smile.

"Like you, Richard. I cried. I cried at the trial, and I know you saw me. Even when you sat on the witness stand falsely pointing me out as the rapist and killer, I witnessed your surprise. Not even my lawyer picked up on it. The hitch in your speech, the widening of your eyes. You wondered, Richard. I knew from your voice and eyes how much you wondered about a man who you claimed butchered your parents, the same man who could cry over your testimony."

The weight of the gun increases in my hand beneath the flow of Clayton's words.

"You're checking my wallet, checking my driver's license. Checking my photograph in particular. You're wondering about me, Richard. You're wondering what you really saw when you were a boy."

"I saw what you did to Momma. I saw you kill them both."

Clayton moves his *Living Bible* over his chest, and his blue stare freezes the air between us. "Do you think you could repeat word for word what we've said here tonight? I mean, word for word? You'd get the gist of it right, of course, but you couldn't repeat word for word what we've said. What makes you think our eyes are any different from our ears, especially with you back then, a child so traumatized? Your trauma so intense it exists even now." He leans toward me over the table, his *Living Bible,* aloft at his shoulder, floats with his hand. "What you saw through your eyes blinded by fear and hate was the gist of things. A skinny white boy with swastikas, raping and killing. But you didn't see the word for word. No, sir. It wasn't me. But it's okay if you still want to believe the gist of things rather than the word for word."

"Why would it be okay with you?"

Clayton twists his head toward the cross in his neck. "All I want is for you to give me a chance to prove you're wrong." My gun, now dangling in tangled fingertips, aims loosely toward the floor. "Your eyes overlooked something tonight, Richard."

Clayton sets his *Living Bible* on the table, pats it gently, then reaches inside his coat to open his wallet. He removes the Dollar-Mart receipt and lays it in his palm as if it were the last bit of food on earth. "Look at the color of the paper, how yellow the edges have turned." He motions it toward me. I set my gun on my lap and take it. "Look at it more closely, Richard. It's not just a receipt but a credit card receipt, and it's quite old. The name is mine. The signature mine. And the date and time."

I stare into the paper cupped in his hand, and both seem to pull on me as if dragging me unwillingly into a different aspect of the past. He sets the thin paper on the table.

"He showed me," Auntie Doria says. "That's the reason I let

him past the soda bottles. Because of his paper, and you. Certainly not because of his so-called preaching." Her criticism of his faith, though, sounds more cautious than before. "I let him in, and I called you. You needed to see for yourself."

"In prison," Clayton says, "every inmate wants a DNA test, the guilty as much as the innocent. The guilty because they're bored and have nothing to lose; they believe mistakes can be made with anything. But for the innocent, we know we need something, something extra besides wanting a DNA test before a lawyer will give you his time for free. In my case it was this receipt. It proved things enough to give me hope and a willing lawyer. The DNA test proved the rest and set me free."

He punches each word through his lips. "I did not rape your mother. I did not kill your parents. I am here to help you find out who did."

"Why didn't this receipt come out at the trial?"

"The police took it when they arrested me. I told my lawyer back then, but he said it couldn't be found, and he wasn't particularly interested in believing me over cops he'd gone fishing with for so many years. You know how things go, Richard."

"How'd you get it now?"

"There are things you don't understand about this town. Howard Riddy got it for me."

"And the note on my car, the paper taken from Fred Schumacher's office?"

"Riddy." Clayton smiles. "There are things a man can get his hands on when everyone thinks you're a harmless old nut. Even pieces of paper the authorities want hidden."

"Seems to me this receipt proves your guilt. You were arrested in the neighborhood within the hour of my 911 call. The receipt is a forged piece of bullshit. So your story's bullshit."

"The DNA test proved up my innocence, and so the truth of the receipt has been confirmed. What did my pardon conclude?

Yes. 'Henry Clayton's innocence has become irrefutable.' Cops can lie, Richard, are you prepared to deny that? Two cops arrested me, and they made one big lie about when and where. The receipt, if you'll give in a half inch and think about it, proves corruption. How deep it goes is part of what I need to help you find out."

I never saw Clayton smile during the trial; I anticipate the brightness of it to fade away now. When it does, I inspect his face, its shape and texture. Older. Creased. The high cheekbones have fallen within a heavier man. But it's him. And the boy within me, hidden within the folds of a tablecloth, inspects him as well.

"You've convinced everyone who matters you're innocent. What do you want with me?"

Clayton groans a bit, as if my question grips at his heart. "Because," he says, "the Lord has commanded me through Matthew. I do not question our Lord."

I look into the shadows in this small kitchen, toward Auntie Doria. "Richie child," she says. "Regardless of anything else, how much longer can you stand to live the way you have? This could be your salvation."

The sound of my salvation from Auntie Doria's lips in response to the arrival of Henry Clayton strikes me as the sound of smoke solidifying into human flesh. The boy inside me clenches his fists even as I speak.

"All right, Auntie. All right."

Clayton lifts his stare toward the ceiling over Auntie Doria's kitchen and praises Jesus. Makes Auntie Doria hiss like her ancient teakettle. I look toward the paper, the receipt, and read again the words aiding Clayton's effort to move me in a direction I could never have imagined. Henry Clayton's computer-printed name, and his signature below it, on a credit card receipt. Created the date of the murders, less than an hour before the murders began. From a Dollar-Mart store in Nebraska, at least a seven-hour drive from Red River Falls.

"You keep the receipt," Clayton says, his head twisting toward his scar. "Like you said, I've been proven innocent to the people who matter. I don't need it anymore."

I fold the receipt once and slip it in my shirt pocket. "I said all right. I said so twice. Give me a couple of days to adjust to this." Auntie Doria nods her head.

Clayton's voice turns adamant. "Check out whatever you want, but don't keep me waiting. Even the Lord moves away from people who witness His miracles yet remain nonbelievers. And, you know, it really wasn't nice of you to wait so long to thank me for the daffodils."

"I still haven't thanked you."

"I have confidence, Richard. You will thank me. You will one day want to walk the extra mile for me. I already told you that's from Matthew." He winks at Auntie Doria. "And I got my numbers straightened out now."

"Leave this house," I say, raising my gun.

Clayton closes his eyes momentarily, then stands. "You know how to reach me." With his walk through the kitchen and darkened living room, his lips silently imitate prayer. I close the front door after he leaves. While Auntie Doria resets the soda bottles, I watch Clayton through the front window; he moves away in the glow of the yellow-orange porch light, the cement walk beneath him appearing absorbed to his ankles. Moments later his white head and dark suit splinter into shades of gray, flesh misting back into smoke until he vanishes.

Auntie Doria calls for me from her kitchen, frozen at the table. Her stare also has frozen toward the space Henry Clayton recently occupied. "He left his bible behind."

It's a ragged-looking thing from the Red River Falls Lord of Light Community Church. Vinyl cover curled at the corners, shredded along its front edge. Unimpressive without Clayton and his dark suit.

There's nothing to say to Auntie Doria about her doubts. Her words sound empty, as if a child's voice calls out lost from the depth of a cave. "He got it wrong about Matthew, Richie. He's got it all wrong."

12

I've always respected Auntie Doria's views on the Bible, but not in the way she had once hoped. Over the years, I've learned to keep my distance and my cynicism sealed up.

It's my appeasement of her faith more than anything else. The plastic smile I give her, the polite cough, forms of autopilot the secular switch on to survive in an environment of constantly vocal Good Christians. My perception of facts immunizes me against proselytizing, even Auntie Doria's. I've never challenged her out loud, although her expression of faith succeeds only in feeding my doubt, confirms my long-ago conversion from agnostic to atheist.

Respect for Auntie Doria, and love, made me attend St. Rita of Cascia church all those years I lived with her, never missing a Sunday. But I never believed, not after what I saw. I know, of course, that Auntie Doria has understood this about me for a long time.

She asks me to stay the night moments before I would have asked to stay. Our reasons feel similar, although she expresses her concerns about Clayton with her faith.

"It's Matthew 22:21, not 22:20," she says. "The Lord's words about giving to Caesar what belongs to Caesar. A preacher doesn't quote the numbers and get it wrong and say he's a preacher, that's what I know."

"He admitted he got the number wrong."

"It's more than just the numbers. Matthew 22:21 is about

Jesus surviving a test from the Pharisees. A test among all kinds of tests and trickery that meant life or death. Only the shallow and snake oil salesmen think it's simply about paying taxes or obeying man's laws."

There's a scent of ambivalence in her breath, her agonizing over whether she has helped me or irreparably harmed me. I can't appease her. It's impossible to say to Auntie Doria that the Christian Bible is just an ancient book.

I bring my hand to my chest, to the pocket holding the paper proving Henry Clayton was at least seven hours away from Red River Falls the night of Momma's rape and my parents' murders. "What should I do?"

For once I can clearly see her eyes tonight. The depth of their brownness. The permanent way they hold my image. "You can't keep living the way you do. It's hardly living at all."

I smile. "No guidance from Scripture, about loving my enemy?"

"No," she says. "It's not easy to know what Clayton is to you."

Reaching for Auntie Doria, holding her, I feel her shivering doubt mixed with hope. The expression of faith in this home, and the uncompromising, opposing views birthed from the same Scripture. Any particular way to be a Christian inevitably causes disgust in all the other ways to be a Christian. Devotion to particular versions of faith not only makes the world's turmoil possible, but inevitable. A similar battle has begun between my faith in what I witnessed from under the table as a child, and what I've witnessed tonight as a man. A civil war beneath my skin.

"No," I say. "I'm not happy the way I am."

She squeezes me close to her breast. "Praise Jesus," she says.

Before she leaves me for sleep, I smile my plastic smile into her eyes filled with faith. It remains the best I can do.

13

I ask for Jack's help while visiting Momma's and Poppa's graves Tuesday morning. He's insulted when I tell him he doesn't have to feel obligated. "Of course I'm obligated," he says, but doesn't explain why. A more normal man, I suppose, would already know why.

"What does Clayton look like?"

"Like the man who killed my parents."

"What's your impression of him?"

"He's a born-again Christian."

"Oh?" Jack says, brushing a leaf off Momma's headstone. "Which kind?"

"There are kinds?"

Jack rises and falls on the balls of his feet at a slow tempo. "You know, I'm a born-again." He faces Momma's gravestone, unaffected by my surprise, still rising and falling on his feet. "You should ask me about me sometimes. Over three years as squad partners, you'd think you'd know about me. I doubt you'd know anything about me unless I volunteered information."

"You're always volunteering."

"There are two kinds, really. The good kind and the not-so-good kind."

"Seems to me the good kind is the one the good kind says he happens to be."

"It's got nothing to do with denomination." Jack angles

toward Poppa's headstone. "The not-so-good kind are more noisy about it on the surface and quiet about it in practice in their private lives. You know, the ones divorced three times before they're forty, the ones whose children have turned away from them and all they can do is blame the other parent whenever they can. The ones who talk about themselves and never ask questions about others. The ones who constantly smile yet never think anything's funny. You know the kind I'm talking about."

I cough, a *yes* kind of a cough.

"The noisy ones think they're not so noisy because they're the kind of people who think they know everything about omnipotence, so how can what they have to say be noise?"

"But the jokes you make about religion, worse than Drano's."

"Satan didn't create swearing, good laughs, or good alcohol. At least I don't think Satan did."

"Well," I say. "I didn't know there are quiet born-again Christians."

"That's because we're quiet." Jack jabs his elbow into my ribs. "Here I am. Exhibit A."

"Now aren't you committing the sin of saying you're the good kind, just like the not-so-good kinds do?"

Jack doesn't move, focused on Poppa's headstone. "True faith is personal, not for public display. But you asked me about myself. Finally. So I answered. I'll let others decide whether I'm the good kind or not. Especially when my time comes. I'll be judged about it then."

"You've never asked me to join your church. Aren't you supposed to do that?"

"When I think you're ready I'll ask. For now, I'm not asking."

Rejected by a proselytizer for over three years. Now there's something to think about. Thought it would be a relief, so why does it bother me now, especially coming from Jack?

"Which kind of born-again is Clayton?" Jack asks.

"Auntie Doria has her doubts. The doubtful kind."

Jack reaches into his shirt pocket, removes Clayton's Dollar-Mart receipt and studies it some more. "Looks authentic. Seeing this must have been like a kick to your balls." Jack cocks his head. "Two days ago, my boy kicked me in the balls."

"Tyler's head doesn't come up much past your knees."

"What I meant to say was, he kicked a ball into my balls. Sent me reeling to the floor."

"Oh."

My flowers, the freshest red roses from Auntie Doria's shop, rest between Momma and Poppa's headstones. I'm grateful for the absence of daffodils and notes from Clayton. Grateful to have been left alone for a few days since Clayton's appearance at Auntie Doria's house. Jack grunts through his mouth and nose.

"Never thought a sperm of mine would grow up one day and kick a ball into my balls."

I watch this man, watching me. Obviously grateful when he's able to make a man like me laugh. A good born-again Christian. Quiet about it. I'm a witness to this secular miracle.

"After shift tomorrow," Jack says, offering me the receipt. I stuff it in my shirt pocket. "We'll get started."

He closes his eyes, moves his lips, a silent Amen to the gravestones, then raises his chin and opens his eyes. I turn from the graves and take the lead toward our squad car dim in morning fog.

Wonderment overtakes me concerning the absence of ghosts. This would have been the best time, the best place, for ghosts. Perhaps they have abandoned me. The less painful conclusion, though, is that they were chased away, banished by evidence of the secular resurrection of Henry Clayton.

14

When I was in high school, one evening well after dusk, I was observed running laps around the track. A coach with a stopwatch clocking my mile. "I saw you on the way to my car," he said, and gushed over his watch. "Four-twenty-three. A mile in four-twenty-three." He leaned against the fence separating us, asked me what year I was in.

I didn't answer. You're a white boy, was all I thought. Years of practice at isolation helped me make him disappear, easy to ignore.

"Sophomore?" he called out. "Why haven't I seen you before? We could really use you on the track team. Hey, boy, there could be a scholarship in your future."

I had planned another two miles around the track. Instead I jogged away from the track to a dirt path toward home while this white boy's praise turned to anger, anger to hate, until hate expressed itself as nigger.

Like my father did when he was in high school, I ran. His path to college through a track scholarship wasn't mine to take. Running took me to a better kind of isolation than I had previously known. A place of complete euphoria where my heart, lungs and legs performed without effort, and my mind lost itself in the feel of the wind. I'd run forever if I could. I'd die trying to run forever, to hold on to euphoria. Often I'd come home after one of my runs, forget about Auntie Doria's soda bottles inside the front door, and send them skittering in pieces over her floor. She cleaned up the glass without complaint, hoping sleep would overtake me. Instead I stayed awake in bed, concentrating on the euphoria running gave me. Sometimes, yes, it worked, by carrying me to a place between sleep and wakefulness where all I saw was the whiteness of my bedroom ceiling. So I ran to exhaustion before bed each night in the hope of running away from my nightmare in sleep. And it worked often enough to keep me running.

I found out, though. Some teachers and coaches took offense at a boy with a talent who refused to lend himself to the high school's cause. The large boy who wouldn't play football. The lanky boy with a ninety-mile-an-hour arm who preferred to work after school for his family than play ball. I learned my lesson in the hallway outside the cafeteria. White boys and dark brown boys taught me with their fists and their feet. The coach who had timed me at the track came by to watch, said nothing, and let the boys walk away as if I had accidentally pummeled my head against their feet and fists. Students in the cafeteria glanced at me over their lunches and stayed in their chairs the ten minutes it took before I could stand on my own.

I dove deeper into isolation. Finished high school as a home-schooled boy, taught by Auntie Doria between flower and plant sales at *Naiveté*. Inside Auntie's shop, I dissolved into Momma's books, at a desk in the back room among the humid scents of floral arrangements and potting soil. I read them carefully, imagined the moment when Momma's eyes traveled over the same words, her hands turning the pages I turned. It gave me a vivid sense we were together again, in words, thought, and touch, though separated by time.

She had underlined in places that struck me as odd. For example, she underlined "nigger" in *The Adventures of Huckleberry Finn* each time the word appeared, and she left a note in a margin in the last chapter: *The slave owners certainly didn't call their slaves African-American Jim,* Momma wrote. *Know the truth about history, make it accurate no matter how painful, to better shape the present and future.* This is where I saw Poppa's handwriting below Momma's, the only place he wrote in any of Momma's books. *But Diane, dear. This sort of thing really pisses the black man off.*

I smiled at their exchange, pictured Momma and Poppa debating this single, most vile word, with cups of tea in their hands while listening to a piano concerto play softly on the stereo. From her chair at the store counter, partly hidden behind red gladioli, Auntie Doria spoke of Momma and Poppa as perfect examples of something she called the human multiplication equation. It's a simple formula, she insisted, able to measure a person's worth. According to Auntie, imagine multiplying Momma and Poppa until there are millions and billions of them, to the point where they make up the entire population of the earth. Then consider what the earth would be like. How peaceful, clean, enjoyable, and forgiving. Auntie believed if all the world were populated by Momma and Poppa, billions of times over, the earth would still be the Garden of Eden. I consider this the best thing Auntie, or anyone, has ever said about them.

These days I run for the same reason that got me beat up in high school. To find precious isolation in a place of euphoria. But I've gone beyond a single purpose. My route takes me east of *Naiveté,* across the street of racial separation into the neighborhoods of white parents and their children. A biracial man running down white boy streets after sundown, in gray shorts and shirt, sweating. I carry my wallet inside my water pack, a couple of dollars and a cell phone. When I'm asked to stop running by Red River Falls cops in their squad car, I flip my wallet, show my badge, and rattle off a few names from the commander's office. After three years on the force, I don't have to flip the badge anymore. From behind, they stop me. When they see my face, the white boy officers look disappointed, mutter my name, and drive off.

I find joy in this. It adds to the euphoria of running. I suppose it's similar to Momma and Poppa's debate over that hated word from *Huckleberry Finn,* whether it should be erased off the pages or modified to appease sensibilities, or whether it should be studied and examined in order to help wipe out the hate that birthed it.

I study the white boys driving by me, how they slow their cars, angle their eyes toward me, then drive off. Some to smile and wave. Others blast their acidic white boy rock and roll on their stereos, screaming a song's unintelligible lyrics at me. Still others show fear, and more than a few utter the word. If I could, I would tell Momma and Poppa the experience a biracial man has running down a white boy's street these days is not entirely different from what Jim experienced as an escaped slave floating on a raft down the Mississippi in the 1840s. Regardless of the reaction white boys display, decent, indifferent, or repulsive, I'm identified first by my skin.

A quick bleat from a squad car's siren goes off behind me while I run down the center of the road. I'm three blocks from *Naiveté,* a final stretch of white-boy neighborhood before I cross the divide. Slowing, I'm careful to unhook my water pack so as not to imply I'm reaching for a gun. Another bleat of the siren, a short flash of MARS lights, the squad car pulls beside me.

"Stop running," I hear. I turn and find a face darker than mine behind the wheel.

"What the hell are you doing?" Larry Grimes says. I look into his window; he's without a squad partner. "Get in."

"Why?"

He nods toward some white boys gathering under a streetlight at the next corner. Teenagers with buzzed hair, shirts off.

From here, on a couple of boys, I can make out the markings below their right ears.

"I've been trailing you for a few miles now," Grimes says. "Get in the goddamn squad car. Now."

15

Larry Grimes secures his gun and police belt inside the squad car and pops open the trunk. He digs through emergency equipment and some towels. Although it's nearing seven, four hours into second shift, his uniform is crisp, his body strong and compact inside it. When he stands, he hands me a baseball glove and a ball, slips his left hand into another glove.

"What about the bat?"

Grimes slams the trunk shut. "It's for something else," he says. "The mitts and ball only make it look like a baseball bat."

He waves me over to the first diamond in Farrow Park, takes the mound while I stand behind home plate. The park is an oasis of green. Four groomed and lighted baseball diamonds, a spray park, an elaborate playground for children, a gazebo band shell, and narrow crushed limestone paths meandering the park's borders among forest trees. It provides space for community picnics and flea markets, as well as Fourth of July fireworks and fall harvest festivals, and it sits on the western edge of Red River Falls where neither black nor white holds a monopoly. It's a place Red River Falls intended for equilibrium, proof of possibilities and peace through government expenditure and constant maintenance. More often it's a place requiring extra police attention.

For the first few pitches, Grimes throws easily. Soon we're in a rhythm, the slap of the ball into our gloves predictable. I lower into a catcher's crouch, Grimes's pitching motion increasingly polished. It becomes obvious he's had experience at this beyond boyhood pickup games, perhaps tempted by the promise of a scholarship the way I once was, and he either took the opportunity or was taught a similar lesson.

While he throws, Grimes's face appears blank, mouth closed, eyes emotionless. His skin shifts from dark brown to black beneath the artificial lights; his deep blue uniform turns just as black. Caught in the trance of his pitching rhythm, I see him as a space where a person is supposed to be, a shadow detached from its body.

He breaks rhythm, extends his gloved hand toward me, then reaches his other hand back and fires the ball. A sting to my hand, and I ask him, throwing the ball back, "How fast?" Saying nothing, he fires again, faster this time, more of a sting. His pitches come more quickly, centered down the middle of the plate. His eyes close with each pitch, face drawn tight, and he throws fire.

I hold the ball, shake my hand out of the mitt. "Take it easy on me!" But the next ball comes as fast, and with the next, he puts a curve on it, flying it high into my chest and knocking me on the ground.

He comes down from the mound, stands over me, hardly breathing, his face dry and relaxed. "How old am I?" he asks.

"I'd guess you're in your late thirties."

"No guessing. How old?"

"I don't know. Not exactly."

"Am I married? Any kids?"

"I have no idea."

He kicks at the ground near my hip, spins away toward the squad car. Brushing myself off, I follow. My left hand aches from the sting of his pitches, and I wonder if he had planned this as some sort of penalty. At the trunk, tossing the mitts and ball inside, closing it with a slam, he walks around me and stops at the driver's door. "This shift is my last patrol," he says. "As of eleven-thirty tonight, I've quit." He watches me rub at my sore hand. "I'll drive you home."

From Farrow Park toward the divide, he already knows where I live. His jaw works at something. A thought he's been meaning to say. I tell him he's got a hell of a fastball and a wicked curve.

"Double A," he says. "As far as I got."

"Why are you quitting?"

"I'm forty-one," he says, glancing at me. "I have two kids. A daughter who's ten, another daughter who's eight. I was married for eleven years, been a widower for six." He rattles this information off like he's reading a list. Even the next thing he says sounds as though it comes from a machine. "In your three years on the force you've never asked me a thing. You've never learned a thing about me. It's clear you've never thought to try."

"So you asked me to play catch with you, to get to know me better?"

I've made him laugh, and he winds his head about with his laughter. "Those white boys down the block were waiting for you."

"How would you know?"

"Because I know."

"Can you be more specific?"

"No." He brightens and fades as we drive past streetlights. "You're an ass, Hill. You always have been. You come and you go not giving a shit about anything or anyone. Do your job and go. There's no smiling, not even on the surface."

"I don't owe you an explanation."

"I'm not asking for one. I'm not taking notes on your opinions."

"Then why are you bothering to warn me about some white boys?"

"Because," he says. "I'm a cop."

"So I'm part of your job description?"

"That's all."

We reach the dividing street, from white to black, and move away from his patrol zone two miles from Momma and Poppa's house. "What did those white boys want with me?"

"They wanted to hurt you. They wouldn't mind to see you dead."

"Do you know why?"

He laughs again, this time a helpless burst from his gut. "With those white boys, there are lots of reasons. With you in particular, it's because of Henry Clayton."

Grimes pulls to the side of the road a mile from the house. He turns to watch me, studies me, and shakes his head. "You look like I've run you over."

Taken the strength out of me is more accurate. Replaced it with something alien. "At least tell me about Henry Clayton."

The squad car moves forward again. Its modest acceleration eases me back against the seat. Grimes says nothing until he parks in front of Momma and Poppa's house. "I've been on the Red River Falls police force for eight years. For eight years I've shown my smile to the white boys. I've listened to their stories, laughed at their jokes, gone to their weddings, and cried at their grandparents' funerals. I know their middle names, know when to slip them a birthday card." He looks out his window at Momma and Poppa's house. "I've watched you. I know about you. I've known what you're about since you came to the force. The thing is, you've got it backwards. I've disappeared by blending in. You've made yourself stand out by standing alone. I'm the invisible man, not you."

He rubs at his face, watches me now with some small level of compassion. "I'm considered one of the boys on the force, second shift, even if I'm black, especially since I'm black. The white boys know me as a black man who goes along to get along. I'm invisible and I'm able to hear things you can't because no one thinks I'm paying attention."

"Do you care?"

"I care enough to quit."

"How does that help me?"

"It doesn't. I'm quitting so I don't have to deal with it anymore."

"What about Clayton?"

"He's why I'm telling you to quit and move away. It's your answer, same as mine."

"You won't tell me why?"

He hangs his hands over the steering wheel, his eyes turned to glass as if looking inward. "There's something about Red River Falls. A mood, desperation or apathy, I really don't know. It allows old ways to exist, maybe because its roots are so deep. Otherwise, no, I can't tell you why."

"Then you should've left me alone tonight," I say, reaching for the door handle. "Run away. Keep your bullshit to yourself."

He grabs my shirt, squeezes it in his hands and pulls me back toward him. "I'd die for my daughters. So you better damn well believe I'd let another man die if that's what it takes to keep them safe." He holds me as if ordering me to witness his face, its blend of despair and conviction. Before me is a man with a look similar to Poppa's, so determined to sacrifice himself for the sake of his child, to keep his child a secret from the hands of a madman. Grimes softens his grip, brushes his hands over my shirt.

I'm compelled to ask him, "How'd your wife die?"

"It's too late for you to ask me now."

"All right," I say, and step from the squad.

Before driving off, Grimes tells me again, in earnest, to move away from Red River Falls. I see only his arms and chest through the squad's windows. Whether his face reveals his resignation about my future, I cannot see. He's a man who turned invisible by finding out what he could about people, so it's likely he understands what I'll do. Despite what he says about Red River Falls in general, and the secrets he must keep about Henry Clayton in particular, Larry Grimes knows he will leave town with his daughters, and I will stay behind.

Morning shift starts with an announcement. Sgt. Larry Grimes has resigned effective immediately. Jack, on the chair beside me, shakes his head and mutters "Good man" in a way noncommittal to whether he describes the man or the fact of his leaving. The rest of the morning shift officers show no reaction. Drano in particular nudges his elbow into Blond Boy to take note of brown hair dye dripping down the neck of the officer in front of them.

Warrant review handouts, reports on areas of increased criminal activity, a reminder to obey the traffic laws if we expect the citizens to do the same. All routine. All of this by rote.

Larry Grimes has left no footprints here after eight years on the Red River Falls police force. It proves he understands the truth about invisibility. I'm convinced. My life since Momma's and Poppa's murders has been a mistake, making me not an invisible man, but an easy target.

Jack elbows my ribs. He whispers, "After shift today, we'll check on Clayton's receipt."

16

The late model gold Mercedes was going fifty in a twenty-five down Fedder Street.

Cops speed, and not just while off duty. We speed to start our shift, and we speed to traffic court to testify about speeding tickets. Then we speed away when our day in court is over. We understand the need, or at least the urge, to drive over the speed limit. Still, we have a thing about speeding in a residential zone, especially twenty-five over on radar in a residential zone. Quad Com sends the driver's information to our squad's computer screen. Ezra Davis, white female, fifty-six, valid DL, plates, insurance, and registration. No felonies. Address checks out. One misdemeanor domestic battery charge, dropped. Likely her husband felt guilty about lying to the police, so he took the fifth or didn't show up to court on trial day.

Jack winks and warns me to be on guard. He hands me her license. "Fifty-six, five foot three, hundred and fifteen pounds. But her look—she looks like she can take you."

"Turn the MARS lights off. You're attracting the neighborhood."

I return her license at her window. She talks in a respectful tone. "I thought the speed limit was forty-five. Perhaps I was distracted." I look down the street of bungalows and cars parked at the curbs restricting travel. Fedder should be a one-way street.

"Six more miles an hour over, Ms. Davis, and this would be a misdemeanor reckless driving instead of a traffic ticket. One child stepping out between cars, and it'd be a whole new problem for you."

She faces her steering wheel, hands at ten and two, expressionless. This happens often enough. Some drivers are polite from beginning to end, others aggravated. Still others, like this one, don't make up their minds throughout the whole stop. "I'm not allowed to give you a warning at this much over in a residential neighborhood, Ms. Davis, but I'm glad it's nothing worse. I'll be happy to tell the judge you were polite and apologetic. Obviously then, with your record, you'll get supervision."

A smile. "I know who you are," she says.

"Yes, Ms. Davis?"

"I've lived in Red River Falls for thirty-seven years." She looks at me, her face round and pleasant, youthful for fifty-six. Her smile broadens. She's a rare type, a wealthy white woman looking at my eyes rather than the blur of my skin color. "I'm sorry."

"I know you are, Ms. Davis."

"Yes, for the ticket. But what I mean is, about what happened to you."

I step back, believing she's confused, and check the front of the car to make sure it has a plate. It does, and I see the sticker on the bumper: *How Am I Driving?* Makes me wonder why she'd have it on the front bumper, and on a new Mercedes. Back at the window, I extend her copy of the ticket. "It's been on all the area radio stations the last ten minutes, Officer Hill. I'm sure it will make CNN in another fifteen."

"What will?"

"The history of what happened. Your parents. And you." There's a tear gathered on the side of her nose. "You'd be surprised how many people in Red River Falls remember you. I'm so sorry," she says, and reaches through her window to touch my arm. The ticket withdraws in my hand, crumples into my palm. "Are you sure, Officer Hill? I have no motive beyond my condolences. Supervision will be fine."

"Go. Just go."

Teenagers gather close by on the walk. The Mercedes pulls away from the curb, slowly at first as if giving me a respectful opportunity to change my mind. Jack waves me over to the squad. Inside, he watches me closely. "Are you all right?"

"I don't know. Why don't you tell me if I'm all right."

Jack speaks to dispatch. "Officer Hill's back with me. Repeat what you said."

The voice through the speaker could be one of three people, I've never bothered to match our dispatchers' names with their voices. "Homicide at 2171 Volker Lane. Victim's age: seventy-eight. Name: Howard Riddy. Suspect apprehended inside the residence. Male white. Mid-to-late thirties. Shaved head. Tattoos—black swastika below his right ear. Two on his back."

I switch our dispatch radio off. Although Clayton's swastikas have been torn out, I need to ask Jack. "Is it Clayton?"

"No one's saying yet. Similar murder technique. Single shot to the head. Hacked body parts."

I sense, I don't know. I don't sense anything at all. My face has gone numb, the familiar tension gone. "Can we go to Volker?"

Jack scratches at his chin. "Are you sure?"

"Not really."

Jack shifts our squad into gear. "Okay."

I stare at the glove box and feel Jack's warmth. This time I am the one who has reached to Jack, my hand pressed to his shoulder.

17

Local newspaper and radio reporters have found out about Howard Riddy's murder before dispatch and Quad Com. I have nothing against reporters. Just like I have nothing against lawyers. It's our own fault they do what they do. Their actions are reflections of our actions. If everyone would act reasonably, reporters and lawyers would act reasonably. Perhaps. With a town mascot like Howard Riddy, shot in the head, his limbs separated and set neatly in the blood around his torso on his trampoline, it's hard to expect reporters to flock anywhere else.

Looking out the picture window, I watch reporters stand with their mouths moving expressively over their microphones, some with cameramen focused on them, then to Riddy's house. Neighbors wander out from their homes and crowd behind them, to the side, a few mixed in. This includes the association president, the screamer from the porch next door. Likely she'll say Riddy was a quiet old guy, kept to himself mostly. A nice gentleman. All of it a lie and a betrayal to her true feelings. Murder, after all, is a bad time to badmouth a neighbor to the media.

All of this madness, this explosion of interest, held back by the likes of Blond Boy, Drano, other officers called in from second and third shift, and wooden street barricades. My vision fogs over the scene, my mind still rattled from the lunacy of the questions lobbed at me as soon as Jack and I arrived. "Does this convince you of Henry Clayton's exoneration, Officer Hill?"

"Could this prove who really killed your parents, Officer Hill?" "Will you participate in the interrogation of the suspect, Officer Hill?"

"Officer Hill, how do you feel?"

I blink to wash away the fog, focus again on the current madness. How do I feel?—Why do reporters always ask such a question, scream such a question over the heads of others? Mothers of murdered children, husbands of cancer-stricken wives. *How do you feel?* What kind of person is incapable of already knowing the answer to this question? Maybe I don't like reporters after all. Behind me, crime scene preservation officers flash their cameras at a slower pace than a few moments before. Voices mumble as if sneaking in discussions about golf during a church service.

How could I have missed the strong memories of strangers for so many years? All of them interested in what happened sixteen years ago to Momma and Poppa. One reporter pressed a cameraman's camera lens toward the ground, instructed him to leave me alone with a stern "That's enough!" Not to her microphone, but to me, she said, "Are you all right, Officer Hill?"

I looked her face over, plain with high-arching eyebrows, white skin, reddened cheeks and red-brown hair. Irish, I suppose, and her eyes focused intently on mine. "I'm not all right."

She apologized, lowered her stare, and yelled at other reporters to leave me alone. I took note of the call letters on her shirt. WVOL AM. I'll remember her if I ever decide to speak to a reporter.

A crime scene photographer flashes his camera and laughs. All the photos of Marilyn Riddy seem to streak by, like a flock of birds leaving for another place. Men in suits mill about, work at notepads and iPods, cameras head toward their cases. Somewhere a phone rings. Jack stands off in a corner of the room, one arm pressed over his chest, his hand pulling lightly at his lips. He stares at the center of the room, the crowd of us circling the trampoline. Riddy's remains depress its red-stained tarp, taken apart the same way Momma and Poppa were. Drops of blood drip to the floor.

The eyes of investigators occasionally flash at me, then focus back on their work. They know there's no need for me to be here, apart from my history, but they don't object. I stay out of their way.

Walking around the room toward Jack, I'm distracted by the sight of Howard Riddy. The separation between thigh and hip, an arm from its shoulder. Riddy's head, turned toward me and separated from his neck, is not what I expect. Eyes closed. Lips together without a hint of final emotion or agony. Skin still smooth, bloodless and tan. Peaceful. Even the bullet's small entry wound at his temple appears as though it's a mistake.

Beside Jack, I say, "Where's Schumacher?"

"He can't come."

"Grandstanding for the press is his homicide routine."

"Not this one. Conflict of interest with his son."

Marilyn Riddy's pictures seem to return, the same flock of birds silent in the wind, landing once more to feed. "Schumacher's oldest boy has always given him trouble," Jack says. His fingers continue to work at his lips. "It's an embarrassment to any prosecutor, let alone the elected prosecutor. It proves bad apples can happen in any family, but I wasn't aware it had gotten this bad."

"You're thinking about your son?"

Jack's face remains aimed toward Riddy, but his eyes corner toward me. "I'm always thinking about Tyler."

"Then who's going to lead this prosecution if not Schumacher?"

"He'll have to ask another county to step in, or the attorney general's office. Maybe a private attorney will take the case on as special prosecutor."

"Jack," I say, and the walls, the pictures of Marilyn Riddy, feel as though they have pulled toward me. "Why?"

"Prentiss Schumacher is thirty-seven. Shaved head. Tattoos. Swastikas, one below his right ear, two others on his back. He's had them over twenty years." Jack inhales deeply, then turns to me. "He's been arrested for the murder of Howard Riddy. He's the one who was found here, blood on his hands, hunting blade at his feet, gun in his pocket. Fred Schumacher's son."

"Is he talking?"

"Said two things. I was set up. I want my lawyer. Not a word more."

In hundreds of photos, Marilyn Riddy reflects what I'm feeling, anguish far too overwhelming to put into words. "Let's get out of here."

"Are you all right?"

A popular question lately. "Better. I don't know. Maybe a bit better."

"One more thing," Jack says. "The photograph we took from Riddy. Prentiss Schumacher's in it. He stands to the right of Henry Clayton."

The pavement running past 2171 Volker feels as though it has shifted. Neighbors and reporters have moved another direction. At the squad car, I turn to look for a reason. I see him, a book in his hand held aloft. A replacement bible, I suppose, for the one he forgot. Such a thing would horrify Auntie Doria.

Beside a thick-necked man in a suit, Clayton stands on something that makes him taller than the rest. Microphones rise to him, he speaks over them, and they fall only to rise again for another answer to another question. Through the air, the vibration of Clayton's voice reaches me. Exoneration. Now complete in all aspects.

He gives me an utterly tranquil look over outstretched microphones, a message of the most definite kind. In his way, he tells me. He has done what Jesus in Matthew had instructed him to do.

So quickly. So soon. He has walked the extra mile and doesn't need me anymore.

18

Zookeeper's voice shatters through the speaker beside the booking room door like tin cans tumbling over pavement. "If it's Officer Hill with you, I've got orders to keep him out."

"From who?" Jack says.

"Everybody. The chief, the prosecutor's office. My mother's bridge club."

Jack glances back at me, my duffel bag over my shoulders. "Zookeeper," Jack says. "You know I've got things on you."

"Nothing big enough for this."

I step around Jack, stretch toward the speaker. "Turn the cameras off and let me in."

"Officer Hill?"

"Zookeeper. You know what I've got on you."

Hesitation, a sound of crumpling paper. "Not fair. It's not fair."

Jack's elbow nudges against my ribs. "Shee-it. What do you have on Zookeeper?"

The metal door vibrates with the buzzer, and I pull it open. Zookeeper's voice growls beneath the noise. "Cameras off. I'm taking a fifteen minute siesta on the crapper." He adds, "I've got a timer on my watch."

"If you don't tell me what you've got on Zookeeper," Jack says, following me in, "I'm turning around."

I grip my duffel bag tighter passing Zookeeper's station, abandoned now, the sound of the bathroom door in back shutting with a click of the lock. Fluorescent light glows off the metal booking desk, concrete floor, and cinder block walls. Electrified air, the entire space, and my teeth feel as though they're grinding cold metal. Overhead, cameras aimed at the row of cages have turned blind, the usual glowing red dots beside the lenses absent. Zookeeper will note in his booking logs some sort of mechanical malfunction, source unknown, and will blame the wiring in the outdated building, obviously unreliable with newer technology plugged in everywhere. He's done it before when cops wanted privacy with a suspect.

Jack's steps continue behind me; he sighs with my silence.

I stop at the cage, Riddy's former cage. Seems both poetic and inevitable for Prentiss Schumacher to have arrived there too. But I don't look in right away. Instead I listen for the breathing. I'm the boy under the table, coward under cloth, knowing Momma and Poppa are dead while their murderer remains a while to admire his work. My eyes close, ears tuned to a murderer's breathing, as distinctive as a fingerprint.

The breaths in the cage jar against my memory, and I turn to face him.

"Mud cop. What the fuck do you want?"

Prentiss Schumacher sits on the bench inside the cage, shirtless, blue jeans tight and worn, his feet drawn up under his thighs, arms wrapped around his knees, head down. Like the rest of this space, his shaved head glows fluorescent.

"I want you to look at me."

"Took a glance at you already. Now you can go to hell."

"Look directly at me."

"This ain't no lineup, mud cop."

"Why don't you just call me nigger?"

Prentiss Schumacher grunts a laugh for his own benefit. "I'm reformed."

"Looks like dried blood on your fingertips," Jack says, gripping the bars. "Want to tell us about that?"

"You can't do this, I know my rights. I've taken the fifth, Heat. Asked for my lawyer."

"Heat. My middle name's Heathrow," Jack whispers, and nods to indicate this is another thing about him I should have learned long ago.

There's a familiarity in Jack's voice, warmth in his eyes, when he addresses this wrecked man in a cage. "Of course, Prentiss. That's the beauty of the law and our situation here right now. Everyone knows you've asked for a lawyer, so you can confess to a hundred murders right now, how you chopped old ladies into pieces, and there's nothing any cop can do to use it against you." Jack slackens his body against the bars. "I'm no cop standing here, Prentiss. It's me. Uncle Heat."

"What about mud cop?"

"Call him Officer Hill, Prentiss. If you want me to help you, you've got to let Officer Hill take a look at you."

Prentiss rolls his head side to side in the cradle of his arms. "A mud man and a Jew want to save me."

"On my grandmother's side," Jack says. "Her mother was half Jewish."

I say, "Great grandfather the last time you mentioned it."

Prentiss Schumacher stretches his legs off the bench to the floor, unwraps his arms, giving him the hopeless appearance of a man trying to take flight. His neck and head are the last to unfurl. "The percentage of matzo balls in your blood doesn't matter, Uncle Heat."

"I'm not saying it does."

Jack studies my reaction. "You're uncertain."

"Turn around slowly," I say.

Prentiss bites at his lips, stands, and makes a comment about the loveliness of his ass, but he turns. The swastika on his neck, below the right ear, a second one centered between his shoulder blades, and a third at his hips. The thinness of his body, sixteen years later, resembles the memory as much as it resembles his father's squeezed shape. Although my heartbeat sounds in my ears, the sight of Prentiss Schumacher does no more than confuse. His appearance is like a statue made from a mold, an imitation of an original. There's no rage igniting the boy inside me, no immediate fury rising to the surface.

"Are you willing to take a DNA test?"

Prentiss Schumacher's eyes narrow at me. "Why should I?"

"If you're so damn innocent, you wouldn't ask why."

"I'm not saying I'm innocent. I'm saying I didn't kill anybody." He kicks at the floor and shakes his head. "Have you ever heard of a plantation cocktail?"

"Never."

" 'Cause you'd be the drinker, not the maker." Prentiss holds on to the bars, leans into his arms. "At the Hall we always make this toast when the meeting finishes up. Praise our cause, raise empty glasses, and spit into them. I mean spit. Not just once, but six, seven times."

"Doesn't sound like much of a cocktail," I say.

"Here's the point. A bunch of us work at restaurants, or have kids working at restaurants. A regular thing. We wait for your kind to show up, or Mexicans or something. Then we take the glasses from the Hall, add drinks to the spit, and serve." Prentiss laughs, turns from the bars toward the bench seat. "Plantation cocktail."

"What makes you think Clayton would single you out?" Jack says.

"He set me up for Riddy's murder, didn't he?"

"That's what you're saying."

"It's what I know, Uncle Heat. Clayton's busy saving his own ass. Cleaning up some loose ends is what he's doing." Sitting, Prentiss curls over his knees. "My dad's the chief prosecutor, and I'm the apple from the tree. Clayton hates prosecutors." Eyes focused on me, he says, "Go figure."

"You don't know," Jack says. "You're guessing."

"I'm not taking no DNA test."

"You won't have a choice."

"God bless America, Uncle Heat. Right?"

I ask, "Where's the Hall located?"

"Look it up in the Yellow Pages, mud cop. It'll be right above the listings for hardware stores."

My hands, unclenched, almost relaxed, pull a photograph from my duffel bag. "Take a look at this."

"Whatever for?"

"Do it."

Prentiss flashes his eyes at Jack. "Is this all right?"

Jack nods. "None of this is happening, Prentiss. Remember."

There's a nod shared between them, some sort of established trust. Prentiss steps to the bars, sticks his nose through, leans toward the photograph. Twelve boys gathered in Riddy's house, dressed as Prentiss Schumacher has dressed today. Taking a step back, he laughs. "That's me. Next to Clayton. Third from the left end."

Jack eyes the photograph. "Was this your entire group?"

"At the time? Hardly. Maybe half. Half didn't want to mess with Riddy. The rest of us did, or we thought we did back then. Horny old fuck. But the pay wasn't bad."

"The swastikas," I say. "The way you dress."

"Our club uniform. Required."

"Were you still messing with the old man?" Jack asks.

"Messing how?"

"You know what I mean."

Anguish covers Prentiss' face. "I'm not saying. Not even under these circumstances." He reconsiders, speaks softly, "Not today. There won't be any proof of it today." He approaches the bars, again presses his face between steel, and glares at me. "I would have loved to have done what Clayton did to your parents, but I didn't, you understand, mud cop? I'm a man of certain beliefs, but no action." A smile, his white teeth so upper middle class. "I'm like my old man in that way. A real coward. Go ask Heat, he'll say so."

I'm caught in the strength of his stare, and it's as though I'm held there, forced to examine every angry feature. "Clayton's been exonerated."

"Hell, mud man. You don't sound convinced."

My fingertips loosen around the photograph, and it falls. "No."

"I heard," Prentiss says, hissing through his lips, "your momma was a good lay. Heard it from Clayton himself."

Jack reaches through the bars to Prentiss' arm. "It's all right," I insist. "I can handle this."

Prentiss lowers his chin toward his bicep engulfed within Jack's grip. "Uncle Heat," he says. Hardly a man's voice at all. "Uncle Heat. I didn't kill Howard Riddy. I didn't kill anybody. Ever."

My eyes, more willingly now, move over Prentiss Schumacher's face, withdrawing portions of flesh to drape over past images. Curvature of chin, mouth, nose, and brow. Slant of eyes, placement of ears, jaw and cheekbone. I'm forced to wonder about jurors, all of them convinced enough to not only convict a man, but also convinced without any doubt at all to the point of ordering him to die. Over and over, perhaps hundreds now, such men are exonerated by a science of perfection; perfect, as Auntie Doria would say, because DNA is not the science of mortals, but the artistry of God. So often I've witnessed prosecutors and defense lawyers argue over the truth of a case in a courtroom, both sides motivated by the desire to win. Sometimes this desire is fueled by a blinding belief in a cause, but more often by politics, or by something worse; jurors listen and shift uncomfortably in their chairs, as if demonstrating how easily they move from one opinion to another, until at last something overtakes them. Perhaps anger. Anger and expediency.

But my excuse is what? What is my blinding belief? Visions, of course. Memories so deeply ingrained to the point of animation within my own skin. Swastikas so shocking. Bare torso, jeans, a mere uniform among boys on the verge of manhood. Muscular shoulders and back, narrow hips, typical of youth. A voice mutilated by inspired hatred. And me, a small boy thrown into a system that demanded sworn testimony of my most personal and horrific images before a mass of strangers. All of us collected in a room of wood polished to the sheen of ice, and a dozen pairs of probing eyes of white men and women passing judgment over my credibility. A process intended to create certainty out of chaos also made tears swarm over Henry Clayton's eyes.

Removing layer upon layer of memory, I'm again drawn back to that night under the table. For the first time, though, I work to erase what I can of the influences of men and their system of justice. A white boy naked over Momma. Poppa forced to watch. Swastikas. Chaotic voices. Never did I stare into the murderer's eyes like I stare into Prentiss Schumacher's at this moment. My knees begin to buckle, and Jack's arms stop my fall.

"What the hell?" Prentiss says. His voice rises. "You know it wasn't me! He knows it wasn't me, Uncle Heat!"

I gather myself together, straighten, Jack's mouth at my ear. "What is it, Rich?"

Like approaching thunder, a voice booms from the outside and rolls into this room. "Where are you, Zookeeper? Buzz me in!" A distant shout from the bathroom. Zookeeper rushing out. "Goddamn, Jack. It's my job on the line!"

Jack hurries me toward the booking room door, Prentiss Schumacher's voice chasing after me. "Tell my father, Uncle Heat. Tell my father he knows it wasn't me!"

Buzzer activated, heavy sounds of the door lock mechanism grinding. Jack asks me again. "What?"

I can't answer. Can't speak. No breath yet, not enough to say a word.

The door emits a firm chain of clicks and swings open, slams against the outer wall. On the other side, Marla Weist stands behind Fred Schumacher. His mouth moves, brow furrows. All I can make out is the depth of his rage, and Jack's soothing voice failing to calm the situation.

Somehow I'm outside the booking room with Jack; Marla and Fred gone inside. Zookeeper's whisper through the speaker sounds more than pitiful. "If I go down, you boys go down with me."

19

We wait in chairs outside the booking room. Seems like hours. Jack doesn't say a word. I finally gain the ability, and need, to talk.

"I have nothing on Zookeeper," I admit. "He thinks I'm dangerous, like the rest of you think I'm dangerous."

Jack rests his head against the wall behind us. I press the glow light on my watch just to do it.

The booking room door goes through its tribulations. Fred Schumacher walks to us, Marla again positioning herself behind him, her piled hair climbing higher where Fred's head leaves off. There's an unexpected calm about him, his voice less dramatic. He holds my duffel bag and the photograph out to me. "You dropped these," he says. "We really need to talk."

I once heard a defense attorney argue in court during a motion to suppress a confession that the 1970s decor of the Red River Falls Police Department interrogation room is proof enough of police threat and coercion. Dark paneling, worn shag carpet, a dark table with metal legs and delaminating top, coned lighting cans stacked on a vertical post, and off-pink plastic chairs shaped like soup ladles. It was one of my cases, and the attorney was being serious.

Fred stands and paces behind one of the soup ladle chairs. He pauses every few steps, eyes Jack and me seated on the other side of the table as if trying to figure out how to reach over an uncrossable expanse. Seated on Fred's side of the table, Marla holds a notepad and pen. She looks as though she would rather have a cavity drilled.

"What?" Jack begins.

Fred booms at him. "Say nothing, Officer Harter."

He's half Jack's width, but Fred shuts him down using the depth of his voice. "I'm telling you, I don't want you to say another word. You're still on duty, yet you're here instead of on the streets doing your job. Your shift commander is left in the dark about your whereabouts; maybe you're bleeding to death somewhere but he doesn't know. You've convinced Zookeeper to break rules in a way any defense attorney would have a field day with. And you're here interrogating a man who has already shouted all the way to the police station that he won't talk without his lawyer."

Jack coughs, smiles at Marla's hair, and raises his hand.

"You insist on being an ass," Fred says.

"May I say more than another word?" Jack doesn't wait for an answer, heaving his elbows half across the table. "Who is Prentiss' lawyer gonna be?"

Fred Schumacher hesitates, pinches at his lips.

"Shee-it," Jack says, leaning back. "It's you. You're going to be your son's lawyer."

"I didn't say that."

"But you're thinking it."

Jack glances at Marla, her pen still over her pad of paper. "So what's the situation here?" Jack says. "Are you the secretary for Red River Falls' elected prosecutor in a homicide prosecution, or are you taking notes for the defense? I mean, which side am I talking to right now?"

Fred Schumacher stiffens his back, his hands work at his suit collar and tie. There's a sudden give in him, a lurch forward, almost prostrate over the table before Jack. He drops into his chair. Remarkable how his face, dropped into the cup of his hands, reminds me of Prentiss in the cage. His is still a booming voice, now inconsistent with his situation. "Who else can I trust? He's my son."

"You want to ask me something specific, Mr. Schumacher," I say. All three turn to me, mouths slack as if surprised to hear I can speak. "Let me ask you some questions first."

Fred closes his eyes momentarily and nods.

"He'll test positive for gunpowder burns on his hands?"

"Prentiss owns several guns, all legal. Shoots almost every day at a firing range." Fred clears his throat and looks away. "Probably, but it doesn't prove he shot Riddy."

"His prints will be on the knife handle and in the house?"

"Likely all over the house. Says he picked the knife up after the fact. Not so unusual."

"Will there be a DNA match?"

"I don't know if perpetrator DNA is part of the crime scene or what's been found in Riddy's house. Prentiss has been there before. Many times. I never approved, but it's a fact."

"Riddy's murder is not the DNA match I'm asking about."

"Oh." Fred lifts his head wearily. "I can't say."

"What was Prentiss doing at Riddy's house?"

"It's privileged information." Fred raises his hands to keep me from leaving, which is exactly what I thought to do. "It's more than that, Officer Hill. It's something I had hoped to look into before giving the information out. Clayton told him to go to Riddy's."

"Why?"

"Prentiss doesn't know. He didn't ask."

"DNA exonerated Henry Clayton. My testimony, math equations, that's what you told me. Seems to me Riddy's murder puts an exclamation point on Clayton's innocence, at least it's the way things appear right now." I witness a diminished man.

Squeezed more than usual, his thinness lost inside his suit. "You want to ask me for my cooperation to help your son."

With a halting motion, he brings his hand to his chin. "Yes."

I shift forward in my chair. "Where does Prentiss get his hatred from?"

"What do you mean?"

"Last night I saw some white boys with their shirts off. Some had swastikas on their necks like your son's. I also noticed older whites out there with them. Parents most likely. They didn't seem to give a damn whether their sons had the Third Reich displayed on their bodies. So I have to ask, does Prentiss get his hatred from you? Do you call me mud cop behind my back, and ease over the word 'nigger' in your conversations with other white boys? Did your babies grow up smiling at you when you said the words?"

Fred stands and raises his palms above the table. His lips move but no sound comes out; he bows his head.

"What I saw in a cage was a thirty-seven-year-old man with tattooed hatred and a sneer to match. And I see how much he resembles his father."

Marla looks down at her lap. Jack smiles and turns easily to Fred. "I'd kind of like to hear a response to that myself."

"I," Fred begins, and falters. "You have no right. He's my son."

"Your son's a skinhead. And you're asking this mud cop to help you set him free for a murder today, and perhaps a rape and two murders from sixteen years ago. Just so you remember, Schumacher, they're my momma and my poppa in the ground. I believe I do have a right."

Fred reaches for his chair and sits. When he speaks, he cocks his head toward Marla. "Yes. I've said things I regret. Yes. I've heard things I let go."

"You allowed swastikas to exist in your home, you did nothing to change his attitude."

"He's an adult. I can't force him to do anything."

"He's your son. From what I've seen of him, it's a sure bet he's asked you for money and a place to stay, very much like a child. You give him these things, probably more. But you never put conditions on your fatherhood."

"Don't lecture me until you're a father yourself."

"I don't have to be shot to know bullets hurt, and I don't have to be a father to know he's screwed up. Someone killed my parents, maybe the same man who killed Riddy. You want to know if I think it's your son." Schumacher's stare wanders, and I pause to catch it in mine. "Even if Prentiss isn't the one who pulled the trigger, wouldn't you agree accountability travels a long way in this situation?"

"Are you saying it wasn't Prentiss?"

"You haven't answered my question."

"Nobody's perfect, Officer Hill. But I'm devout. I'm a good Christian."

Jack rolls his eyes. "Can we leave that out of this discussion?"

"Richard," Marla says, her hands folded over her notepad. "Please. Do you believe Prentiss murdered your parents?"

Soft, giving, her voice touches me, as it always has before, with gentle strokes.

"Marla," I say. "I don't know."

With what I lived through, and the indelible images burned into my brain whether awake or in restless sleep, it's an answer that matters. Fred Schumacher has no idea how profound it is for me to have spoken my doubt. He pounds his fists on the table and booms at me, "Is that it?"

Marla coughs politely into her hand. "Fred," she says. "It's a good start."

"As a father, I know I could've done better. Prentiss insists he didn't kill anybody."

"Still," I say. "From my perspective, even if he's innocent of rape and murder, wouldn't it be better if a man like your son stayed behind bars?"

Schumacher stands, fixes his suit and tie. "I'm issuing a press release tomorrow. My resignation takes effect at the end of the month. You may despise Prentiss and hate me for creating him. But considering your history and recent events, we find ourselves tied together."

He leaves, takes Marla with him in the tow of his wake. Jack and I remain with thirty-five minutes officially left in our shift. We're in no hurry to get up.

"So," Jack says. "The lamb becomes the lion?"

"Feels like failure."

"Come to dinner tonight. We'll talk it over."

"Jack."

"C'mon."

"I can't."

"You always say no."

"Not always."

"One time in three years doesn't count, especially since you canceled." Jack stretches his legs, eases low in his chair. "Tyler said something last night. Really threw me. He changed his mind about what he wants to be when he grows up."

"Sock puppet thing didn't work out?"

"Yeah. Well, this time he's convinced himself, waved a whisk broom over his head like a magic wand to prove it. When he grows up, he wants to be a mommy."

"Oh."

"Theresa gave me a parenting book with a chapter explaining why I shouldn't worry." He stands and shakes the hems of his pants loose from his socks. "You haven't seen Tyler since he learned to walk. Pictures don't count."

"I'm not good with kids, almost as bad with adults."

"Let me tell you something about Fred Schumacher. He was an assistant prosecutor for ten years before he ran for chief prosecutor and lost by thirty-seven votes. Then he played lackey to the winner for two years before getting forced out over some political excuse. In private practice, he defended the same people he used to prosecute. Not so unusual, tons of lawyers choose the same career path and get used to it. Not Fred. Fred couldn't stand it to the point of vomiting after winning a trial."

"Divorce, real estate, personal injury. A lawyer has plenty of choices."

"That's not how Fred's built." Jack rubs at his neck, looks at something on the ceiling. "The second time he ran for chief prosecutor, he went into debt spending a fortune to win election to a job paying less than half of what he made at a private firm. What you saw just now was an apology. Don't you understand? A man who gives up a career he adores for the sake of his son, a son like Prentiss at that, you have no idea. Think what you want to, but what you witnessed just now was a man choosing fatherhood over a cherished career. No less than what your father would've done for you." He claps his hands together before I can respond. "You haven't experienced the pain of a bullet until you've actually been shot, and you don't know a father's heart until you've had your own wrapped in the arms of your own child. On this subject, don't even try to argue with me."

"You think I should give an alliance with Fred and Prentiss Schumacher serious thought?"

"It's what I think."

"What will Fred do if Prentiss's DNA matches any of the crimes?"

"Don't know." Jack shuffles his feet over the worn carpet. "We can check Clayton's receipt out tomorrow. Right now, I think dinner at my house is more important."

I press my hand on my breast pocket, feel the rectangular outline of Clayton's Dollar-Mart receipt, and slip it out to take yet another look at its words and numbers. "What's Theresa making for dinner?"

"Probably Chinese. Definitely delivery. The Yellow Pages are the cooks in my house. Dinner's at six. You have over two hours to learn how to smile."

We sit several minutes longer and my mind's so busy, perhaps I've forgotten how to think. Jack, however, finds ways to flit his thoughts about.

"I wonder," he says, "if there's something going on between Marla and Fred."

Jack watches me handle Clayton's Dollar-Mart receipt and set it on the table. He begins to reach for it but I snatch it back up, and our silence pretends the moment didn't happen. This bit of paper is something for me to possess, a foolish dog guarding a meatless bone. "It's me here," Jack says.

"I know."

"I wasn't going to tear it up."

"Promise me you won't tell Fred about it."

"See you at six," Jack says.

"At six."

The receipt feels cold in my hand.

We leave the interview room, Jack in the lead, still rubbing at the back of his neck. And I know, given the words we've chosen, we haven't promised each other a thing.

20

What I have learned.

It's not a question. Not a thought of self-reflection. It's a fact.

The thing I have learned is the danger of certainty. Religious faith is an obvious example, but also the claims of science. Neither belief in God nor genetic science has been able to prove who did and who did not murder Momma and Poppa.

The trial I experienced as a boy was not a search for the certainty of truth, but what a prosecutor could show with an actor's talent and persuasive flair. Perhaps assisted by dishonesty.

Most of all, though, I have lost my childish certainty in Momma and Poppa. They were unable to provide their young son the most precious gift a child inherently desires. The belief they would live forever.

Such an odd feeling, to let go of certainty as if such a decision could give my thoughts room to fly, open up endless possibilities, and find truth exposed when the clutter is cleared away. After discarding any notion of certainty, I find what I have left may be worse. The fear there may be nothing for me to learn at all.

When Auntie Doria's eyes glow within her church, and her face beams receiving the words of a sermon, it's as though she has something definite to hold on to. Faith, so untouchable, made of smoke, born from centuries of hearsay, politics, and superstition, is like a steel bar overhead she grasps, and a platform of reinforced concrete she firmly plants her feet upon. It makes no difference to her if, with her final breath of life, she learns the God of her faith proves false. For Auntie Doria, and I suspect for others like her, belief in faith makes God real enough here on earth.

Although I can't bring myself to Auntie Doria's faith, I acknowledge my jealousy of the calm and confidence it gives her. Her ability to peacefully sleep night after night. Her complete certainty in something so impossible for any human being to comprehend is like an insect claiming it can explain the human mind. But I never sleep a peaceful sleep, nor does my running euphoria provide moments of complete calm or restfulness. At best, on occasion, I reach an unsatisfying numbness, a doubter's version of purgatory.

Faith, I suppose, is like a narcotic. It causes people to ignore facts that could lead them to doubt, or to question authority. Auntie Doria's faith shields her from pain of all sorts. At the same time such faith provides a service to a man like Henry Clayton, who uses it as some sort of line in the sand he can cross over and claim to be reborn. A person apart from whom he once was. In this way, in his own mind, Clayton avoids the consequences and blame for his past.

What I have learned, then, is that certainty and uncertainty are equally undesirable. So I am caught in a middle that has no name. At best I can describe my position as emptiness. A moment when the bottom has fallen out of my life and I stand on nothing.

It's well past six in the evening. Jack has likely called my house, and Auntie Doria, a dozen times by now, wondering where I am. Dinner is getting cold. His son complains about hunger, and a decision will soon be made to start eating without me. Here, in the attic storage room of the Red River Falls Police Department, sunlight through roof vents grows dim. My skin shifts from light brown toward black, and I sit on a metal filing box, disintegrating into the darkness. Henry Clayton's receipt in one hand; in the other, a computer disk categorized neatly from nearly sixteen years ago. Labeled, *Henry Clayton: Evidence Record.*

All of it obvious. Even a choice of obsolete computers and electrical outlets has been provided for me in this room. I could power up the computer again, slip in the case file disk, and glare at the information one more time. I could wonder some more about Jack, his familiarity with the Schumacher family, especially with Prentiss. How he sought me out three years ago to be his squad partner when nobody else was willing. And his claim of being a born-again Christian.

Like certainty and uncertainty, I know everything about Jack Harter I need to know, or I know nothing about him at all. Each choice feels equally undesirable.

What I lack is faith. What I now have is computer-driven proof that the police knew about Henry Clayton's receipt. That Clayton was buying cigarettes in a Dollar-Mart store seven hours away from Red River Falls at the time of my parents' murders. And it was Jack Harter, a rookie cop back then, who categorized this evidence in a multiple homicide investigation. Two months before Henry Clayton was sentenced to die.

I already know my plans. Tonight, I'll sit in my recliner chair in my living room, surrounded by Momma's books. Henry Clayton's receipt and the computer disk will rest on top of my television set, and I'll stare at them until the sun comes up. After several cups of caffeine and a shower, I'll look at my reflection in the bathroom mirror. Then I'll confirm what I have learned: not only am I a man who stands on nothing, but also a man who has no place to go.

When this moment arrives in the morning, I'll decide to make the call.

21

Her name is Sydney Brey, and she talks from her side of our restaurant booth like a woman approaching her thirties who hasn't entirely left her teens. Flair of hands, gum-popping between sentences. Smiling the whole time she talks. She adds to her word count with "like" and "you know." And people don't say things. They "go."

I watch her lips move, the easy way her hands flip long, reddish-brown hair from her eyes. She wears a mannish dress shirt with WVOL printed green over her breast pocket, untucked over tan jeans. Our lunch arrived ten minutes ago, served by a waiter who strained not to notice her paleness and my brown skin at the same table. The food on our plates remains uneaten. Mine because ordering it was a formality. Hers because there's too much one-sided talking going on.

I knew this could be a mistake the moment I thought to reach her at the radio station. She insisted on Blarney's Island, a restaurant overstuffed with Irish symbolism, inside Red River Falls' only enclosed shopping mall. The sounds of the lunch crowd, their talk, clanking of forks on heavy plates, and the hurry of servers and busboys, rise and fall like a song without a melody. I'm enveloped inside this noise, alone with her and her conversational clutter. She drifts from one topic to the next, sentences unfinished and floating off to the next with yet another "like" or "you know." I don't hear most of it, and work up the nerve to interrupt.

"You asked about me."

She falters, catches her breath. "What?"

"Outside Riddy's house. You put your microphone down, told a cameraman to back off. Then you asked me if I was all right."

"I couldn't be a reporter in Red River Falls and not know your history." Sydney's eyes flit to the side then back toward me. "It was obviously the right thing to do." Her voice transitions to a more exacting tone. "You haven't listened to a thing I've been talking about."

"Yes."

"Yes what?"

I hesitate, interlace my fingers over my plate. "You said hello. Told me your name. Something about job applications to radio stations in Chicago."

"New York. Anything else?"

"Not really."

Her constant smile fades, and she takes a bite of her hamburger, wipes her lips with her napkin. "You know what I thought? I thought this lunch was like a first date." I wait for her smile to return, a laugh to prove the joke. Instead the power of her stare, the squeeze of her lips, and the way she holds this look, this edge-of-anger look, complete her transformation into something formidable. "A date, you know? That's right. Something like a date."

The directness she throws across the table forces me to evaluate her in another kind of way. Auntie Doria would insist it's the natural way for a man to look at a young woman. Sydney Brey has a plain face. Nothing extraordinary about it except all the pieces seem to fit. It's as though her hair must be that length and reddish-brown color, and has to fall beside her eyes and cheeks just the way it does. The smallness of her nose, the subtle W shape of her lips, and the downward tilt of her eyes beneath thin eyebrows rising into the form of a question. All of her features appear as though they have to exist this particular way.

"I've been inspected," she observes.

A busboy gathers dishes and utensils from a table across the room, and they bang as if he jumbles them beside my ears. Someone has turned the volume and bass up on other conversations, and the air around me feels thick with their voices.

"I didn't ask you to lunch for a date. I asked to meet you because I need your help."

Her eyes nearly close watching her fingers tap on the table. "That was the other possibility I considered," she says. "When I first saw you on the street, you looked desperate. Like an immediate first impression."

"My first impression usually scares people away."

"Well then. You've improved."

I take a bite from my sandwich, struggle to swallow. Eating allows me to consider her some more. "What kind of investigative reporter are you? I mean, are you any good at it?"

"That's like asking a crappy doctor and a great doctor the same question. Won't their answers be the same?"

"Can you maintain a confidence?"

"Of course I can maintain a confidence. Right up to the moment I give it away on the radio the first chance I get. I'm kidding, you know. Mostly kidding." She lowers her chin. "What sort of secret are you keeping?"

"Several."

"Give me one. No off-the-record crap."

"It has to be off the record."

"Bullshit," she says, and pushes her plate away. "There's no record so there's no record to be off of. We're not in a courtroom. I'm not recording our conversation. And, for the record, it's not even a date. The only fact I've got here is this lunch has been a waste of my time. And my burger's overdone."

She gathers herself up to go, napkin to lips, a final sip of water. To stop her, I shift my duffel bag from my booth seat to my lap. "Like are you ever going to tell me what's inside that nasty-looking thing?"

I touch at the corners of the picture frame inside the bag. "A year ago I arrested a man for stabbing a drifter in the thigh. At the trial, the defense lawyer argued his client's Christian beliefs, how his devotion to the Christian Bible motivated him to get this drifter off drugs and into rehab. At least that's how it read in the newspaper."

"A story? You're sending me off with a cop war story?" Sydney Brey crumples her napkin in her hand. "You'd think at least I could've gotten a decent burger out of this non-date thing."

"The lawyer's client wasn't Christian, he was Muslim. Very devout. No apology from the reporter, no retraction from the newspaper. No matter how many times the lawyer insisted he was misquoted, it didn't matter to his client, his client's friends, or the mosque his client belonged to. The words he never said were in print twenty thousand times over, and they have made his life miserable." I remove my hand from the bag, shove my plate into hers. "So I'll ask you again. What kind of investigative reporter are you?"

"You really want to know?" she says, slapping her purse on the table. "Here goes. I exist to make lawyers look good by comparison, you know? People want to tell me their big story only if they're off the imaginary record. Let me tell you something, I've got a goldfish to feed and yoga sessions four times a week. So I'm not a reporter inclined to go to jail for the sake of protecting a source. That's in style for federal prosecutors these days, you know."

"I'm not asking you to report an unsupported story. I'm asking you to keep a story quiet until you can help me prove it."

Her hair covers the corners of her eyes, narrows her face.

"Let me give you my precise job description. A news radio investigative reporter in Red River Falls doesn't have all day to follow off-the-record leads." She tilts her head and shrugs. "My news stories arrive off the national wire services and the police scanner I carry between work and my apartment. Each story thrives for a moment, peaks, then fades away to make room for the fresh stories waiting in line for a few minutes of airtime. The only consistent broadcasts in news radio are the commercial breaks."

"You're telling me you're a hack?"

"I'm telling you I'm a news radio pro. Traffic reports air every ten minutes, the weather every fifteen, sports twice an hour, national news for five minutes at the top and bottom of the hour, plus the minutes per hour mandated for playful banter between the anchors to attract and keep loyal listeners. Subtract all of it and the commercial breaks from sixty minutes, and consider how much time that leaves for someone like me to report investigative news."

The check arrives and I take it, search through my wallet for cash and find only a five and a single. I leave a credit card for a fourteen dollar tab. Sydney Brey thanks me, pleasantly enough, although she appears slumped in her chair as if defeated by her own career description.

"You're like a firefly," I say. "You flit around and flash your light in one spot, then you're off to somewhere else in the night to flash another bit of light."

"I admit it," she says. "But you're stuck in the same spot you were sixteen years ago, you know? It's amazing to think we've landed at the same lunch table."

"I had hoped to trust you."

"I had hoped for a date and a better burger. Guess we're both leaving disappointed."

My lunch plate in my hands lifts barely an inch, then slams

back to the table. A sudden silence. A silence of stares and gaping mouths, their tangible pressure against my skin. I focus on the jagged crack in the porcelain, and the plate separates into halves in my hands. Lunchtime conversations recover, stares drift away, and my isolation returns.

Sydney Brey stays calm at the sight of my anger. "Maybe I really didn't think this was a date."

"I'm sorry. Don't go, not just yet." I press the pieces together and study the jagged crack. "You know about my parents' murders?"

"I'm an aspiring New York news radio reporter stuck in Red River Falls. What else is there in this town to study?" She takes the broken plate from my hands, separates the pieces and stacks them at the edge of our table. "Tell me something vital. Something you think I don't know about your parents' murders." She sighs. "Off the goddamn record."

Her eyes open wide, bright gray, and she waits. I imagine her as an object I'm about to trip over. Unlike something unseen, I'm aware of this hazard. What remains unknown is how I'll fall. There's an energy behind me pushing me along.

Sydney whispers, "C'mon. No date, my burger sucks, serves me right ordering a burger in an Irish-mall restaurant. At least make this worthwhile, for both of us."

"No. I can't." These are the words I say, so ingrained from my years fighting off visits to child psychologists. Their probing questions failed against my isolation. Their increasing efforts only strengthened my shield. At least the visits motivated me to study hard, get good grades, and run, to prove how well-adjusted a boy I was, given my circumstances, to persuade Auntie Doria to stop subjecting me to formal therapy. For Sydney Brey my words flow easily, inspired in part by Larry Grimes, my urgency, and by Sydney herself.

"Sixteen years ago someone buried evidence that would have

acquitted Henry Clayton. I'm not saying who."

"Because you don't know."

"I'm not sure. That's not your test."

"You're testing me? How do I pass your test?"

"By listening to me and telling no one."

"For how long?"

"Twenty-four hours."

"That's not very long."

"To someone in your profession, I suspect it's an eternity."

She smiles. "It depends on the secret."

The waiter arrives, takes the bill and credit card. Hesitates at the sight of the broken plate before he walks away.

"I'm certain who killed them," I begin, and close my eyes. I put myself back under the table, shielded within the cloth, my hand reaching out to lift the edge of the cloth off the floor. Momma's legs are spread apart, forced that way by the white boy wedging himself between them. Her head turns away from me. He's forcing a kiss on Momma's lips. Her arms and hands make foolish motions even as he moves over her. I wonder where she should put her hands, why she doesn't bite him or strike at him. Clench her fists or claw at his face. Instead Momma raises her left hand. It's as though she knows I'm watching her, this ridiculous position of her left arm held straight off the floor, her left hand outstretched, directing me to watch, lowering it toward the white boy raping her. Beside the swastika. Her fingers press beside the swastika on his back.

"Henry Clayton raped Momma. Henry Clayton killed my parents." Momma rolls her head toward me, her fingers now circling counterclockwise around the swastika; her head nods as though she believes I understand a particular message, then she lets her left hand collapse to the floor.

"But it wasn't Henry Clayton." Sydney talks so slowly, her response resembles a question. When I open my eyes, she bursts through Momma's fading image. "The DNA. Riddy's murder. Odds are it was Schumacher's son."

"It was Clayton."

"The DNA makes Clayton's exoneration rock solid. And if the police intentionally buried some evidence which would have freed him sixteen years ago, why did they let this DNA thing go forward?"

"It's been sixteen years." I open my duffel bag, lay the Dollar-Mart receipt and photograph stolen from Riddy's home before her. "Imagine what can change over sixteen years."

I pay the tab, leave a fourteen dollar tip for a fourteen dollar tab on the credit card bill. My apology for the plate. Sydney Brey continues to study the old receipt in particular, glancing at the photograph only to display her disgust.

"This receipt proves the DNA was right," she says.

"Take the receipt and photograph home."

She slides her hands around the frame. "I don't understand."

On the back of my copy of the tab, I write my phone number and give it to her.

"Which impresses me more?" she says. "Trusting me with your credit card number or your direct line?"

"It's my home phone." I fold my duffel bag together, note how fresh its emptiness feels, as if I've accomplished something. "Call me when the secret strikes you. Something in the photograph an investigative reporter might find important."

She stands, gathers both receipts and the photograph. "Try to have a good afternoon, Officer Hill," she says in a tone close to pity. A doubting kiss on my cheek. The brush of her lips, though, causes me to flinch toward her breath.

"Call me when you know."

She clutches the photograph to her chest. "Now those sound like words from a first date."

I make myself more clear. "Call me when you're ready to be

an investigative reporter."

Her smile had returned, but it's gone again. Turning, she walks away as if she was passing by and had never sat at this booth. I watch the bounce of her long hair against her back, the way her hips move beneath the hem of her WVOL shirttail.

Lunch crowd noise overtakes the air I inhale. My fingertips at the rough edges of the broken plate. For now, there's nothing for me to do but wonder about Sydney Brey.

22

Running tonight feels as though I've slipped into a current determined to take me somewhere unknown. Although I race along white boy streets in every direction, the wind remains at my back. Arms frantic, knees lifting high. I'm a target here. Larry Grimes has made it clear. I move as fast as I ever ran during my best days in high school. It's not euphoria I obtain as much as it is strength, a feeling I have the power to control the uncontrollable, with the wind constantly at my back regardless of the choices I've made.

From a sidewalk, a lone white boy eyes me; shirt off, he displays his teenaged musculature, his teenaged invulnerability. I drift off the center of the street toward him, block his way and stop. He tries to step around me. I block his path again. "Problem?" he asks, his voice harsh. I step closer, keep my eyes on his until he can no longer hold my stare.

"That's right," I say. "Turn away when I come down your street."

Moving toward him, I bump my shoulder against his, send him stumbling backwards. He says nothing, recovers, and continues along the walk, glancing back at me with a look similar to fear.

The wind steady at my back and my feet light upon forbidden streets. I don't know why I approached that white boy the way I did, other than it felt necessary to do it, as much as it feels necessary to run along Leaper Street to the cemetery. The gate there is locked and I pace at the entrance, listening for the sound of the Falls through my breathing and rush of passing cars.

Tumbling water emulates distant whispers, especially this night, and the outer edge of its mist reaches my skin. Within the faint sound and touch of the Falls, I'm able to discern Charlie Watts's childish voice worrying about river ghosts. "They're here, Rich. They're really here." I think of Poppa. Poppa sits down with me to explain Hitchcock's meaning of the glowing glass of milk Cary Grant carried up the stairs in *Suspicion.* And Momma. She reads the opening passage aloud from *A Prayer for Owen Meany,* as if the words prove the existence of a good and purposeful God.

From the gate at Leaper Street Cemetery, along the switchback miles through white and black territories, always with the wind at my back. Faster now, legs pumping, I'm inspired not by the wind itself but by what it carries. Touches of cold, like icy fingers. Ghosts. Whether from the river, or from Momma and Poppa's house, or from within me, the ghosts I thought had abandoned me have returned.

They're not chasing me, not when I think more thoughtfully about their touches at my back. Rather it's clear, their purpose is to push me forward.

By midnight, Jack has left six messages on my answering machine. One to the next, it's a downward flow of emotion. Cheery reminder to concern, to anger, then to something worse than disgust. Auntie Doria has left three messages. In each she tells me to call Jack, she's worried, and she loves me. There's no downward flow with Auntie's emotions.

Oaken doors and heavy curtains seal Momma and Poppa's house, impenetrable to nighttime's artificial lights. The rooms are like recesses deep within a vast cave. Utter darkness creates a sensation of infinity to opened eyes, even as the same darkness clothes me in claustrophobia. My fall toward uncertainty and the return of ghosts cause uneasiness about whether I've slid the deadbolts fully across, although I remember doing so once, then again to help me create certainty. I wonder whether spaces exist between doors and doorjambs, or between joining curtains, wide enough for Jack or Henry Clayton to peer through and discover me in the black. The phone rings on the nightstand beside my easy chair in the living room, igniting a small, rectangular light. The numbers within the rectangle show me it's twenty minutes past midnight, and Jack's calling once more. This seventh time, he doesn't leave a message. The chair's cupping shape holds me like a baby in a cradle. I'm a child fighting off sleep out of fear I'll miss something in the night. Something exciting. Something adults keep from the kids. A mystery perhaps. Or an answer to a question I've only recently learned to ask.

When the phone rings again, I'm caught moments into my nightmare. The cloth under which I watch Momma and Poppa, and Henry Clayton, is within reach, then pulls away. The green-yellow rectangle on the phone flashes *Caller Unknown.*

After the third ring, I press the receiver against my mouth and ear, and I wait.

"Officer Hill? Are you going to say hello?" She sounds different, more deliberate, and her voice through the phone carries her breath against my cheek.

"Tell me what you found."

With Sydney Brey's words I'm brought back in time. Not under the table; I'm outside the protective sweep of cloth, standing beside Momma, her body forced to the floor. I'm alongside her left hand's foolish stretch toward the ceiling. Momma's fingers drop toward the white boy's back, touch his skin beside the swastika there, begin their odd circling motion.

"The arms of the swastika tattoos in the photograph," Sydney says, "all break to the left. Clockwise swastikas. Except for the tattoos on one man."

I whisper, "Henry Clayton."

"Are you saying Henry Clayton stands second from the left end?"

I grunt something, and wonder if she can sense how firmly I press the phone to my face, whether she knows her words flow over me, and through my skin.

"Clayton's," she says in a rush, "are the only ones breaking to the right. Counterclockwise swastikas."

Dreaming images fade, and the black in this room overwhelms me. "The man who killed your parents, are you saying his tattoos were counterclockwise swastikas?" Her pace slows. "You're still convinced Henry Clayton murdered your parents."

I'm caught in the possibility of what Momma knew. She didn't speak to me in order to help me survive. She understood the end of her future and Poppa's future were already determined by their attacker, yet she kept her motherhood unspoiled. A brilliant woman who, even in torture, made a gesture as far from ridiculous as it was desperate to a son she loved and sacrificed herself for. She accepted the risk of a terrified boy who could grow into a man far too angry to grasp her final message. The passage of time, before I came to understand, has made inevitable the doubting by others. It shows in Sydney's pessimistic tone when she asks me again whether I'm sure.

"Neo-Nazis use the clockwise swastika," I say. "Typically. It's something Momma knew."

"I can't tell for sure, you know, but is that Prentiss Schumacher standing next to Clayton?"

"Yes."

"Have you told his father about the counterclockwise swastika?"

"No."

"Have you told anybody?"

"Just you."

"Ever? During the trial?"

"Nobody."

"A memory you tell nobody about for over sixteen years until you find this photograph, versus a proof-positive DNA exoneration and a computer-generated receipt made at the time of the murders." She coughs in the unnecessary way people use to delay conversation. "It could be a problem."

"Is it a problem with you?"

"It's virginal to be the first one you tell. I mean, I'm sorry to say it like this. I can't imagine what you've lived through. But it's like firing up the investigative reporter in me, you know? I thought you might like to hear me say so."

"At the moment, I don't regret telling you."

"You didn't tell me. I figured it out." She draws in a long breath. "I suppose you want me to keep this thing secret. I can go a week. It may kill me, but maybe I can go two weeks, so give me some credit. I've already passed your damn test."

So many things to reveal after sharing one secret. Undoing one brick in my fortress encourages more secrets to flow. Caution gets the better of me. I acknowledge what she's done with silence.

"Richard," she says. "I'm calling you Richard from now on. The thing is, you have to deal with the receipt and Clayton's DNA. Especially together."

I ease the phone from my face, wipe my sleeve over my brow. "Give me those two weeks. Maybe a month."

"A month?" She hums something, perhaps a moan of frustration. "It'll be a new record for me." She says in a soft way that draws me back to her kiss, "Only because it's you. Bye for now."

Rote memory takes my body through the dark, upstairs to

bed. How odd it is to be aware of sleep's approach. To be able to wonder, even after sleep comes, about a miracle. A miracle, at least, for me.

A new dream.

No hiding under a table, no peering under cloth to view rape and murder. A dream, not viewed through the eyes of the child I once was, but through the eyes of the man I've become.

A moving image lasting less than a minute, then repeating. I'm compelled to study her, concentrate on something new about her each time it replays. She kisses me softly on my cheek, smiles, and turns. She walks away with Riddy's photograph clutched in her arms.

Her face is more appealing than plain.

I've learned without any doubt just how beautiful Sydney Brey is when she walks, and what it feels like to leave my desolate place, to walk beside her.

23

The dragging repetition of arraignment court, the defendant-by-defendant explanation of constitutional rights and obligations, shifts toward a perverse excitement whenever a homicide defendant first appears.

Prosecutors and defense attorneys. Victims' rights groups and court watchers. All are strangers to the actual story. They watch through attentive eyes, lips slightly parted, and display their sympathy in silence. I perceived during Henry Clayton's trial that it was a sympathy more for their particular cause than for the suffering of a boy.

Auntie Doria brought me to Henry Clayton's arraignment. She insisted. Said it was necessary out of respect for Momma and Poppa. She rushed me into the courtroom through a narrow passage of parting spectators. We were taken by prosecutors to seats in front of the bar, claiming they needed to surround me, to protect me. I suspected they simply wanted a chance to be part of some portion of the case, to have their names in the newspapers, or be included in an artist's rendition of the scene. Reporters did what they could to press closer toward me, leaned ridiculously far over the crowded pews in front of them to glimpse sadness or despair, a visual they could dramatically describe in their opening paragraphs. Auntie Doria shook me when I yawned, tsked at me, and repeated, "Stand tall for Momma and Poppa. Show this devil you're unafraid."

For Prentiss Schumacher's arraignment on the murder of

Howard Riddy, a fresh suspect in the murders of Momma and Poppa, and in Momma's rape, I've worn my police uniform. Although absent and unexcused from shift, I wear the uniform in order to earn a seat from the bailiff in front of the bar, a few feet, I realize, from where I sat beside Auntie Doria sixteen years ago.

I cannot help but notice how little has changed. The same courtroom, authoritative in its polished cherry wood, the doweled banisters, judicial bench, witness stand, and bar separating spectators from case participants and court staff. Humidity from the crowd of people overwhelms both the air-conditioning and the flow from twin ceiling fans. Sunlight angles through arching windows on the east wall and reflects off the haze in this room to create a light fog. The only surprise for me is the sense of dimension. Rather than shrink this place, both my adult height and the crowd seem to stretch it, expand its length and width beyond my recollections as a boy.

The case is called and guards unlock the metal door to the holding cell beside the clerk's desk. Three more guards appear, two at Schumacher's sides, another behind him. Chains bind his ankles. His hands clasp through cuffs and connect to his waist through a belt made of thick leather. He's forced to walk toward the bench using a toddler's shuffle to the Christmassy jingle of his ankle chains. Dressed in a light blue jumpsuit, *Red River Falls Corrections* printed in red letters over the back, Prentiss Schumacher appears paler than he looked under the fluorescent lights in police lockup. Thin, gaunt, obviously a white boy gone a night without sleep. The thick stubble of beard coating his jaw, his closely shaven scalp combine to give his head the appearance of being attached to his body upside down. Two arms of the swastika tattooed to the side of his neck reach over the V of his collar. Arms with angles to the left. Clockwise swastikas.

Prentiss Schumacher walks by without any indication he sees me, or cares to. His father, however, rising from the prosecutor's table, buttons his suit coat and looks hopefully at me for several seconds, then nods. He walks to the left of his son, where prosecutors typically stand, before Judge Warren Brooker sitting on high at his bench.

Judge Brooker's white skin flares beneath his mass of gray hair. His fingers work at the corners of the few pages in a thin court file destined to grow thick. "Where's the defense attorney?"

"The defense attorney hasn't been determined yet." Fred Schumacher's voice has turned shallow.

"It's clear, though. You can't prosecute this. Your office can't prosecute this. We'll need to appoint a special prosecutor before I can arraign this defendant."

"I demand a trial now." A hush rushes through the courtroom at the cool sound of Prentiss Schumacher. "I'm not agreeing to any continuances. As long as I'm locked up, you have ninety days from yesterday to prosecute me."

"I don't prosecute a thing." Judge Brooker folds his hands over the court file. "Has your daddy been busy giving you some legal advice?"

Prentiss turns a bit toward his father. Fred ignores the gesture.

"The prosecution," Fred Schumacher says, "requests an order compelling immediate sampling and expedited examination of this defendant's DNA."

Prentiss moves toward the judge's bench, stiffens when guards grab his arms. "No DNA!" Sharp to his father. "We didn't discuss it, Dad. I'm not agreeing to DNA."

"What's going on here, Fred?" Judge Brooker stands from his chair. "You can't ask for anything. You and your office have a blatant conflict with this entire prosecution."

"Your Honor, this defendant hasn't waived a single day of his statutory right to speedy trial. As an officer of the court, regardless of anything else, I am obligated to point out two unavoidable facts. First, by the time a special prosecutor is found and approved, perhaps more than half the statutory speedy trial time will go by without a single step taken toward working up the case. Second, a defendant in a homicide case, with blood all over the scene, does not have the right to object to a motion for DNA sampling. Even if this defendant's mother, girlfriend, and his kindergarten teacher were here making the request, a judge would simply look foolish in this situation if he failed to order the DNA testing on the court's own motion." Fred Schumacher's voice recovers some of its strength. "Nobody wants to be the judge responsible for the release of a defendant charged with murder because of a statutory speedy trial problem."

Prentiss, near tears, has to be held up by the guards. "I can't believe you, Dad. What are you trying to do?"

Judge Brooker presses his hands on his bench. "How long have we known each other, Fred?"

"Over twenty-five years."

"And how many rounds of golf have we played together?"

"I couldn't count them at this point."

"Reporters are taking notes as we speak."

"I'm sure they are."

"You know what I have to do?"

"I understand completely."

"All right." Judge Brooker straightens, raises his voice to the courtroom. "I'm ordering the appointment of the public defender's office until and unless private counsel is retained. I'm also ordering the sheriff's office to arrange for an immediate DNA sampling to be transported to the proper authorities for comparison with the available evidence. Last," he says, and turns to stare directly at Fred Schumacher. "I'm ordering the court reporter to prepare the transcript record here this morning and forward it to the Attorney Disciplinary Board. I have no choice, Fred. You've done this in open court."

"I suggest an arraignment date with the public defender's office present as soon as possible," Fred says. "Speedy trial time to run on the prosecution's case."

"Fine. Tomorrow morning." Judge Brooker looks as though he has something more to say to Fred. He presses his lips together, faces his bailiff. "Let me know when the masses clear. Then we can start the other cases. I'll be in chambers."

Prentiss Schumacher has collapsed into silence; he's escorted by his guards, returns to holding without acknowledging his father. I sit, lost in the sounds of people standing and filing out the back of the courtroom. A cough alerts me to Fred Schumacher. He stands in front of my chair, extending the court order he's drafted.

"You might be making a mistake," I say.

"This order's for the expedited DNA examination. I'll make sure it's compared to the DNA evidence preserved in your mother's rape test kit." He nearly shoves the order into my hands. "I doubt there's any perpetrator DNA evidence to compare in Riddy's case."

Word for word as Judge Brooker ordered, Fred Schumacher has faithfully put it in writing.

"I want you to be there," he adds. "I want you to be there when the DNA is drawn from Prentiss, its transport to the crime lab, and when the forensic comparison is made. They won't let you inside the lab, but you'll hear first."

"What's your point?"

"I want you to be sure, just as much as I want to be sure. I don't want any doubts." Fred Schumacher pauses to catch his breath. "Under these circumstances, I trust you most of all."

"Why didn't you discuss this order with your son?"

"I didn't need to. The law doesn't allow a defendant to object.

Besides, with his test, we'll know."

"You sound convinced."

"I am," he says. "It's DNA."

"You trust it more than you trust your son?"

"Prentiss? Do you mean to be absurd?"

I glance away from him toward the emptying courtroom. Drano leans against the back wall. Sydney Brey sits, her hands folded over the backrest in front of her, inspects her watch and mouths she has a deadline to make.

"Where's Marla?" I ask, turning back to Schumacher. It's a question that further pulls on his face.

"She had to take care of other things in the office."

"You believe your son's guilty."

He lowers his head, rolls the court order into a tube. "What I want to say to you, Officer Hill. What I have to say." He walks to the bailiff, hands her the order for Judge Brooker to sign, and waits until she's gone into chambers. He angles himself, peers over his shoulder. "Last night, I arranged for a preliminary print comparison on the knife. My son's fingerprints came back on the handle and the blade."

"He gave an explanation for that possibility."

"He also has an explanation for Riddy's watch, jewelry, and the money officers found in his pockets. You didn't know. Neither did I. I had to find out from the evidence inspector. Then Prentiss decided to give me an explanation for the things he stole. Early this morning. I may be a father, but I'm also a seasoned prosecutor. Too many clever explanations from a defendant only make the obvious explanation more true."

Fred Schumacher's past has caught up to him in the form of his son. How thoroughly it defeats him. Shoulders rolled forward, his voice particularly hollow. Yet I'm unable to give sympathy to this man, and I'm unwilling to tell him what I've shared with Sydney Brey. I turn to look for her. She's gone.

"I want you to transport the DNA sample," he says. "I want you to be there when the truth comes out about your parents' murderer. I'll make the arrangements and contact you. Don't think I'm unaware of the problems created by sending the victims' son along with the evidence, but I don't give a damn. As the boy's father, I can't think of a better way to make the results conclusive beyond all doubt." He shrugs. "Besides, Prentiss still insists he's innocent."

My muscles stiffen at the touch of Fred Schumacher's hand on my shoulder, and I wait for him to leave the courtroom before I turn to go. Drano blocks my path.

"Did you think we were unaware of your little lunch date with Ms. Brey?"

Stepping around him, refusing to acknowledge his presence, I'm out the courtroom with Drano at my heels. "You can't ignore me on this, Hill."

Drano follows as I hurry along the corridor to the stairwell. He breathes more rapidly, strains to keep up with my rush down the stairs. "You have to come with me. I'm saying this as a police officer."

"You're arresting me?"

"I suppose I am. Yeah. I am."

At the exit doors, I stop to face him. "For what?"

"Theft. Official misconduct. For collecting a paycheck even though you blew off work without permission."

"I haven't collected my paycheck yet."

Drano wipes sweat off his brow. "Attempted theft. Now I'll have to add resisting. You know how it goes."

"You're an idiot," I say, and leave the courthouse.

Nearing the bottom of the courthouse steps, I turn toward Drano, watch him at the top step with his arms folded over his chest. "Actually," he says, "my job was to slow you down. Where you're standing right now is perfect."

Drano's stare rises over my head, to his left, and when I turn, Jack pulls up in our squad car on the courthouse drive. He rises from the squad, his stare unemotional on mine, voice even. "Did Drano tell you you're under arrest?"

"He did."

"Get in back."

Drano says, "He wouldn't believe me."

Jack levels a scowl at Drano, steps to the back passenger door and opens it. Waves me over. "Don't make me force you in, Rich. Make this easy. If you try to run, I've got cops in every direction, and you know how much they like you." Jack lowers his chin, says my name as if it were a final warning before a greater punishment.

Drano pushes me toward the squad. "Cuffs?"

Jack grumbles. "Do I have to tell you to shut up?"

"Just asking."

I should run, take my chances. Other officers mill about on the walk, typical outside the courthouse as the morning court calls progress. Some glance at us as if we're engaged in an odd demonstration. Jack's hands are on me, removing my service revolver, at my shoulder, directing me into the back of our squad. "There we go," he says, closing the door. "No trouble here."

Jack gets behind the wheel and Drano opens the front passenger door. "What do you think you're doing?" Jack asks.

Drano freezes with one leg in the squad. "I'm getting in."

"Why?"

" 'Cause we're assigned partners today. We're a team." Drano tries to smile, at me, then at Jack. "What's going on?"

"I'm having a private conversation with Rich. Please remove yourself and close the door."

"I thought we were making an arrest."

Jack steps on the gas and lurches the squad away from Drano, closing the front passenger door with our acceleration. "Here's my first complaint about you," Jack says. "With your disappearance, shift command teamed me up with Drano."

I squint through the protective cage separating arrestees from cops, hear the locking of rear doors I can't open from inside. "Do you really have other officers involved in this abduction?"

"Just Drano. The rest were an educated coincidence."

"What does Drano know about this?"

"Same as with everything else in the world. Nothing." Jack's eyes momentarily focus on mine in the rearview mirror. "He thought this would be a friendly hazing."

Our squad turns from the courthouse parking lot, left, away from town. In silence we pass by miles of corn and soybean fields until the lines disappear from the road. Fields of wild grass reach to the horizon. Jack presses on the brakes, steers toward the gravel shoulder.

"My second of so many complaints about you," he says, "has to do with me. Me and Henry Clayton."

24

Jack stops the squad. Gets out. He paces over gravel on the shoulder. I can't see his face, but his figure, dark in his uniform, passes by the windows. A back door opens and Jack's hands are on me, dragging me out. I'm shoved over the trunk and, when I stand, Jack grips me at the collar, his face turned gray, looming over me.

"What're you thinking?" he says, and draws a fist back. "You stand my family up and force me to partner with Drano, did you really believe I'm not going to find out what you're up to?"

I stare over his head, at the blue in the sky, smell heat off the road. Jack pulls me toward him, demands an answer, and growls when I stay silent. The back of his hand lands against my jaw, the force sending me to the gravel at Jack's feet. One of his boots moves back and I prepare myself for the blow. I'm lifted, tossed to the gravel again. Digging my feet in the ground, I lunge at him. Jack moves to the side and throws my momentum to the road. I taste blood in my mouth. Feel it run over my chin. The broken asphalt ahead of me leads to an eternity. I run toward it.

"Rich! You're moving like an old man. Besides, I've got the squad car here."

My body aches from the punishment; my left knee in particular throbs with every step. There's no sense in running, or standing for that matter. I crawl on the shoulder toward tall grass. The sound of a trigger drawn back startles me; Jack, braced at the hood of the squad, raises his service revolver overhead. I imagine the report like an explosion, tearing at my ears, slamming against the horizon as if I were prey encased in its echo. At the edge of the grass, I grip my hands around gravel, and wait. The shot never comes. A car door closes, the forward movement of the squad so patient . . .

Jack steps out, his boots near my head. "You know how I hate running, and if I actually shot in the air, I'd have to explain the spent bullet. Fill out all sorts of reports. I thought cocking the trigger would do the trick."

On my side, knees to chest, I hesitate. Wait for Jack's next move. I'm lifted, forced to stand against the squad's front quarter panel. His hands gently brush my uniform, and he tells me to lick the blood off my lips. "Of course now we'll have to come up with a story for your appearance."

He leans beside me against the squad, tells me to relax and returns my service revolver to my holster. "It seems," he says in a controlled voice, "you've been nosing around without my knowledge. Actually I roughed you up 'cause you've been such a tight-ass partner far too long, I had to get it out of my system."

"Is it out?"

"Pretty much."

"Couldn't you have gone to your born-again church to pray and turn the other cheek?"

"I suppose, but I thought knocking some sense into you would be more satisfying." He grins at raw skin over his knuckles.

"What's with you and Henry Clayton?"

"Well now. There's the problem. An A-disk is missing from evidence archives. And it seems the A-disk has given you an answer about me and Clayton, something to make you blow off dinner with my family."

"It begs for more answers to more questions."

"A three-year cop walks into evidence archives and walks out with an evidence disk from a closed murder case. Real easy. His partner finds out only because the partner knows about a peculiar Dollar-Mart receipt, and he's pissed off about being stood up. C'mon, Rich. You've got to know our archive security doesn't exist, not like it is with the active evidence room. A delete button here, a little addition of words there."

"Are you saying someone tampered with the A-disk?"

There's a sudden sadness in Jack's voice, a slump to his shoulders. He steps away from the squad, spins about with his arms outstretched. "I wasn't even a rookie cop back then. I was a police cadet, one cadet out of three at the time. Each of us hoped for a permanent job. A police officer, Rich. A cop is all I ever wanted to be. Here was this double homicide and a media frenzy. I was almost a kid myself back then, and it was a cadet's dream to be involved, so cut me some slack."

"Why was the receipt never disclosed to Clayton's attorney?"

"Maybe it was, you don't know."

"Are you saying Clayton's own lawyer hid this evidence?"

"I don't know what I'm saying. I mean, what I'm telling you is I can't have my own squad partner run from me. This is exactly the sort of thing we need to talk about."

I fold my arms, look away from him.

"You're confiding in a reporter."

"She's never spied on me. Never dragged me away from the courthouse. She's never beat the crap out of me on a country road."

"You blew my whole family off. You took advantage of my invitation to my family's dinner table just so you could check out Clayton's receipt behind my back."

"A missed invitation to dinner? Is that what this mugging is all about?"

"A full-course Chinese dinner."

"It was delivery."

"Someone had to place the order. Someone had to pay for it." Jack shakes his head, looks down the road. "I covered for you at morning shift. Just so you know, you've got a bad case of the shits."

Jack steps to the road with his fingers at his lips. "I wasn't there for Clayton's arrest. Those cops are dead now. Artie Duncan and David Waller. Good men. Waller retired and passed away over a year ago. Artie was a huge man. German stock. Taller than me and about fifty pounds heavier. It may have been fat, but it sure looked like brawn packed into his uniform. Artie gave me the receipt to put into evidence after the trial, told me to keep my mouth shut about it, that it didn't matter anyway. He knew who he arrested within an hour of your 911 call. He knew it was a bullshit piece of paper. Nobody argued with Artie Duncan, and I sure as hell wasn't going to ask him any questions about the receipt."

"You back-dated the evidence entry?"

"Artie's order. I obeyed my supervising officer. Now, I suppose, so no one could accuse him."

"He didn't mind putting the risk on you."

Jack sighs. "I realize that."

"But how does the receipt exist?"

"First tell me if you still believe Clayton murdered your parents, or Schumacher's boy. Maybe somebody else?" Jack looks toward the southern horizon, his eyes seemingly hazed over. "You still aren't ready to tell me."

"No."

"But you know something."

"Nothing you need to hear."

"You told the reporter?"

"She has my phone number."

Jack hangs his head and stares at the street. "Artie didn't give me the receipt until after Clayton's sentencing. About two months after. By then, nobody was looking."

"You didn't have to obey a bullshit order. You didn't have to commit a crime."

"Being a cop is all I ever wanted to be, even if it's in Red River Falls. A new job, a new wife with two miscarriages under our belt. I was told to keep my mouth shut not only for career advancement but to get my job in the first place. Artie decided which cadet was in and which cadet was out. That's the way things operated back then."

"It was a test for you. Keep your mouth shut, and you get your dream job."

"Clayton was a convicted man sentenced to die. Nobody but other skinheads gave two shits about him, and they didn't seem to care much either. At the time, it didn't feel like a big deal."

"You never bothered to consider how Artie Duncan got the receipt, or why."

Jack blinks quickly, rubs at the back of his neck. "I considered, but considering didn't get me anywhere."

"So you partnered with me to make sure your secret remained secret."

"You came to the police force already pissed off at the world. I partnered with you because no one else would have you."

"How did Clayton get the receipt out of archives?"

"Riddy. He's the logical answer." Jack sits on the hood, sheet metal bending under his weight. "Riddy loved to do favors for the young men in his life. And the archives, just as you proved, are easy in, easy out. The old fart walked around the department like he owned the place. He probably had no other motive than to drive us all nuts."

"The receipt is garbage, but garbage won Clayton a DNA test."

Jack slides off the hood, moves toward me, doesn't see my

hand fisted at my side. When he's in range, I swing and strike, watch his bulk fall to the earth.

"Clayton's a free man now," I say, standing over him. "What the hell did you help set in motion all those years ago?" Head and neck begin to rise from the ground, my heel at his right shoulder, shoves him back down. "This was about my parents. All you wanted to do was keep your goddamn job."

"Don't you think I know?" He groans at my feet, brings his hands to his nose. "I think it's broken. Now we're gonna have to explain this too."

"Tell shift command we got in a fight over a Chinese delivery dinner. We both lost."

"Could work," Jack says.

I sit in the squad, press my tongue against the wound in my mouth. Jack makes his way to the driver's side, lowers himself behind the steering wheel. He starts the engine, turns the squad around toward Red River Falls, and stalls in the road.

From here, the town resembles a dark mound in the distance. I glance at Jack, at the swipe of blood over his upper lip. His eyes, though aimed toward the road, have a familiar look, something I've recognized in the mirror. He's in the past, reviewing memories, comparing them with other possibilities that would have changed the present.

"What?" he says.

"Nothing."

"You're staring at me like you'd rather see me dead."

"What did you expect?"

He shakes his head. "It wasn't all about keeping my job."

"Drive," I say. "Just drive."

He doesn't drive; he hangs his left arm over the steering wheel, leans toward me with a sick-dog look drawn across his face. Another secret to tell, more slow poison bottled up inside needing to come out before it kills him.

"Someone else knows about the receipt. She knows because I told her a week after I archived it. I told her because the job didn't feel like it was worth it after all. Auntie Doria. She's known for almost as long as I have."

There's no change in his pitiful expression. No reaction to my disbelief. Of course he knows, as well as I do. I could confront Auntie Doria, and she wouldn't lie to me if I asked her for the truth with her hand pressed on her bible.

"Why'd you tell her?"

"After the sentencing I saw you as the worst kind of victim. What struck me hardest, what I remember about you the most, was the stranglehold you had on Auntie Doria's hand. To you she was the world's last life preserver. The image haunted me. It didn't take long before keeping the receipt a secret didn't feel like it was worth my job anymore, but I figured it wasn't my decision to make."

"So you asked Auntie Doria what to do?"

"I introduced myself to her at the flower shop. Bought a bouquet for Theresa too." He shifts our squad into gear, leaves his foot pressed on the brake pedal. "I've kept it secret because Auntie Doria insisted. She believed it would be best for you." He watches me closely, seems to understand my silence, then drives us toward Red River Falls.

Jack talks so softly, as if unaware his voice begs forgiveness. "After that, I started going to church again."

"Why is it all you drunks, thieves, and liars get religion and think your rebirth excuses everything? You're like kids caught cheating at a game, insisting on a do-over. For some reason you think it gives you the right to lecture to the rest of us who never drank, stole, or lied in the first place."

I'm without the energy to forgive. I listen to his words, how their plainness is overpowered by their meaning.

"We didn't know back then," Jack persists. "Who the hell

could know? A perfect science would one day set that son-of-a-bitch free."

25

Jack drops me off at Momma and Poppa's house. We make no gestures, polite or otherwise. I assume he'll say nothing, just go. It's not unlike him, though, when he says before driving off, "Tomorrow morning, at shift, I expect you'll be over your case of the shits."

I stop on the front walk and stare at the house I own. It doesn't belong to me, not in the way that matters, and it never will. It's Momma and Poppa's home, and a young boy's. The past possesses it, like a museum, far too preserved despite the changes I've made to its interior. Echoes, memories, and the smell of its bones cannot be decorated away. It's not as though I haven't sensed this emotion before, but in the depths of other, more urgent emotions, somehow this one got lost. Now the thought seems to scream at me, inverting itself into an opposite perspective. A two-story cube of bricks grips my life within its corners. This house clearly owns me.

A plastic grocery bag leans against the front porch railing. It contains the Dollar-Mart receipt and Riddy's photograph; a note posted on the screen door asks me in pretty lettering whether I listened to the recent newscasts on WVOL. *Waiting to find out in back.*

Sydney Brey sits on the grass in the backyard, her shoulders against the brick below the kitchen window. "You really need some landscaping. It's all grass, if you can call this stuff grass. And you could really use a bench or something, you know?"

She inspects the swelling on my face, stands to take a closer look. Her fingers, now with a touch of my blood on them. "What happened?"

"A fight over dinner."

She smiles. "You don't eat out very well."

"No."

"Was it always this empty back here?"

I move to the center of the lawn, point toward the pale wood fence at the back of the yard. "There used to be a swing set over here. If you feel for them, you'll find the depressions in the ground, where we'd sit on swings and drag our feet."

"With your friends or your parents?"

Her question surprises me. Why would anyone care about my past before the moment that defined my present? Pleasant memories are there, but my nightmare makes them hard to talk about, painful to recollect out loud knowing how everything ended. "Both," I say. "I had a lot of friends at one time in my life."

"Really?" she says.

"Kids don't notice black skin and white skin so much, and skin like mine, somewhere in the middle. Not the way adults tend to. But, you know, parents teach things and kids grow up."

Sydney steps closer and dabs more blood off my lips with her sleeve. "My closet's full of these WVOL shirts. It's embarrassing, but they're free to underpaid employees." I try not to think about her in my dream, or the way the dream makes me feel. Why do I find this so difficult? "You haven't been allowed to grow up," she says. "Or maybe you grew up in one instant, far too early. Either way, the result is the same."

"How's that?"

"Innocence should be lost in small pieces. When it's taken from you all at once, you feel yourself separated from the rest of humanity." Her eyes look purposeful, proving she believes what she's saying. "Your parents loved you, and the neighborhood children loved them. They came here to play, and became your friends. Did you have a best friend?"

"Charlie Watts."

"The drummer for the Rolling Stones was your best friend?"

"A boy whose mother worshiped the Rolling Stones was my best friend."

"What happened to him?"

I walk to one of the depressions in the grass, feel where Charlie Watts fell off the swing during my seventh birthday party, landed on his back, and cried in Momma's arms until she made him laugh. That's when I learned my friends felt the same way I did about Momma. The best mother on the block. Maybe in the galaxy. "You're not entitled to know," I say to Sydney. Not in any emotional way. Just stating the fact.

"I've kept my word. Everything you've told me remains a secret."

"Charlie Watts isn't a secret." I leave the small hollow in the earth, move toward Sydney. "It's something you're not entitled to know."

"I'll figure it out someday. I'm pretty good at figuring people out."

Before I can ask it, she knows my question. "I have two, living, loving parents. I'm the girl who avoided teenage angst. I grew up never telling either of them I hated them, so I never had to apologize like most children have to. Never spanked, never felt ignored even with two brothers and a sister. It's like you'd gag at my life's story."

She scans my backyard for something. Perhaps imagining, as I now do, this space filled with children, and my parents there to soak up our energy.

"But things aren't so perfect in my life. I'm kind of a runaway bride. Such a surprise coming from the daughter of practically perfect parents and their practically perfect marriage. You'd think I'd figure the man out while we were dating, but it didn't hit me until we wrote our own wedding vows. I read his and gushed. He read mine and corrected it."

"Corrected your wedding vow?"

"Edited or corrected, whatever. His blue ink was everywhere over my pink. Comments in the margins. It seemed like a good time to shove off, you know? Even if it was the morning of the ceremony." She tilts her head. Watches me sympathetically. "Big deal, right? I mean, in comparison to your life."

She returns her fingers to my lips, touches them and laughs. "I believe I've made you smile."

"It's probably a reaction to the pain in my mouth."

"You should get into food fights more often."

What would she say if I were to tell her I dream of her, tell her my dream plays for me now even though she's here? Maybe because she's here. Her smile makes her face turn childlike. Yet she's a woman capable of ending a marriage the day it's supposed to begin. A woman who, despite her idyllic childhood, probes my history using an improbable insight. She proves she's formidable, someone I should have on my side. The thought to confess my dream is there, and I should thank her for it in a way an interested man ordinarily would. But this is too new. The sensation she creates is too new. An anger inside me rises to object. I'm neither deserving nor entitled, especially with what remains unresolved.

I look to the ground. "I saw you at the arraignment, realized you had a deadline. But I didn't hear your newscast. I was too busy food-fighting."

"You can hear the replay on WVOL, twenty-three and fifty-three minutes after the hour, every hour for the next five hours. Then the evening news kicks it off the air for good."

"What did your report say?"

"The usual. Nothing important."

"What do you mean?"

"Richard," she says, touching my arm. "I saw part of Prentiss Schumacher's swastika on his neck for myself. Clockwise. I kept your secret. I'm keeping my side of the bargain."

"I thought you would."

"You had your doubts."

When I look at her this time, I linger over her eyes. "It wasn't doubt. It was fear."

She walks toward the side of the house. Stopping short of the small stoop at the side door, she transforms into her serious self. "I did a little bit of research. On DNA. There's plenty on the Internet. Some of it on what could go wrong. Genetic alleles, amplification factors, evidence storage errors, misinterpretations of population percentages. Most of it's far too scientific for my bachelors-in-liberal-arts brain to comprehend."

"I seriously doubt Henry Clayton would understand any of it too."

"Agreed. But I did find a story from England that should interest you. It seems there was this rape involving a woman who couldn't identify the man who did it to her. The semen was there, and severe injuries too. There was no doubt she was a victim of a violent attack, and her village was in an uproar to catch the guy. DNA criminal forensics had begun to flourish then, and a test was run on the semen. It came back to a man with a small rap sheet living eighty miles away. She couldn't identify him in court, and he had a dozen witnesses testify to his whereabouts the evening of the rape. He couldn't have done it. Even so, the DNA evidence said he was the one."

She watches me closely, a reporter checking for a reaction. "The jury convicted him anyway. I mean, after all, it was DNA evidence, and DNA forensics is foolproof."

"Did you come here to tell me my memories are mistaken?"

"What is it with you? First you assumed I fulfilled the role of a heartless reporter. Now you assume I'm done with the story, you know? I'm not even at the most important part. Here's the thing. This perfect science got more perfect after the case. Isn't that a silly thing to say? How can you improve on something already perfect? You can't, unless it's not perfect at all. Do you get what I'm saying?"

"Have you ever heard of a plantation cocktail?"

"A bar drink?"

"More of a possible explanation."

Her hand reaches for the screen door. "Never heard of it." She tugs at the screen and it jars open.

"Please," I say. She misunderstands my urgency at the sight of the door.

"What? I'm not invited in?"

"Finish your story."

She folds her arms over her chest, and the screen door closes. "It seems at the time of the trial there was a six allele test. There's that word again, but please don't ask me what an allele is, you know? All I can grasp is that it has something to do with what scientists count and compare. Well, the science improved to a ten-allele count, then a thirteen-allele count, and it turns out this man's DNA didn't match the rapist's semen using this improved technology."

"I sincerely doubt the crime lab used old technology with Clayton's DNA."

"Richard," she says. "You should note how I'm beginning my sentences with your name when you annoy me. It's better than swearing, you know? The point is this. People want to believe in something perfect. With life imprisonment and the death penalty, people want to believe there's a perfect science guaranteed to get the right guy, so they can sleep at night and not have to worry."

"How does this story help my situation?"

"Richard!" she says, halts and smiles. "That was a real fuck-you kind of Richard. Look, I don't know about Clayton's DNA test. I don't know about his damn receipt. But I saw for my own eyes Prentiss Schumacher's clockwise swastika and the photograph with Clayton's counterclockwise swastika. The whole idea the battle here is between a perfect science versus your imperfect human memory is bullshit. The fact is, nothing can be perfect when human beings are involved. Garbage in, garbage out. Laziness. Corruption. Take your pick."

"The shock of an eight-year-old boy. Believing in his mind's eye what he still wishes to believe sixteen years later."

"There's that," she says. "Look, I'm not the one to determine what's true. I'm telling you that a perfect science can never be perfect if there's room for improvement. Even if the machine is perfect, it's bound to fail at some point when people are at the controls." She reaches for the screen door again, my hand grabs hers.

"I'm sorry," I say, lifting her hand off the door handle. "I don't let people in this house except for Auntie Doria. It's too hard for me."

"I'm not surprised," she says. She stares at the door, then higher up toward the second story, at a window with the curtains pulled slightly apart. "But I have to go in."

"Don't."

"What? Kitchen a little messy?" Sydney opens the screen door, turns the handle on the interior wood door, and pushes through. I rest my hand on my service revolver, follow her in past doors I have always kept locked since I bought the place, for which I have never had a key.

26

At the threshold to the kitchen, Sydney remarks, "Cleaner than mine, although that's not necessarily a compliment."

No marks on the jamb.

"Please leave the house," I say. "You should respect my wishes."

"You've asked a lot from me." As if that's reason enough, she continues on. She passes through the hall running by a bedroom and a den. She pauses along the way at pictures on the wall. In particular at a photo of Momma and Poppa side by side on the swings; Momma large weeks before my birth, Poppa with a wrench in his hand after tightening the last bolt on the swing set. She's turned to kiss him, lips puckered into a tight circle against his cheek. "Your father was a handsome man," she says. "Like you. Although you get your tight-ass smile from your mother."

Hand on my holster belt, I push by her to check the den, bedroom, and living room. No one else is present, nothing disturbed. Sydney's preoccupied with the wealth of shelving packed full of Momma's books. "You've read all these?"

"Most," I say, and notice on the bottom shelf, the tilting of one title against another. A space caused by a missing book.

"Impressive. Are you a college boy?"

"Community college. An associate's degree in criminal justice. There wasn't enough money left in the trust fund for anything more after I bought the house."

"What possessed you to buy it, you know, after everything?

"Everybody asks me about the house."

"Is that your answer? No answer at all, like the mysterious case of the vanishing Charlie Watts?"

"Please," I say. "You need to leave." I listen for an invading sound. A breath, a creak beneath a step.

"You keep it neat. I suppose out of respect." She turns back toward the hallway, but her stare lingers on my face. "May I go upstairs?"

"No."

Sydney smiles, her eyes ablaze. "It's not what you're thinking."

"I'm not thinking anything. Do you have to use the bathroom?"

"No."

"You can't go upstairs."

She returns to the living room. Frowns at the sag in the recliner facing the TV. "Guess I should've said I needed to use the bathroom."

"Sydney, you should leave now."

"You started your sentence with my name. Are you swearing at me?"

"You could take it that way."

"No unusual smells, rotting flesh, chemicals, or otherwise. You're a strange man, but there's nothing to call the police or mental health center about." A familiar kiss on my cheek, what I've replayed so often in my mind. "I'm not necessarily believing you over DNA," she says. "But you have one month less one day before I go with a story. It'll either be about a man unable to accept the truth, or a man who kicked the crap out of DNA forensics."

Standing near the front door, she examines the room a final time. Watches me by the dining room table, suddenly quiet. "Is that the table?"

"No."

"What happened to the table?"

"I don't remember."

"Sure you do. You kept it, sold it, or burned it." She stops chiding me, brings her hands to her chest the moment she focuses on the floor. An involuntary catching of breath. Sydney stares at a time and place from the past and the sins committed on the floor we stand upon. There is nothing to say, respectful of Momma and Poppa. This room cannot tolerate expressions of sympathy, nor encouragement for the future.

She's gone; quietly leaving me, finally. She waves from her car, an aging Mustang. I turn from the window and listen. Again I examine the gap between books on the lower shelf. A minor space nearly filled by the leaning of other volumes.

At the foot of the stairs, I wait. I had always thought I could hear an ant crawl across the sidewalk on the other side of the street. It's a gift developed during an overly introspective life. I can hear everything move but a shadow.

Twelve steps to the second floor, each with its own sound. A muffled crush of carpet. A groan from a floorboard. How the sounds amplify themselves now. I close the space in the curtain covering the window overlooking the side door and wonder what the eyes peering through had witnessed. Wonder what had been heard.

Although I feel myself float upstairs, this house belies my approach. And when I turn into the bedroom, Henry Clayton stares straight at me from the wooden rocker he has turned to face the door. He smiles beneath his shining scalp, wearing his preacher's clothing and a look of expectation. His left hand holds up a worn copy of *A Tale of Two Cities.*

"Did you know I read this book three times in prison? It really pissed me off, especially the coincidence of a man looking like the protagonist's twin. Someone to save the day through self-sacrifice. Every second on death row, I wished to God to create my own twin to save the day for me. Even offered to donate a rib." He tosses the book on my bed, folds his arms in his lap. "But I guess I got something better."

My hand rests on my service revolver. "How'd you get in here?"

"Consider this, Officer Hill. My pants and coat are such a common brand, any thread left behind would be meaningless. Obviously, unless I take off my clothes, I don't have any hair to leave either. And if I take the clean handkerchief I've got in my pocket and wipe off the arms on this chair, there'll be no usable prints left to discover. Only this book remains, which I intend to take with me so I can read it a fourth time. You see? I never was here at all."

"I'm a witness."

"Then arrest me. Find out for yourself who'll believe you. Maybe your Auntie Doria, but only because she loves you blindly." He eyes my weapon. "Relax," he says. "I'm here to advise you."

"No longer helping me?"

"I gave you the unrepentant Prentiss Schumacher. The helping part is over. It's time to advise you against continuing down the wrong road. To convince you to stop talking to the wrong people. Your reporter friend in particular is like the Pharisees. She'll lead you astray from the Kingdom of Truth."

"Why did you obliterate your tattoos the way you did?"

He smiles. "You're not entitled to know."

Henry Clayton presses his fingertips on the chair's wooden arms. "Here's evidence of my presence left behind. But there were no stolen keys or signs of forced entry. You invited me into your home. If anyone asks, I'm a new friend of Officer Richard Hill's since the truth of his parents' murders came out. The former accuser and the once accused, together in peace. All I have done is work to follow the example of Jesus and battled my way into your Jerusalem despite the risk of death."

"Things didn't go so well for Jesus in Jerusalem."

"Only to a nonbeliever." Clayton rises from the chair, assumes a calm stance before me. "Jesus lives on forever."

In his presence, I'm forced to keep my eyes opened, though the urge to relive the nightmare intensifies. My search is no longer for the truth but to find confirmation of the truth. Every cell in my body is repulsed by his presence here, in the house Momma and Poppa still possess. My revulsion magnifies hearing Clayton say in such earnestness, "I didn't kill your Momma and Poppa. I didn't rape such a good woman."

When I ask, "Who did?" my question brings a smile to Clayton's face. I don't know why I asked it; I already know his answer.

"We should pray together for Prentiss Schumacher's soul."

"Why don't we discuss it and Riddy's convenient murder over a plantation cocktail?"

Clayton's head flinches to the right, a tic toward his scar. "Does it have alcohol? I don't drink alcohol anymore."

"I've never heard a preacher lie so naturally like you do."

His head tilts, and there's a loss of serenity in his voice. "I heard you've been talking to a reporter. Today I witnessed it for myself. She's fuel for your doubt, encouraged notions in you which should have died long ago and been replaced by peace in the truth."

"She's just someone I'm interested in."

"I don't need a DNA test to prove that's a lie. Understand I have eyes everywhere in Red River Falls. They teach me how fast you run, the path you take, the length and color of your shorts and shirt, the way your sweat catches on your eyebrows. You have so many vulnerabilities. Auntie Doria, Jack Harter and his wife and son, and now this Sydney Brey. They're safe because I say so. Because you, like any man, can be reborn into a new life. As a true believer, my purpose is to lead you to the Kingdom."

While he talks, Clayton approaches me, and it's as though he achieves composure through his own words. Head straight, serenity regained, he lifts his hands toward my arms. His calm imitates his appearance at the trial. Disconnected, off into the future, a wealth of moisture and pity showing in his eyes.

"Have you read John's Revelation, Officer Hill?"

"Twice."

"My suspicion is you studied John's Revelation as a boy to prepare for a written exam. But you didn't read it with your heart. If you read John's Revelation with your heart, you would know your risk. You would know the risk of everybody on earth, especially people you love. You would understand it's the same fate shared by Jesus Christ's enemies. Their horrible end has been prophesied in John's Revelation, and the danger increases the longer you doubt me."

"My own End Of Days by doubting you? Doesn't sound quite born-again of you, or preacherly. It sounds more like the words of a man taking God's name in vain."

Clayton's smile vanishes. I've said the wrong thing; the opposite of what a self-professed apostle of God expects to hear. It's as though I've slapped him, his serenity instantly submerged, replaced as quickly by an inside-out surge of rage. It warps his face into the shape I saw as a boy. I'm caught gaping at him, frozen. He jumps me before I can raise my gun.

"You've been injured," Clayton says. "I can easily add to the damage."

He presses me against the wall, grips my throat, his face twisting toward mine. He holds me there, his eyes fluttering shut. With his next breath, there's an easing to his grip, a return toward serenity. "Whatever I was then, that's not me now." Clayton's hands relax, pat at my shoulders. "This man you see was never in this house when you were a boy." Turning to the bed, he lifts *A Tale of Two Cities* and stuffs it inside his coat, then wipes his handkerchief over the arms of the chair. Henry Clayton stands before me, as he once stood in the courtroom while the jury rendered its verdict, and, later, his death sentence. Detached. Calm. There's no show, no acknowledgment, of his violence. His voice, soft like the lamb's, proves his confidence in his innocence. "I haven't been here today. I've been reborn. And I shall lead you to your rebirth."

He passes by me, hurries down the stairs. I follow and watch him open the front door using his cloth on the handle. "Prentiss Schumacher killed Howard Riddy, and he killed your parents. How you believe otherwise is a symptom of your unforgiven sins, something you'll face eternal damnation for. Your salvation is through me. Through the truth. Through the proper conviction of Prentiss Schumacher." He watches me, his serenity in full control of his body and face. "Allow me to help you, Richard."

"What are you afraid of if I refuse?"

Clayton hesitates, eyes a grocery bag leaning against the porch, then raises his nose to the air. He inhales sweet summer smells and leaves without answering my question.

From Momma and Poppa's house, down the main walk, his steps move easily as if to demonstrate his lack of concern. He visited me once before at Auntie Doria's. Sent flowers to Momma's and Poppa's graves. Offered to help me find the real murderer. He's got plenty of witnesses to support his claim of innocence, and his own DNA exonerated him. He can insist he was here to console me about Prentiss Schumacher and to seek out his peace with me. I am the one to be discounted. I am still the traumatized boy, fanatical possessor of a discredited memory, a believer in the existence of something so vile as a plantation cocktail, convinced it could have been used by a man like Henry Clayton to defeat perfection.

On the surface of things, Clayton's presence in this house declared his innocence, and conveyed a threat should I refuse to play along with Prentiss Schumacher's prosecution. Below the surface, though, he proved his ability to relapse into the man who existed before his professed rebirth into Christianity. Perhaps he relapses when he wants to, or perhaps it's beyond his control. More importantly, despite his government-certified exoneration, he has proven he is a man still in fear of the boy under the table.

Locking the front door, the grocery bag and its contents pressed to my chest, I turn around and wait. The images will come. They always do when I linger over the spot. Rather than Momma, I focus on Poppa. Hands behind his back, a cord looped around the radiator. Mouth gagged. Sweat runs over his face, blends hopelessly with his tears. Clayton, finished with Momma, approaches Poppa with a blade. Poppa has already succumbed at this point. He wants to die.

Clayton's expertise in the barbaric act is clear; and there's the fact of how long I hid clutching my knees under the table, fighting off the revealing sounds terror makes. My expertise. Clayton lingered after he murdered Momma and Poppa for so long I believed my silence would fail before he would run off. I have always believed Clayton waited so he could observe, so he could take pride in his crimes.

Something to talk to Sydney about. I'll consider telling Jack too. What happened here today, and what the police and prosecutors marveled over at the time of the murders, and again at the trial.

It's what the defense had argued a great deal about to the

jury in Clayton's defense, that such violence occurred over an extended period of time. Yet no fingerprints were left behind.

27

Dinner at Auntie Doria's this evening brings a couple surprises. For one, we're eating outside on the back deck despite the threat of rain. Auntie Doria barbecues over a grill. The grill, until now, looked fresh out of the box.

She's invited guests, her other surprise. Two women, one never married with a daughter, the other divorced with a son. Both women in their twenties. Also a married couple from three doors over, the Miltons, who are a month shy of their forty-fourth wedding anniversary, Mr. Milton reminds me again rather sadly; they are a vision of marital happiness but for the hurtful things they say to each other. We gather in folding chairs around a wrought-iron circular table, and watch Auntie Doria barbecue to avoid watching each other.

The daughter and son appear to be about the same age, perhaps seven, and run off to play within a collection of backyards. An agreement was reached long ago among the neighbors. No fences allowed in order to create a makeshift park to substitute for the lack of a nearby public park or field. Children here have a protective place to expend their energy, to play their made-up games. Let the whites too afraid of their own neighborhoods do the organized sports thing. Here, the children rush out of houses spaced side to side, and houses facing back to back; boys and girls argue over which game to play and, once decided, they argue over who should be the captains and who should make the rules. These children, all of them, laugh when they play their games, they get lost within their imaginary adventures. Living with Auntie Doria, I was the one exception to this rule.

Most of the homes are old and small, like Auntie Doria's, repaired well enough in a do-it-yourself sort of way. Each with an inexpensive beauty. Colorful knickknacks hang from eaves and trees. Pastel paint covers window trim over whitewashed clapboards. Garage sale wagons, Victrola trumpets, and ceramic drainpipes put to use as flowerpots and vegetable gardens. Auntie Doria hangs wind chimes, a series of foot-long crosses, from two hooks in her eave over the back deck. A hand-sized portrait photograph of Denzel Washington, laminated within clear strips of Plexiglas, hangs among them.

None of the hangings on any of the homes hangs quite right. There's a slight tilt to each house, in random directions, adding charm to the area, like cottages on a hillside without the hill. And the faces on the people, their collective shades of brown, possess a charm of their own.

Charlene, the mother of the girl, looks doubtfully at Denzel's image spinning in the breeze. She's packed herself into faded jeans and a pink top, and constantly contorts her face, an actress before an imaginary movie camera, performing with a vengeance. Her mouth and eyebrows in particular stretch and compress like rubber, as if everything around her is repulsive. "Your man Denzel is getting kind of old," she calls out to Auntie Doria.

Auntie Doria glares over her glasses. Smoke from the hamburgers has put red in her eyes. "Nothing old about Denzel. Never will be. He's what you call a classic good-looker, honey. Don't say anything otherwise about Denzel."

Charlene bends her face toward Leslie, the divorced mother of the boy. "Classic is another word for old," Charlene says, and sends her lips scrunching to the left side of her face.

"Quiet," Leslie says, and blinks at Mr. Milton. Leslie is the prettier of the two; at least she doesn't contort herself, and I can tell what she looks like despite the fact she sits under a hat more resembling a chandelier. Deep brown skin over her oval face, full lips and hair cropped short to her neck. Lovely, I admit to myself. I'm sure Auntie Doria wants me to notice her.

Large in his UPS uniform, Mr. Milton hunches over the table. He doesn't care about Denzel or any of the women at the table, particularly Mrs. Milton. "When's my burger gonna be done, Doria?" he barks. "It's a sure thing I'll fall over from hunger before I get to eat." Mrs. Milton looks away, somewhere, I suppose, as long as her husband is not in her line of sight.

Auntie Doria brings a plate of four burgers to the table. "It's all I could fit on the Smoky Joe at one time. One of you will have to wait for my next batch."

"I can wait, Auntie," I say.

She sets the plate on the table and rubs my shoulders. "So polite, my Richie child. What a man should be like. Don't you think so, Leslie?" Leslie forces a nod. "What do you think, Charlene?" Charlene's lips remain scrunched to the left. When she nods at me, she looks as though she bites into a lemon.

The others grab their burgers and toasted buns. Mrs. Milton lets hers sit on her plate. Rather than eat, she watches the children play. Beneath what's obviously a wig, and the weight of boredom layered over her bones, she displays a pathetic jealousy.

"Don't you wish you could still run like those kids?" Mrs. Milton smiles at me. "Maybe you still can. This old lady sure can't."

"You can cook," Mr. Milton says. "Better than this burger."

Mrs. Milton slaps at his shoulder. "Don't be rude. You're a guest here."

"What do you do for work?" Charlene asks.

"I'm a police officer."

"Cop," she says. "A detective?"

"Patrol officer."

"Oh."

I turn away so I can't see what new, horrible shape her face has become.

"I'd like to play tag with the children," Mrs. Milton says in earnest. "Anybody want to play tag?"

Mr. Milton insists through his chewing, "Shut up and eat your burger."

"Would you like to play tag, Officer Hill?" Leslie says. Auntie Doria moves behind Leslie, rubs her shoulders and smiles at me; clearly she's the one Auntie Doria prefers.

"I injured my knee today at work."

"The right side of your cheek looks a little puffy too," Charlene says.

"I arrested a resister today. Part of the job."

"You should play tag anyway," Auntie Doria says. "Your sore knee gives the ladies a chance to catch you, is all." Auntie Doria walks around the table back to me. Grabs my left arm and pulls to raise me up. "C'mon, Richie child. Play with these girls."

Heat comes to my skin. Auntie Doria recognizes the emotion in my eyes, and hushes in my ear, "Don't give me none of that, child. This is a party. I've invited the Miltons and some lovely girls here for you to talk to, and they want to play a silly game. Don't go on and ruin it."

Hushed or not, everybody hears, and everybody looks at me, silent, even Mr. Milton, who starts on Mrs. Milton's burger. "C'mon, Richie," Auntie Doria says, lightening her tone. "The girls want to play a game of tag with you."

I stand quickly from my chair, rise over Auntie Doria, and scold her. "I'm seeing someone, Auntie Doria. I'm already seeing a girl."

Auntie Doria's mouth hangs open, and her glasses, stuffed

up high to the bridge of her nose, magnifies her eyes and the hurt I've caused her.

"Probably some gnarly white girl," Charlene says. "And here I am by myself, the sweetest dark chocolate there is."

Auntie Doria rushes into her house. I'm left standing with my arms stretching out toward her.

"I'll take care of the burgers," Mr. Milton says, and heads for the Smoky Joe.

Mrs. Milton shakes her head at no one in particular. "I never should have said a thing about a tag game."

Leslie excuses herself to leave, calls for her son.

"I'm just talking here," Charlene says, whose face suddenly hangs loose. "Just letting off some of the frustration is all. Didn't mean anything personal by it."

Auntie Doria sits on her living room couch, eyes opened but otherwise appearing asleep. All the lights are off, and the cloudy August evening casts a candlelight's shade through the windows. "I thought you would be happy for me," I say, sitting beside her.

"I am."

"What's the matter then? Why'd you run off?"

"You didn't tell me nothing about a girlfriend. You went along so I could make a fool of myself in front of my neighbors."

"It wasn't something I meant. This just happened over the last two days."

"Who is she?"

"Someone from a news station."

"Um hmm." Auntie Doria looks across the room, lost in the glow of the windows. "Why do you suppose I go to church all the time? Why do you think I pray in the mornings, before our meals, and bedtime, and every chance I get in between?"

"You're a believer, Auntie. You've been a believer since I've known you."

"Richie child, you don't appreciate the half of it. I promise every day to the good Lord I'll take care of you the best way I know how. And I promise your Momma and Poppa the same thing every time I put my hands together and ask the Lord to hear me. Do you have any idea the burden placed on me, to receive the trust from your parents' good souls in heaven?"

I take Auntie Doria's hands. Press them to my face. "I couldn't know. There's no way a man like me could know."

"A good answer. An honest one. But you owe me. You owe me the truth, and you're obligated to share everything with me 'cause I'm bleeding for you, son. That's right, you might as well be my son for all the nights I stay up worrying about you. Remember, though, I wouldn't change my life for the world, honey. You better believe it right now."

"Auntie, it's just so hard being a man around you when you treat me like a child."

"You'll always be your Momma's and your Poppa's child, but you're my child too. I won't feel any different if I see you live to a hundred, so you better get used to it." She kisses my hands over hers. "Tell me, do you really have a girlfriend?"

"I don't know yet."

"Don't know? Have you told her how you feel?"

"Not in so many words."

"What words have you used?"

"No words, Auntie. But I assume she knows how I feel."

"When it comes to love, women can't always be good mind-readers, especially when the man's skull is so thick. You better go and tell her before she's off marrying another man, and you're still sitting around assuming." She studies me, bangs her glasses to the bridge of her nose. "This woman does exist, right? You're not making things up, are you?"

"She's real."

"Praise be. Take me out to the porch, I haven't had my burger yet."

"Auntie," I say, holding tightly to her hands. "You knew about Henry Clayton's receipt long before he showed up at your door."

She settles back in the couch. Glances at me, then turns to her living room windows. "Who's telling you such things?"

"Do I have to get your bible?"

"Bible or no," she says, swaying her head, "I've already said how I feel about you. Felt the same way about you from the start. It's best you don't question me on something like this. If you do, you'll be questioning my love for you. You'll simply destroy my heart. Absolutely you will, if you keep on asking."

"Don't let Henry Clayton in here under any circumstances. No matter what he tells you. Keep your doors locked. And I'm getting you a cell phone."

"You can buy me a cell phone all you want, but I'm not putting it to my ear. They're cancer-causers, if you've been reading things like I have. I'll keep my pop bottles against the doors and windows at night. Works as good as any fancy alarm. Always has."

I hold her face, kiss her forehead and each cheek. Touching her, I know my vulnerability, suffer the power Henry Clayton has over me.

"Take me outside, child. Mr. Milton's like a meat-eating vacuum cleaner."

Auntie Doria flutters by my side walking through her house. On the back deck, it's as though nothing worrisome has happened between us.

"Charlene's gone home," Leslie says. Leslie's burger has two small bites in it, a curve of lipstick on her napkin.

"The woman's gone off to play tag with the kids," Mr. Milton says. "Not the funny-faced girl. My wife. She's actually gone off to play tag with them kids."

Auntie Doria looks toward the yard and smiles at the sight of the children using Mrs. Milton as something to run around.

"There's thunder in the distance," I say to Leslie. "Better call your son in."

"My wife can stay out and play in the storm," Mr. Milton says. He eyes the burger on Leslie's plate. "She can attract the lightning away from the little ones."

Leslie coughs, her hat brim scraping at my ear. "I live at the end of the block. Your auntie knows my address and phone number." She smiles at me, full lips over white teeth. "You make your auntie's Denzel Washington look like a third runner-up in a man contest. Call me if things don't work out with the other girl."

Leslie gathers her son, says her goodbyes to Auntie Doria and Mrs. Milton caught in a circle of wound-up children. I consider Sydney Brey and wonder why I talked about her the way I did to Auntie Doria. Even if I didn't say Sydney's name out loud, it felt good. It felt like I told the truth.

Below descending clouds, I realize what's going on. With each small step I take toward happiness, I increase the risk, and scope, of my vulnerability. It's best, then, to imagine the dream of Sydney Brey. Making it real is not something I should do, and it certainly isn't something Sydney can afford. It's too hard already worrying about Auntie Doria.

28

Drano hisses under his breath during morning roll call, harrumphs like an old man unable to speak his anger. Seems he expected more from Jack, and my firing or resignation, not the calm we display sitting next to each other.

Jack's nose isn't broken, but it's noticeably swollen, as is the right side of my face. Nobody says a thing about it. Shift command mentions nothing about my absence yesterday, nor what happened outside the courthouse after Prentiss Schumacher's arraignment. Drano raises his hand to ask something, all the while glaring at me. Then his hand falters and scratches some phony itch on his neck.

On our way to our squad car, Drano intercepts Jack. "Like I give a shit anymore."

"You've never given a shit."

In our car, we pull out from the station lot and head toward Leaper Street. "It's Tuesday," Jack says. Withdrawn the rest of the way, he drives us toward the cemetery.

Standing at their graves feels unique this morning. Perhaps it's the break in the humidity, the fresh smell beneath these ancient trees after last evening's rain. I'm compelled to touch Momma's gravestone, then Poppa's. To have believed there was nothing here for me has been a mistake. It's got nothing to do with Auntie Doria's sort of faith; neither is it the whispering of the Falls, nor the cold touches of river ghosts. It's the tangible strength of the headstones. The words etched into them declare who lies here, how long they lived, that they were beloved parents. My standing here, admiring these stones, is an announcement to the world of something unbreakable.

Jack looks at his shoes, rocking on and off his toes, muttering his amens. I remove Clayton's receipt from my breast pocket, the A-disk from my pants pocket and hand them to him. He takes them, smoothly putting them in his breast pocket without comment.

In our squad, he shifts into gear. We barely move before he brakes and puts the squad back in park, checks his watch, then dials a pre-set number on his private cell.

"It's me," he says into the phone. "I want you to make a demand." Jack's eyes focus steadily ahead. "I'm heading out of jurisdiction to check something on Riddy's murder. Nebraska. A six- or seven-hour drive each way. Call the chief and tell him it's urgent. I'm going with or without authorization, but I would prefer authorization." He glances at me, then goes back to his phone. "He's with me, yes. All right, I'll tell him. No need to thank us, Fred. It's our pleasure. Say hi to Prentiss for me."

Jack hangs up, gets us rolling again. "Prentiss Schumacher was arraigned this morning," he says. "The DNA sample will be taken on Thursday at county jail. Noon. Fred expects you to be there."

Jack stops the squad before turning left onto Leaper Street, and waits there despite the lack of traffic. "Before I left the house this morning," he says, "Tyler had a bad case of the stinky toots. Theresa asked him what's the matter. The boy said, 'I think I got a gas station in my tummy.' I wanted to tell you earlier, but it wouldn't have been polite in front of your Momma and Poppa."

"I'm glad your nose isn't broken."

"I'm glad you still have all your teeth."

We're quiet heading out of town. It isn't until we pass the point of yesterday's fight when I thank him. He wants to know why.

"For Auntie Doria," I say. "For keeping your word to her."

Jack hands me his cell phone. "Call information," he says. "Make sure this Dollar-Mart's still in business, and what it's selling. We'll need to buy some underwear, toothbrushes and paste for the trip home."

29

Being at peace with Jack isn't the same thing as being comfortable with him. The surprising thing about Jack, though, is his ability to keep a secret for sixteen years. It took the threat of lost friendship, with me of all people, and his trust in my memory of Momma's and Poppa's murders before he could break his promise to Auntie Doria. My discomfort with him now is knowing he's a better man than I ever thought possible.

The drive to Delton, Nebraska is like being trapped in a loop of boredom. Stretches of farms over flat land, an occasional town not lasting longer than a count to twenty at forty-five miles per hour. Then repeat. Along the way, Jack calls Theresa on his cell phone every hour. Each time he tells her he loves her, then asks to speak to Tyler; tells him he loves him too.

A mileage sign reads six miles to Delton. I realize I've spent the trip counting. The number of calls to Theresa, the seconds it takes to drive through barely-there towns, our food stops and gas station bathrooms. The miles to Delton, Nebraska.

When we reach its city limits, Delton proves it's the exception to the small town rule. Far too many homes to count, businesses at strip malls, packed parking lots, and a population sign claiming 45,900 souls. There's no apparent explanation for its existence or its size. In this way, it reminds me of Red River Falls.

Jack finds the Dollar-Mart on the main drag. Gray brick all around streaked with black near its flat roof. A neon-lit logo over the entrance needs the "M" bulb replaced. A substantial building looking more like a warehouse than a retail store. At four in the afternoon, its lot is nearly full.

We park in the loading zone up front. "You look like you need to use the bathroom again," Jack says.

I nod.

"Probably nerves."

"We're fighting DNA evidence at a Dollar-Mart store."

Jack slips his cell phone in his shirt pocket, releases his seat belt. "Let me tell you about perfection. Playmates of the year are airbrushed, and I've heard if you scratch at the Mona Lisa, you might find the numbers on the canvas telling DaVinci where to put her smile. Whenever people get overconfident, it always leads to disaster. It's the error caused by human certainty."

"You've got bread crumbs on your mouth."

"I know what I'm talking about," Jack says, and leaves the squad without wiping his lips.

We don't have to search for the manager inside the Dollar-Mart. Our uniforms attract him. He's the only man working here wearing a tie, a thin man, taller than Jack, perhaps forty-five, his whiteness tinting blue below the store's lighting. "My name's Davis. Davis Franks. Where's Red River Falls?" he says with the forced smile irritated people often give to cops.

"A suburb of Delton," Jack says. He smiles back the same way.

"Never heard of it."

"You've got a private place to talk?" I say.

He examines our uniforms, focuses on our service revolvers in particular. "All right, gentlemen," he says. "Follow me."

Davis Franks studies the receipt. Flips it front and back, and touches at its edges.

Jack interlaces his fingers over his lap, taps his thumbs

together. "How long have you been manager here?"

I understand the question. The modest-sized office is lavishly furnished as if decorated for a city law firm. Tanned leather groans beneath us, rich wooden trim throughout, a desk for a CEO, not the manager of the Dollar-Mart in Delton, Nebraska. Photographs on the walls are of him, posing in different ways with a hunting rifle.

"I made store manager last year, worked damn hard for it too. I practically live here when I'm not out shooting."

I get to the point. "Is the receipt from this store?"

Franks sets it on his desk and rubs at his eyes. "It's ours."

"Authentic?"

"As far as I can tell. The numbers on top show this store's old code, up to six years ago before Dollar-Mart opened two more stores in Lincoln. It's got the register number, the date and time, credit card information and customer name, all set out in the right places. It's the right price for a pack of cigarettes back then. Plus," he says, "it's got the Dollar-Mart dollar sign symbol running in six font down both sides."

"So that's what it is," Jack says.

"Can't really see how a person could fake all this, or why."

"Where's the employee identification code?"

"Back then they didn't appear on the receipt."

"What about the register itself?" I say. "The receipt was computer-driven. Certainly there's an employee identification code saved on the hard drive."

"Of course. But you'd have to find the right landfill. We've replaced our registers twice since this receipt was generated."

Jack settles back into his chair. Looks at me as if he's about to apologize. "Employee records," I say. "How far back do they go?"

"This store's been here twenty-one years. Employee records are never destroyed."

"We'd like to look at them," Jack says. "Just the months leading up to the receipt, and a few months after."

"The receipt's dated at the start of the Christmas shopping season. We hire temps like crazy that time of year. They come and they go. It won't be like looking through a few pieces of paper."

"We'd like to see them."

"Not just for those months," I say. "For the two years before and the two years after."

Davis Franks swivels his executive chair a bit, a hand at his chin, the other at the receipt on his desk. "Where the hell is Red River Falls really?"

Jack pulls out his wallet. Lays his badge and department ID on the desk.

"You have no authority in Nebraska, any subpoena you've got is worthless," Franks says, pushing Jack's wallet away. "I've got a business to run here. I've got no time to mess with sixteen-year-old employee records. They're likely confidential anyway."

Jack begins to rise from his chair. He's about to use his size, put on his mask of mean cop. With a hand to his forearm, I stop him, and he looks at me as though I've lost my mind.

"Look, Mr. Franks," I say. "This isn't about police business as much as it is about personal business. My personal business. You know we're real cops, maybe not from this state, but cops just the same. We can go to your courts and get an interstate subpoena, but you know how that goes. It drags those confidential records you're talking about through court. Gives you far more work to do when you think about it carefully."

Franks hesitates, considers things, perhaps not liking the idea of being the hunted. I continue on before he reaches a decision.

"The police uniforms we have on are an accident. They were the clothes we were wearing when we made the decision to come here. We're not even sure whether the department will fire us when we get back."

Stretching forward, I'm a beggar at Davis Franks's desk, and my voice makes a sound I haven't heard since Momma and Poppa were alive. A child's helplessness.

"Mr. Franks. My parents were murdered by a young man when I was a boy. I saw it happen then, I see it every day now. It's not as though such a memory could ever fade away. Sometimes I think time only makes it grow stronger. The man who did this has convinced everybody he was at this store sixteen years ago at the time of the murders. Now you can think what you want to because you haven't met me before. Maybe you don't like the way I look, or the fact I'm a cop. But I'm asking you, not as a man or a cop, but as the boy under the table. I'm begging you, Mr. Franks, to let me see those records. The man's name, Henry Clayton, it's on the receipt. But I know where he was. He forced his way into my parents' house, and he raped my momma and murdered them both."

I fall back in my chair, feel the moisture reaching my eyes. "I'm done with my speech. It's what I came here to say. We drove seven hours so I could tell you. Please, Mr. Franks. Give me the answer you know I need to hear, or send me home."

His response exhausts me. "Have you checked out the credit card information on the receipt?"

"Anybody he knew back then could have forged his application."

Davis Franks hardens his jaw. He watches me in an odd way, as if focused on my eyes and someplace else at the same time. "Are you a good actor, Officer Hill?"

"I wouldn't know."

I'm aware of how small I've become in this room. The height of his chair compared to mine, the size of his desk, how tall both he and Jack sit.

"Come back in an hour," Franks says. His words come out so

plainly, it's impossible to comprehend his motivation. Just the same, he agrees. "I should have the documents by then."

"Two years before and two years after," I remind him.

"One hour."

30

Davis Franks leads us to a room in the store's basement. One table, two chairs, and three Dollar-Mart employees dropping off the last of the employee file folders. The young men appear happy to leave the room. Franks lingers, watches us sit behind eight imposing stacks of manila folders.

Jack groans. "Any chance they're in chronological order?"

"Chronological based on what? They're alphabetical for each year based on the hiring date." Franks stretches his head over the files. "Like mountains to climb," he observes. "But we're open twenty-four hours a day, twelve hours on Sundays."

"Thank you, Mr. Franks," I say. "Really."

"You officers need anything else?"

"Underwear," Jack says. "Do you sell underwear at the Dollar-Mart? Maybe a toothbrush and paste would be nice."

"Everything's a dollar or less here, Officer Harter," Franks says, and leaves us to our work.

I open an employee file folder. A dozen pages inside. An application including name, date, and address; an assigned work schedule, tax related papers, papers citing customer complaints and compliments. I ask, "What do you think they put in a dollar tube of toothpaste?"

"I'm wondering about the dollar underwear."

"Maybe this won't take too long."

"What are we looking for?" Jack turns to show me a file stuffed an inch thick with papers. "I mean, exactly."

"The cashier working register seven that day."

Jack scans the pages in his file. "If we're assuming someone working register seven created a bullshit receipt for Clayton, how do we know if it was the day of the murders, the next day, or months later? How do we know for sure it was register seven or that our guy always worked register seven?"

"It couldn't have been made the night of the murders."

"That's the premise." Jack hurries to correct himself. "That's what we know."

"I doubt it was made before the trial. Even assuming Clayton's lawyer sleepwalked through the case, if Clayton had it at the time, he certainly would've made noise about it."

"He'd only cause a stink about it at the trial if he knew it were true, or if he had it forged already." Jack's eyes move over the mass of files. I realize his help has been motivated mostly by loyalty. But now it seems as though he's found his own logic, and it gives a new energy to his voice. "If Clayton waited for Artie Duncan and David Waller to die, they wouldn't be around to oppose Clayton's claim they made up the time and location of the arrest, or forged the booking information."

"Artie Duncan gave you the receipt two months after Clayton was sentenced?"

"About," Jack says. "Don't pin me down to the exact day."

"Imagine a man not only locked in a cell but a cocky young man like Clayton, convicted and sentence to die. He's got nothing left to believe in but his shock at all the white jurors, traitors to his way of thinking. His future becomes a bunch of worthless appeals and the eventual moment he faces. A man like that can get truly inspired to start planning an escape."

"But Clayton didn't escape."

"I think he did. Not the traditional attempt, which is usually short-term and fatal. Clayton worked out a long-term plan to permanently escape, one where the government opened the cell door for him."

Jack frowns at the file in his hand, at the eight piles of employee records imposing themselves on the table. "What do we do with all this?"

"Look for hirings during the two months before sentencing, up to the point when Artie Duncan gave you the receipt."

"Franks said these files were kept alphabetically for the year." Jack checks the top file in each stack. Points to the third from the left. "It's still three feet high, and I doubt we're going to find someone with the last name of Clayton."

"Focus on employees who started and quit during those four months."

A sigh from Jack. "It seemed smarter when we were thinking about doing this, not so smart now that we're actually doing it."

There's a smell to these files. Dust from the past. An archeological dig of sorts. It chills me to think someone came here to touch one of these pages, filled out the forms with the specific intent of freeing forever the man who murdered Momma and Poppa.

When we finish with the stack of files, my watch shows it's past eight-thirty at night. We find no one named Clayton. Jack laments how it could've been a friend, not necessarily family, or someone from the mother's side. There are seventeen files, though, in which someone was hired and fired or quit within the four-month period.

"Seems high," I say.

"It's a Dollar-Mart." Jack scratches at his beard stubble. "What did you expect?"

"Davis Franks has worked here twenty-one years."

"Huh," Jack says at the thought of it. "Guess he had a long-term plan."

"Can't say it didn't pay off for him. Maybe he should be admired."

"I was just thinking I've been a cop for a long time." Jack scratches at his jaw some more. Repeats the same kind of "huh."

"How fast can we check out seventeen addresses recorded more than fifteen years ago?"

Jack pushes himself forward in his chair, arms draped over the stack of seventeen files. Says nothing. There's a cough at the door, Davis Franks in shadow at the threshold. "Bring coffee?" Jack asks.

Franks enters silently, inspects our disheveled appearance. "Those the specific employee files you're interested in?"

"We're guessing," I say.

"May I?"

Jack lifts his arms off the seventeen files and Franks gathers them together. He reads the name on the tab on the top file and tosses it to the floor. He does this six more times before stopping. "This one," he says, setting it on the table. Taps its cover. "This is the one you want."

I spin it about, see the tab with the name. Emily Bates. "Can you tell us why?"

"I've been checking out your story. The Internet prisoner and parole profile lists Henry Clayton, convicted for double homicide just like you said. Exonerated just like you said. I also found Red River Falls newspaper archives. Had to pay for access to its web page." Franks rubs his eyes. "I have to confess, other than showing the last day of employment, this store's employee termination records are not kept on paper. They're not required and the company thinks they're nothing but trouble. We keep two records, computer archives for termination records, paper records for everything else."

"Seems dishonest of you."

"Company policy, Officer Harter."

"I mean you didn't tell us first."

"First I had to check you out for myself."

"What about this Emily Bates?" I say.

"An employee who came and went quickly. In this store's history, she has been the only one fired for tampering with her register's computer, and it made quite a stir in the store at the time. She altered pre-set price codes on her register. Got away with it for two weeks before she was caught."

"What tipped the store off?"

"Cash receipts not matching inventory sold, and the receipts themselves. A closer look at the receipts on the price undersells showed Ms. Bates was using another employee's identification code."

"You said employee codes weren't on your receipts."

"I lied. But it's the first thing I noticed about your receipt." Davis Franks sets the remaining files in his arm on the table with a thud. "It's got the same stolen employee code."

"The Delton police should have arrest records," Jack says. "Probably a booking photo."

"Emily Bates wouldn't admit to a thing. The store decided not to call the police. It was too risky to let out that a cashier was able to tamper with a register's program. The store was glad enough to be rid of her."

"You keep saying 'the store.' Who really made these decisions?"

Franks fails to speak, or look me in the eye.

Jack says, "Well, I'm sure if you had known."

I spin the file toward me. Emily Bates, a pattern of letters more than a name. "Give us a printout on Emily Bates from your computer's termination archives."

"I'll give you a pen, paper, and all the time you need to write down what you want from the file. When you're done, leave it on the table with the others. There are no computer files, gentlemen. You were never here."

Franks' posture sags, tells us it's the best he can do, shuffles his shoes on his way out.

"Your mother and father live in Delton?"

He freezes as though my question yanks a chain around his neck. "I have no idea," he says, glancing over his shoulder. There's a sadness in his eyes that Jack mistakes as a need for more coffee. "Thank you, Mr. Franks," I say. "I surely do thank you."

He nods. Leaves without saying a word.

"You figured him out by the looks of his office," Jack whispers. "And his twenty-one years at the Dollar-Mart."

I breathe in nighttime air outside the Dollar-Mart. The scent from farm fields is thick here. It makes me think of the earth, what lies within it, the schemes people have buried in the past. "It wasn't his office or his years at the Dollar-Mart," I tell Jack. "It's the photographs. They're all of him, and he's always alone."

"Someone had to take them," Jack says.

"Doesn't seem to be anyone he knows." I show him the address from the notes I took on Emily Bates. "Might as well get gas with our directions."

Jack tosses a Dollar-Mart package in the back seat. "Had to buy something," he says. He sits motionless behind the steering wheel, asks me if I'm all right.

"Not really."

Jack starts the engine, pulls away leaving the Dollar-Mart behind us. "No. I didn't think you would be."

31

Cheers rise from a field far down the block. A baseball diamond lit up in the night floats over the darkness of the road, rooftops, and trees. I'd like to watch a ball game. I'd like to be able to sit back and worry about the home team holding on to a slim, ninth-inning lead, or whether the kid selling lemonade has enough left for a second round. Being caught in something so powerful it overwhelms every breath you take serves to prove how important the frivolous things in life really are.

Jack stands behind me on the porch. He wonders out loud who's playing and what the score is. Knocking on the door of the last known address of Emily Bates, I admit I'm wondering the same thing.

A ranch house. Nothing too big, a brick home maintained as an example of fresh suburbia. "I see lights on through the curtains," Jack says. "Try the bell."

There's no need. A whoosh of air, and the front door opens. A short man in cutoffs and T-shirt. Barefoot. One of those white men whose fifties come with enough hair to cover the faces and limbs of three men. He looks annoyed at the police outside his door.

Jack's first with the question, "Does Emily Bates live here?"

"Do I look like someone named Emily Bates? This is the Ross residence. Try next door."

"We have the right address, Mr. Ross," I say. "What we mean to ask is whether an Emily Bates has ever lived here or if you know where she might be?"

Mr. Ross narrows his eyes at our uniforms, then at our faces. "Don't the police in Red River Falls know how to shave?" He touches his own face, ignores the irony growing there.

"It's been a long drive, Mr. Ross," I say. "We apologize for our appearance."

"Let me tell you something." He steps out to his porch, partially closes the door behind him. The beer on his breath is obvious, but his words are clear. "You looking for Emily?"

"Sounds like you know her."

"You find Emily Bates and bring her back to me. I'll take care of the problem for you." Jack and I share a look. "Don't worry, I'm not gonna kill her. I just want the money she owes me."

"How much money?" I say.

"My wife and I bought this house from her twelve years ago. Signed off on the papers, including the home inspection and basement warranty. The first time it rains, I've got a pool in the basement. Cost me seven grand to patch up."

"There are courts for that situation."

"I tried the courts, hired a lawyer and everything. Good luck finding her. I had an investigator try. Heard a rumor she was killed in a car accident in California. Probably another one of her phony stories."

"Do you know anything else about her?"

"No. That's about it." Mr. Ross begins to step back into his house. "Emily Bates," he says, and laughs one of those laughs a man makes when something is far from funny. "If you're looking for her, if she's still alive, you might check out her maiden name."

"I see." I push my foot forward to keep the door from closing. "Do you know what that might be?"

"Get your foot out of my house," he says. I pull it back, and he speaks through the remaining sliver of light. "Is this how things go with cops in Red River Falls?"

"No, Mr. Ross. I do apologize."

"She used her maiden name to skip town on my investigator," he says. "So then I had to pay for the lawyer, investigator, and the flooded basement. Not a lovely woman."

"Who?"

"More like a what," he says before closing the door. "Emily Clayton. She's the bitch you're looking for."

Jack tries to thank him. The door and the deadbolt seal up first.

On a porch in Delton, Nebraska, I think I understand the deafening sound silence makes. It swallows me whole without warning. Suspends my body over the earth, moves my thoughts away from my head. Somewhere a bat cracks against a ball, and there's a joyous roar of people. How small and far away it sounds.

"I think it's time to go home," Jack says, and rests his hands on my shoulders. In this kind of silence, his words and his touch feel miles apart.

Despite the hour we leave for Red River Falls, Jack makes his regular calls to Theresa. Each time they find something to talk about for a few minutes. I have to struggle to find something to say.

"We can stop at a motel."

Jack insists. "I'm fine."

"Let me drive."

"I drive this squad."

"Full shift tomorrow."

Again. "I'm fine. You can sleep."

It's Jack who brings up anything important. "Do you think she's Clayton's mother, his sister, or his wife?" He rolls his head toward me. "Could be an unmarried aunt."

"Doesn't matter."

"No. But she's probably his mother."

"Probably."

Jack's been squirming ever since our last gas fill-up and bathroom break. "You put on Dollar-Mart underwear?"

"Actually it was a buck twenty," Jack says. "Plus tax."

"What crime would you charge Emily Bates Clayton with if you could?"

"I don't know. Aiding and abetting an escape, definitely forgery, identity theft perhaps."

"Not murder?"

"How do you figure?"

"Her son kills my parents. She helps him escape after a jury convicts him. He's exonerated for the murders in part because of what she's done. That's how I figure."

"We'll let Fred deal with it."

"This isn't about Prentiss Schumacher."

"Partially," Jack says. "It's going to have to be."

I don't care for the sound of that, but I know Jack's right. Our notes on Emily Bates Clayton have impact beyond my own purpose. It's the price I pay for Jack's company no matter how valuable his help has been. This information cannot be contained once it's been told even to the smallest degree. Certainly Davis Franks will find out soon enough. Something about the display of sadness I witnessed, as inherent as my own, convinces me Davis Franks won't be surprised when Fred Schumacher shows up with an interstate subpoena.

Staring into the dark beyond the passenger window, I witness my face reflecting back at me, nearly invisible, flying along on the other side of the glass. "If she's his mother," I say, "I can understand. Mine died in a way to protect me. How could I tell another not to save her son from death?"

"You think motherhood is a defense to murder?"

"It depends."

"On what?"

My own ghost through the window studies me eye to eye. "I have no idea." I turn from the ghost to Jack. "If it were your son in Henry Clayton's situation, what would you do?"

Jack begins an answer, falters, and considers some more. "I don't think a father knows until he's actually faced with the dilemma. I'm sure it would be more intense with a mother."

Momma had an answer, so did Poppa. They could have given my presence away, warned me to go for help, taken a chance to save their lives at the risk of mine. Instead they saved me with the sacrifice of their lives. Emily Bates Clayton would likely claim the same motive to justify what she's done. People outside the experience would dismiss her motive. It's not something I find easy to do. Nor can I dismiss Fred Schumacher any longer. Not when it comes to being a father.

"Clayton had his plans," I say. "It explains why nobody from his family showed up at the trial, why he didn't testify. His quiet and pity came from the confidence he had in his white jurors, that they would fail me; then he planned his escape when they failed him."

"I didn't see most of the trial," Jack says. "Cadets worked the night shift back then, and I had to sleep." It's an excuse, I suppose, so Jack doesn't have to admit to being doubtful; better to remain quiet about my ancient observations. He surprises me. "I saw some of it from a back row," he says, clearing his throat. "His silence is the one thing I remember most about Henry Clayton. How it made him look like he was planning something."

Red River Falls' city limits sign welcomes us home nearing four-thirty a.m., still before the first hint of sunrise. Jack complains about his underwear scratching at his crotch, insists it kept him awake for the drive. “Makes it worth the buck twenty.”

32

There's a voice nearby. Muffled. It comes between soft tapping, then repeats. "Open your eyes."

Sydney Brey's nose and lips flatten into phantomlike contortions against my driver's side window. She laughs like a child. "There you are."

While the window rolls down, she asks, "Why didn't you go inside?" We stare at Momma and Poppa's house, then at the wrinkles overtaking my uniform. She leans her face through the window. "Is there something you want to tell me?"

"I called you."

"So you did," she says. "It happens there's something I want to tell you too."

"Where?"

She touches my brow, tugs at my nameplate pin over my shirt pocket. "You can clean yourself up at my place. Follow me."

She walks from my car toward hers, her motion lovely as in my dream. This time she glances back, her eyes bright and her mouth already shaped into a smile. She's caught me. She knows. She has known for a while. Rather than protest the inference, I sit and watch her as before, and she lets me.

Following her car along the streets of Red River Falls feels so natural. It's a *deja vu* of something that has never happened before but was supposed to. There's no pull behind me while I follow, no thought I should remain sequestered inside Momma and Poppa's house. An absence of guilt.

If someone were to ask me to name the streets on the way to Sydney Brey's address, I doubt I could do it. I would be unable to describe her place, whether it was made of brick or wood. An apartment or house. Two stories or one. Her possession of me so sudden, so powerful. She cleanses me beneath her shower with her hands, her lips, and light touches of her tongue. When we kiss, I connect to the energy powering her. Her taste comes with a spark and an indefinable sweetness. Interlaced fingers and limbs, our skin sharing the wetness of water and ourselves.

In her bed, she moves beneath me. I perceive every particle of our skins' touching, an infinite sensation, and the sound of our breathing, the way it proves how we ache to melt within the other. All this I remember. Every detail surpassing my dream.

"You touch me as though you're afraid of hurting me," she says.

"I'm being respectful."

Her eyes appear vulnerable, receptive, moving beneath her lashes as though pouring over my face. "This is your first time," she says. "And don't tell me I'm not entitled to know."

I kiss her lips lightly, rest my head in the soft curve formed by her neck and shoulder. "Was it bad?"

"You were like a honeybee," she laughs. "Checking the subtle details of each petal on a flower before going for the nectar." She floats her fingertips over my back. "Very unusual, but I'm not surprised. It could become addictive."

"Really, Sydney. My virginity would still be none of your business."

She kisses my forehead, holds her lips there. "I suppose not. With you, it feels brand new to me." She asks, "Is sex what you wanted to talk to me about?"

"No."

Disappointed, amused, she rolls on her side, back toward me, pulls the covers over our bodies, and drapes my arm around her. "Sex isn't what I wanted to talk to you about either," she says. "For now, let's keep our mouths sealed. It'll be easier to fall asleep."

There's a warning in what she says, but it's so distant as to be incapable of meaning. My internal quiet, my thoughts singularly of her and nothing else. I'm in the absence of all other things. At peace in a sleep I have never known.

Passion gives way to the practical. I need to get dressed, so I do. Hunger needs to be satisfied, so I eat. She needs to call into work, so she lies. She also cancels a dinner date and tells another lie.

I ask, "Who is he?"

She tucks her hair behind her ears, huddles inside her robe at her kitchen table. "Do you really want me to answer?"

Her hands engulf her coffee cup, raise it to her lips while I say nothing. "You aren't sure. Besides," she says with a grin, "you're not entitled to know."

I drink from my cup. Survey the table. It's filled with the ruin of our appetites. Plates covered with sandwich crumbs and streaks of pancake syrup prove the irrelevance of the time of day. "Your kitchen isn't as disorganized as you said."

"When did I say that?"

"In Momma's kitchen."

Her toes tap lightly against my shins, caress their way to my knees. "Momma's? Isn't it your kitchen?" She gazes over her coffee. "You don't have to answer."

"It's a habit," I say anyway.

"Perhaps a quirk."

It's a more accurate description, I agree. I pick up her cordless phone, press in Jack's home number. A child's voice answers. High-pitched, full of innocence. "Tyler?" I say. "Is your daddy home?" Tyler screams as if I'm an emergency. Jack picks up with an uncertain hello.

"It's me."

"Didn't recognize the number on caller ID. Where are you?"

I stare at Sydney, her eyes catching the moment. The question has been asked. "Sydney Brey's."

"Shee-it. Get anything special?"

"Jack."

"You tell your squad partner first chance you can. Then I get to ask obnoxious questions. You groan and protest, but you answer me anyway. That's how this works, Rich."

Sydney embraces my ankles between hers, leans toward the phone. "The game lasted three hours and Officer Hill scored every inning."

"Heard that. Did you tell her what we found?"

"Everything."

"Sex does that to a man."

"Are we fired?"

"Promoted," Jack says. "Fred would kiss you if he could, if you'd let him. After our now officially authorized road trip, we've been given today off."

"It's good to know since shift's nearly over."

"Fred wants you at County Jail tomorrow at noon. Prentiss's DNA sample. You coming?"

"I made the promise."

"Go back to bed," Jack says. "Maybe this time you can sleep."

I press end call and set the phone on the table. "His voice carries," Sydney says.

"All of Jack carries."

She reaches for my hands, kisses them, and holds them at her lips before letting go. "Why did you really call me? I mean, not this morning. Why did you call me at all? Don't tell me it's what I said outside Riddy's house, and it's got nothing to do with asking for my help to investigate Henry Clayton."

"Of course it does."

"You figured things out for yourself. The rest you got with Jack."

"I'm using you," I say. "I need a reporter who does more than give fluff reports on Easter egg hunts, July Fourth parades, and Christmas pageants. When I'm ready, I need you to report the truth."

"Which would be what you say it is." She shakes her head, raises her hands to defer my response. "Sorry. You know I didn't mean it."

"Remind me how many days I have left."

"Twenty-seven. Then I report your story with what I have."

"Prentiss Schumacher's DNA sampling is tomorrow at noon."

Stacking plates and cups, sweeping crumbs on the table into one pile, Sydney stalls, hides an opinion from me. She gathers her robe tightly around her neck and gives in to something. The other, formidable side of Sydney Brey.

"You called me," she says, "because you needed to. You needed to hear yourself think out loud to a new face."

"That's it?"

"Nearly. You also needed someone like me. Not me in particular, you know. But you're here, and I'm not complaining."

I think to respond. Nothing comes. Her assault is so direct it leaves me exposed, unprepared to argue back. There's nothing to deny; nothing she says needs modification. What remains is whether she has more for me to hear.

Sydney sweeps her hands through her hair, folds her arms over her chest. She begins a prologue describing the necessity, the inevitability, of what I must understand, because she gives a damn about me, and about Momma and Poppa. Then her face blanks and she goes to the meat of her news.

"An innocent man would be just as desperate as a guilty man

to get a DNA test done."

Her words strike me as though they come through the radio, with inflections for an audience, not for a personal conversation with a man she's just slept with. This must be Sydney Brey's intent, and its impact on me is more devastating the more she goes on this way.

"You know an innocent man would be more desperate. And an innocent man's mother would be more willing to commit a crime to help her son get a chance."

"Are you saying you believe Henry Clayton is innocent?"

"I'm insisting you consider what you already know about mothers. You understand motherhood better than most men ever could."

I stand from the table and my chair falls to the floor. Sydney remains calm. Doesn't move. "I'm a news reporter," she says. "I don't do fluff."

"I saw what I saw."

"I know you did."

"Then why won't you believe me?"

"What I believe isn't relevant. Does a defense lawyer care if he knows his client is guilty? He's got a job to do. Same with me, you know?"

"Tell me you believe me."

She blinks. Shows concern, perhaps some regret, but her hardness remains. "I believe in you, Rich."

"Not the same thing."

"It's the answer I'm giving."

"Bullshit."

"You are truthful about what you believe."

"Why do you think I called you?"

"Which time?"

"This morning."

"You needed me," she says. She stands, loosens her robe, and slips around the table to embrace me. "It's all right. I wanted you to call. I was ready to call you."

I hold her as she holds me. Her touch is genuine, yet I'm far from the way I felt when I was so recently in her bed. When I first moved through this place, unaware of anything but her, my mind somehow gathered the practical and the tangible. Stored it away for later use. It's my strength of self-preservation, or perhaps the weakness of my doubt. What do I notice about Sydney Brey now? She lives in the absence of photographs and plants, wall hangings and window treatments. No collection of anything on display, including books. A complete lack of the frivolous I've come to envy. The house she keeps opposes her passion. Sterile. Uninviting. Most of all, temporary.

"Anything else I should know?" I say.

She eases back. Her eyes drift down. "I already told you at our lunch date. I'm a New York news radio reporter stuck in Red River Falls. That's about to change."

"When?"

"A month or two. You can come with."

"Maybe. In time."

With each kiss she gives me, she steals away a piece of this day. How practical I sound. "I need to get into fresh clothes. I need to check in on Auntie Doria."

"Call her from here."

"I'd like to do it in person."

Sydney leads me to her front door. A passionate woman moving through a dispassionate home. "Consider New York," she says at my ear.

"Can I ask you for a favor?"

She gives me a puzzled look. I take it as a yes.

"I want you to arrange a meeting at the Hall."

"You mean the clubhouse where the neo-Nazis have their little get-togethers." She folds her arms over her chest. "Why?"

"Can you do it, give a pretense without letting them know I'm coming with you?"

"Dan Hubert's the lead Neo. I've already interviewed him twice."

"What for?"

"News filler for slow days. Always colorful. Always inspires a lot of e-mails."

"Please arrange it."

"Is that what you had to ask me?"

"Not anymore," I say, and kiss her lips.

She apologizes before I go. Doesn't say for what, and closes the door.

When I had called her, it was to arrange a meeting at the Hall. While I followed her, the thought of her overwhelmed me. She became my world, everything else turned dormant. She's a woman who intuitively knows when to stay away from my pain, when to challenge it, and when to embrace it. Leaving her, I perceive the rest of the world twitching from its sleep. It lumbers toward me like a predator gaining strength, proving my failure, diminishing what I thought I had accomplished in recent days.

Emily Bates Clayton would do what she could to save her son from death, his guilt or innocence has no relevance. It seems cruel that this inherent fact came to me first from Sydney Brey. Her willingness to report this fact apparent, so well-intended for my own sake. Her good cause has put me back under the table. Not only am I witness to the nightmare again, but now I hold on to it as tightly as I can.

33

My path to Auntie Doria's house is a familiar one. I'm surprised Red River Falls doesn't need to patch a canyon-deep rut. When there's no place to go, there's Auntie Doria's. My last refuge as much as it is my first refuge. Auntie will see my uniform and gasp. She'll order me out of it and wash it and iron it along with my socks, T-shirt, and boxers. For an hour or two, she'll make me wear one of her robes, and sit in her kitchen among her crosses and the dozen sets of handsome eyes of Denzel Washington. At some point she'll notice something intangible about me. A scent not my own. My eyes fresh from the sight of a woman. She'll rat-a-tat-tat her questions at me with an excitement that will grind at my despair.

"Not my first time," I'll tell Auntie Doria.

She'll laugh and say, "Looks to me like this time makes the first time nothing more than a handshake with an old nun."

Got it all figured out. I drive to Auntie Doria's house anyway. I look forward to it because, with Auntie, there's no mystery about her like there is with Jack, no split-personality like Sydney Brey's. She's a comforter of consistency, warming me over without prerequisite. Even under her usual assault about women, she manages to make me relax.

How large her modest home appears now. Imposing. The length of sidewalk to her front porch stretches as I make my way, altered by some poltergeist wishing to keep me out. The same mystery has locked her front door.

"Auntie Doria?"

I listen for her dinnertime noises. The way she bangs pots, clatters plates and silverware, as if dinner preparation requires an amateur's drum solo to go along with it. Nothing. I call the flower shop on my cell, perhaps kept open late by a last-minute rush order. Voice mail picks up. A pre-recorded Auntie Doria stumbles over an apology for being closed, gives the store's regular hours, and finishes with, "Goodbye and have a truly bless-ed day."

Activity around other homes in the neighborhood proceeds as normal. Children on porches, cars arriving to park far over the curb, calls for dinner. A woman's angry shout, probably from Mrs. Milton, to get your own goddamn plate of fried chicken.

There's nothing to see through the deck window, or the back door, also locked. All windows closed. An appearance of normality except for the absence of Auntie Doria and her sounds.

I try the front porch door again, press my head to the glass, and there it is. Auntie Doria's music. It comes and fades at my ear with the breeze. Likely she's got her earphones on so as not to disturb the neighbors, and she's cranked up her Christmas iPod, going deaf to the refrain of a rousing gospel chorus. I search my key chain for the old key, the one Auntie Doria gave me the day Children Services awarded her guardianship. The deadbolt fights the warp of weathered wood and unlocks with an audible pop. I push the door open a bit and call her name. Still nothing. Stepping in, I've forgotten about her empty soda bottles and send them clattering over the floor. An effective defense after all. Auntie Doria will tell me so, and I'll have to agree.

There's a smell inside. Food waiting to be prepared. An onion on the cutting board in the kitchen, cherry tomatoes bunched on a plate, and a mix of vegetables in a colander beneath the tap. On her range, a large pot half filled with clear water. The flame beneath it is off. There's a lack of freshness, though, a dullness to the food; not a rotting odor, something closer to malaise.

Empty bottles stand undisturbed against the back door. The patio entrance as well. I call for her at the downstairs bathroom door, then open it slowly. Unoccupied.

If her alarm bottles are set, she must be inside, perhaps folding laundry, taking an accidental nap, distracted by something in need of dusting, all the while listening to her music. It softly comes from upstairs.

I hop over the first step and continue on, calling for her so I don't shock her. When I reach the landing to turn to the final three risers, something behind me grabs my interest. Something I had passed without notice.

A few steps down, I search and find nothing out of the ordinary. Then sunlight through the stairway window strikes an object on the first floor beyond the banister. The smallest flash and it's gone. I move farther down and the light returns and remains steady when I freeze.

I rush to it, run my hand over the wood, then feel a bite into my skin. A sliver of glass. Curved, clear, and sharp. Flecks of colored salt sting at the wound. When I pull the glass from my palm, a spot of blood rises.

Bottles of colored salt are gone from the stairway window where they had stood for nearly sixteen years, on guard, now missing except for one clue. Someone had time to clean up the evidence.

I rush the staircase, turn the corner to the final three steps and leap to the hall. A smear of blood stains the carpet outside Auntie Doria's bedroom. My feet suddenly heavy, I move forward with their plodding banging in my ears. I'm angry at how slowly I move while the seconds race forward. My hands on the bedroom door, shoving it open, then bracing against the jamb. Spirited gospel music plays in conflict with the pumping of my heart. Blood streaks to the left, I step in to follow. Auntie Doria, propped up inside her open closet, clutches her music in her right hand to her chest, earphones caught around her neck, her left hand grasped to the handle of a knife, its blade buried within her abdomen. Blood soaks her apron and shoes.

I fall to the floor. Watch her eyes so still between half-closed lids; they widen with her gasp for breath. I want to run to her but I can't make my limbs move. I want to beg her to open her eyes again, to breathe again. I plead with myself to move. I'm small, veiled within cloth, and make no sound.

Poppa mouths at me to be still, and Momma, her hand no longer swirling toward the swastika, instead motions me back under the table. I've traveled this path too many times. They're angry at me, I know, for disobeying them, but I have to choose another way.

Inching forward, parting cloth. Standing. I call out Henry Clayton's name. He turns, surprised by my approach. He moves toward me with his knife in his hands, then halts. Measures the smallness of me, my eyes unflinching. Something about me catches him off guard. Something from his boyhood, though withered, remains inside the monster he has become. I'm witness to his escape, his stumbling to the front door, cursing at everything on his way out. There's blood at my feet, but not nearly as much as before. Poppa lowers his head, crying for Momma. And Momma stands from the floor, damaged in ways I can never understand. Both of them alive.

"You disobeyed me, child," Momma says. "You could've gotten yourself killed." Her sweet voice, the wondrousness of its long-absent sound, so real it overflows my heart with joy. I run to Momma, bring her to Poppa, and I hold them both close to my body, absorbing their warmth.

Sirens, flashes of light, come through the windows and walls as if I float in the air, and neither brick nor mortar divides me from the outside. My cell phone lies at my feet. I don't remember how it got there, or the call I made, or how I got behind Auntie Doria to sit on the floor with her failing body clasped within my arms.

What I know is I'm crying out for her to live so I can live. How much I will need her, now more than ever, to help me cope with the knowledge that Momma and Poppa may have been wrong. If only I had disobeyed them. Auntie Doria would be in her kitchen cooking, and I could have Momma and Poppa with me now.

34

As a child, when my circumstances still allowed me to be a child, I would sometimes view the world while lying on my back. Outside Momma and Poppa's house on the front lawn, I would just lie there watching the sky. Charlie Watts would often lie beside me and ask me what I'm doing now. I'd say, "Skydiving. The clouds are land, the blue sky the ocean." He'd say, "Cool." Then he'd get worried. "How'd you know you're not gonna crash on land?"

"You always ask me how I know, Charlie Watts. 'Cause I've got my parachute just in case, and I'm not really falling, I'm just playing, and you're ruining the whole thing anyway."

It was easier to do the same thing in my house so Charlie Watts wouldn't find me and bother me with his spoiling questions. I'd wonder about a world where people walked on the ceilings instead of the floors, and how much cleaner it seemed, and how much larger the space would feel. I told Poppa about it once and he laughed that ceiling people might lie on their backs and wonder about floor people. Momma said things only seem bigger to floor people because ceiling people don't use furniture to fill up the space, and after a while all the walking around on the ceiling would turn the paint dirty anyway, so it wouldn't look so clean.

I'd lie there on my back, listening to Poppa watch his movies and Momma turn pages of a book, and I'd wonder about ceiling people for a time. Soon, though, I'd wonder what Charlie

Watts was up to. How much I missed him.

Someone has polished the linoleum floor in the ER waiting room so much it reflects the whole ceiling back up at me. So deep it's as though I can reach into it. From my chair, looking down, I fit in as neither a floor person nor a ceiling person, but a person existing somewhere in between. I long for the playful explanations from Momma and Poppa, and the stupid questions from Charlie Watts. I miss everything about everybody existing up to the moment Henry Clayton made his decision to wreck my future. I wish to reach into the floor and pull Momma and Poppa out, Charlie Watts too; they should be here with me so I could have someone pray for Auntie Doria. I don't know how to pray, and I don't believe in it, but it would be nice right now to have someone pray.

All I do is blame myself for being away from Auntie Doria for so long while she bled towards death, while I chased proof to bolster what I already knew to be true. While she lay dying, I fell into a woman's arms and her bed for my own pleasure. There's blame for me there too. Worst of all, though, is how I blame Momma and Poppa for allowing me to survive. To be fair, they couldn't predict how much I would rather have confronted Henry Clayton when I was a boy than be the man I am now.

Jack's body lands in the chair beside me. He's quiet for a time with his arm over my back. "The doctor been out?"

"Twice."

"Anything definite yet?"

"No."

"You should wash up."

I inspect Auntie Doria's blood dried over my fingers. "In time."

Jack settles his hands on his knees, quiet another moment

while I watch a world within a reflection. "Stop beating yourself up."

"Jack," I snap. I'm straight in my chair, heated. His look is typical of someone who searches for the right words to say about a situation in which the right words do not exist. The draw of his face, its willing lack of strength, pulls me back from anger. He exhales, watches me as if I were about to explode.

"Tell me a Tyler story. Tell me something funny about your son."

"Are you sure?"

I turn back to the floor, the reflections I imagine. "I could really use a Tyler story right now."

"All right," Jack starts. He coughs and pulls at his slacks. "Tyler asked me about buying a sister for him this morning since his mommy was already buying him a brother. Oh, God. I'm sorry, Rich. I'm really sorry. I know now's not the time to be saying this. It's what poured out of my mouth."

"Theresa's pregnant?"

"Sixteen weeks along. The amnio said it was a boy."

I soften to the sound of this, reach for Jack's back, and embrace him. There are words I know to say, so simple, but I falter. Instead I apologize for touching him with Auntie's blood. "It's all right," Jack says. "You're welcome."

We sit for a while, perhaps an hour, Jack in the ER waiting room at Good Shepherd; I'm in the depth of reflections. The doctor arrives showing neither frown nor smile. She looks battle-weary in her blue surgical gown, cap over her head and gauze mask at her neck. Like me, she wears Auntie Doria's blood. "The thing is," she begins, "the stabbing occurred twelve to twenty-four hours before you found her. Whoever did this knew what they were doing. It was meant as a non-fatal wound. The knife's path was deep but avoided all vital organs. It's as though the flesh was pulled far to the side before the single stab. Deep and painful, plenty of bleeding, but not effective if you really meant to kill a person. She probably went into shock from the pain or from other factors, but the length of time she was left untreated almost made her bleed to death."

"Almost?" I say.

"We've repaired the wound, given her transfusions, and waited to see how well she would respond. Her blood pressure's back up, respirations within normal range."

"Can I visit her?"

"Give it another hour or two and we'll see."

The doctor stands there for a moment, then smiles a bit when I thank her before she goes.

"It's an old con game," Jack says. "Prisoners learn how to shank each other to get into prison medical units. Better food. More space. Nurses to look at. That sort of thing."

"There won't be prints in the house, or on the knife," I say. "That's how things go with Clayton."

Jack stands and towers over me. "As long as you're going to blame yourself for everything, 'cause I know that's exactly what you're doing, you might as well blame yourself in the cafeteria. Theresa's pregnant, and I've got sympathy hunger."

There's nothing to see in the floor anymore. Nothing to watch on the ceiling. This middle place is all I've got. Jack reaches to pull me out of my chair. I'm already up.

The thing is, I can't go back to Momma and Poppa's house tonight. The thought of being inside it angers me. Even though I was able to witness Auntie Doria for myself, her steady breathing, her peaceful sleep, I get the same feeling about Auntie Doria's house. As a crime scene, the department wouldn't let me in for a few days in any case.

I consider Sydney Brey. To consider her as the lesser of evils doesn't seem to fit the facts. She can't share the blame I place on myself, and the worst thing I can say about her is she's honest. The best thing to say about her is immeasurable. It allows me to migrate my way back to her address, her sidewalk, to her front door.

There's an added mystery to the moment this late at night. She'll be asleep, wake to a doorbell, come to the door not knowing I'm on the other side. What will her immediate reaction be? I'll catch it and remember it more than anything else. It will be a rare chance to witness a second first impression, and perhaps help me decide my future.

A piece of paper covers the doorbell button. I read the few words written there meant to send me in another direction. More than its words, an indistinct product of a word processor, more than its veiled meaning, the note lets me know its author is inside my head. It reads:

She is safe for as long as you get the message.

A thousand stares are on me at this hour from a thousand different directions. Alleyways and sidewalks shrouded in the night. A streetlamp at a corner a few buildings away intensifies the black everywhere else. There's no reason why I'm alive, why I'm not a victim like Riddy, or Auntie Doria. Of course I'm a victim in a different way. The stares upon me take pleasure in this, feed their own unconscionable purpose. Perhaps if I listen closely enough I'll detect laughter escaping from a defined place. Nothing comes. His location and enjoyment remain undisclosed.

As instructed, I leave Sydney Brey. My walk is slow down the walk. The closing of my car door, more like a slam for the sake of others; I need these stares to witness the certainty of their success.

35

After taking the necessary change of clothes from Momma and Poppa's house, I have made my car into my home. My last meals have been with Sydney and Jack, and what was supposed to be dinner with Auntie Doria. It's minutes before seven-thirty this morning. Among other sedans in the middle stretch of a parking lot surrounding The Lord of Light Community Church, I consider the faith I've found as I watch Henry Clayton arrive. He steps from a minivan, exits with others, surrounded by a circle of faces exalting him. Suits and dresses and polished shoes and equally polished smiles. They gather at the church entrance, maintain their smiles while their lips move over their teeth.

I wait until they go inside, exit my car, and smell the contrast in the air. Freshness of aftershave and perfume, the physical cleanliness of people who have bathed before gathering inside a church on a weekday morning, their spiritual cleanliness, the aroma of their single-mindedness about their faith, energized by prayer before they head off to work. I'm a dark cloud within this aroma, a darkness much deeper than my skin, my uniform, or the determination weighing over my brow.

This church springs taller from the earth as I near, flexes the muscle of its stone and stucco exterior. Artful stained glass, its design without tradition, a mural of colors, glows in the morning sun and demonstrates the fact of its living spirit.

A man at the entrance greets me and opens the door. I notice his white suit made whiter by his thick black hair and the Lord of Light Community Church smile he wears proudly over his face. He nods at my uniform and says, "Not here for business I hope."

"No."

"I suppose the Lord always means business, though."

He waves me forward, gives me a subtle bow. At the threshold, gazing toward the eave of the roof, I'm nearly overwhelmed by the building's size. "This place is as big as a starship," I say. "Imagine the joy if the money this place cost to build had been spent on the needy."

It's the sort of thing I repeated as a child because Charlie Watts had said it first, and I trusted his childish observations because they were too plain and honest to be false. After I moved in with Auntie Doria, I repeated what Charlie had taught me, and I meant it. Auntie Doria threatened to smack me, a threat of no consequence since she never smacked me, and it was obvious from the start she never would. "We need a place to gather, to pray and plan good things," she said. "Where would we be without a place to gather?"

The man at the door stands there attached to his smile, pretending he hasn't heard me. He waves me in one more time.

The scent of outward piety intensifies. It guides me toward the sanctuary doors, and a preacher's voice invites everyone to come forward, one at a time. I stand askance, partially guarded by the entranceway frame. Inside, an expansive half circle of seats separates into six sections like wedges of grapefruit; this space resembles a sports arena and bears little resemblance to the pews in Auntie Doria's Catholic church. Each wedge has its own television screen angled down from the ceiling. Six of them in all, slate green and dull. A stage rises in front, much more than a pulpit, and people gather there in a line before a man in a white suit, shirt, and tie. A woman kneels with the preacher's hands on her head; her words carry unabated, but they're unintelligible. People gather in the aisles, delight in their conversations. Others sit dispersed among auditorium chairs. Henry Clayton, centered in the fifth row, sits beside a man who leans to whisper something in his ear.

My legs move like they couldn't inside Auntie Doria's house. They're light and speedy, make no sound carrying me to the seat behind Clayton. Clayton straightens when I sit, and the man beside him peers back without the congregation's smile of the morning; his face, heavily creased, folds more deeply when Clayton tells him to leave.

We sit there silently but not in silence. One person after another approaches the preacher on the stage. Each takes a turn with the preacher's hands outstretched while words flow in clear syllables from a language as disjointed as it appears inspired.

"Speaking in tongues," Clayton says.

There's no guessing here, my hesitation is not without purpose. Clayton needs to feel my patience, to understand stalking is not a one-way street. I lean forward, reach my hand toward his throat until my index and middle fingers rest below his Adam's apple. "We're in a delicate position," I say. His cross-like scar flames red below his right ear. "My fingers touch a delicate spot."

"I would agree."

"It amazes me how a church is the very place in need of a metal detector, yet I've never known a church to have one." I set my revolver at his back, move the trigger with an audible click.

"How many churches you been to in your life, Officer Hill?"

"As of today? Two."

"You need to get out more."

I press at his neck, his swallow struggles against my fingers.

"The thing is, you've been whittling away at me, taking the important things from me. There's no reason not to admit how effective you've been."

"What I put forth is the truth."

"If I ask, you'll deny stabbing Auntie Doria, so there's no need to ask a liar the question. You'll deny leaving a threatening note at Sydney Brey's. Just as you deny raping my momma, her murder and my poppa's."

"Yes, denial is easy against false accusations. I deny all of it, yes. Jesus said to the people who believed in him, 'You are truly my disciples if you keep obeying my teachings. And you will know the truth, and the truth will set you free.' John: 8:31, 8:32. You're a nonbeliever, so you try to kill me because truth does not find a place in your heart."

"It's interesting, really," I say, and press harder on Clayton's neck; his gasps languish in his throat. "You believe in the Resurrection yet you're so desperate to live, while I suspect this life is all there is yet I'm willing to die. Don't you see the irony?" I ease the pressure over his neck. "Who is Emily Bates Clayton?"

"She's my mother." Clayton places his left hand below his heart. "She's also dead."

"Did you kill her too?"

"Fuck you."

"I'll remind you we're in a church."

"Fuck you anyway."

"Here's the thing. My vulnerability is your vulnerability. If you ever go near the people I care about again, I'll assume you mean to kill them. And without them I have no reason to live, so I might as well kill you anyway."

Clayton moves his hands inside my arm, gently pushes my hand from his neck because I let him. He twists in his chair, eyes the revolver I point at his chest, his smile unaffected. Did he smile through his gasping, his cursing in this church? When he speaks, it's with the urgency of a wronged child. "I wasn't anywhere near the people you care about. I'm an exonerated man. You, Richard, are a lost soul in need of Jesus."

As quickly as I set my revolver in my holster, I stand and drive a fist aimed not only at the scar on his neck, but through it. He stumbles back, falls over row four, catching himself before landing on the floor.

I straighten in this church, satisfied I've wiped the smiles off the faces of the preacher and his congregants on stage.

" 'When you pray,' " I say over Clayton, " 'don't be like the hypocrites who love to pray publicly on street corners and in the synagogues where everyone can see them. I assure you, that is all the reward they will ever get.' "

I'm proof a person can attend church and learn its surface, and quote a selected ambiguity from Scripture for a strictly secular purpose. "Auntie Doria loves those words, Clayton. From Matthew: 6:5."

Struggling to stand, hands at his neck and his voice hoarse, Clayton orders the congregation to let me go. No quote from Scripture, only his pity for my lost soul.

The suspended television screens flash alive. Henry Clayton hovers in the air six times over, arms raised as if martyred on an invisible cross. "Everyone here knows what I am, Richard. Even now I don't show violence. I will not ask for revenge. Perhaps a hundred witnesses, my preacher included. They know where I am every waking moment of the day. You, Officer Hill, are already alone."

I don't run. Instead I ease forward past the entrance and its smiling servant at the door. I'm uncertain where my car is and push the door lock button repeatedly until I'm able to find it from its sound. Breathing as though I'm in full flight, I no longer fear Henry Clayton. I fathom the excitement within me, knowing what I'm willing to do. Marvel in particular at the way my finger began to squeeze the trigger. How close I was to putting a bullet in a man's chest. This is the faith I've discovered within myself, my breathing the result of the rush of pleasure my new faith brings to me, found in a church parking lot the moment I saw Henry Clayton.

36

Fred Schumacher tells me I don't have to be here. There can be a delay for a day or two because of Auntie Doria. I wave him off and take a seat beside him in a room County Jail uses for lineups. White cinder block, a double row of fluorescent lights overhead, and the milky blankness of the one-way mirror when the lights inside the viewing room are off. Feels like a meat locker without the cold or carcasses.

How odd to be on the lineup room's stage. The height lines and numbers like symbols inside a new brand of church. Part of me wishes to extend my hands over Schumacher's head and get him to speak in tongues. One obvious thing about Fred Schumacher, his fatherhood has deepened the lines in his face, weighed down his shoulders.

"Where's Marla?" I ask.

"She's not coming."

"Why not?"

"I'm not sure, really. I expected her to be here."

The door to the general cell block clatters like metal pipes spilling to the floor. In a few seconds, Prentiss Schumacher steps in with two officers. Fred smiles weakly at his son, takes some solace in the absence of cuffs and ankle chains. There's no exchange between them beyond Fred's smile and Prentiss's blank stare.

Lt. Jerry Cassell, a graying corrections supervisor a year from retirement, shares a nod with Fred. Beside him, Deputy Miller, a military type who, when at ease, still walks and turns as though in formation; he usually works narcotics cases, but today he holds a clipboard with a blank evidence sheet and a series of cellophane bags sealed inside a larger clear plastic bag. Looking at his watch, Lt. Cassell calls out, "Two past noon."

Miller writes the time on the evidence sheet, and asks Fred and Prentiss to sign the witness lines.

"All right, Prentiss," Lt. Cassell says. "You ready?"

"No."

"Well, you're looking particularly blue today in your jump-suit, so it'll be pretty easy to figure out who to hold down."

"That won't be necessary," Fred says, and eyes his son for a promise that never comes.

Lt. Cassell takes the large bag from Miller and unseals it along a perforated line, marks the time on the evidence sheet. He removes a pair of latex gloves and stretches them over his hands. Then he removes one of the oblong-shaped cellophane bags, tears it open, and pulls out a small cotton ball on the tip of a six-inch long plastic stick. "Buccal swab," Lt. Cassell says. "The labs like these better than blood. Keeps better." He directs Prentiss to open wide and swipes at the insides of his cheeks. Six times over. Each buccal swab returned to its separate pouch and resealed. Then the six packages are resealed together inside the large plastic bag. "Mark the time at six past twelve hundred hours," Lt Cassell says. Miller writes on the evidence sheet, prepares a numbered evidence sticker, and sticks it to the outside of the bag. Fred and Prentiss again sign as witnesses.

"That's it?" Prentiss says.

Lt. Cassell says, "Done."

"What bullshit." Prentiss gives his father a scowl. Fred stands and rushes toward his son, slaps him across his face. The guards stand there, accepting of the situation; witness no crime here. Prentiss stares into the blankness of the cinder block. "You're too late, Dad. You needed to pay attention long ago."

There's a sadness about him, not toward his father. Rather it's me he looks at, unfocused when he moans, "This is the endgame of Clayton's plan, his plantation cocktail. Do you see how simple it is?"

Lt. Cassell leads Prentiss away through the jumble of the jail door while Miller finishes documenting the DNA sample. "I'm driving this to the lab right now," Miller says. "Officer Hill, you're invited to come with."

"That won't be necessary."

"All right," he says, and documents my refusal before he goes.

Fred stands hovering over his feet. He's unable to look at me or anywhere in this barren room, and his limbs search for a place to belong. "I'm sorry about Prentiss." He settles down long enough to perceive my disinterest. "Why did you agree to come here?"

"To ask you a question. Privately."

"Here we are."

"Did Prentiss ever tell you about a plantation cocktail?"

"He mentioned it before now, yes."

"But you didn't listen."

"Let's see about this test first."

"I don't care about your son's DNA. I want to witness another DNA sample taken from Henry Clayton."

"You can't be serious."

"You heard me."

"No." Fred spins away from me, presses his hands against the wall and leans in. "It can't be done."

"You're the elected prosecutor. You can ask for anything."

"The Attorney Disciplinary Board found probable cause to investigate Judge Brooker's conflicts complaint against me. I can't serve as the elected state's attorney while it's pending."

He drops his hands and turns around. "I knew it would come quickly. I'm not the chief prosecutor anymore. I'm not any kind of attorney anymore. I'm not even allowed to defend a traffic ticket let alone my son."

"Who's in charge?"

"It hasn't been decided yet. Likely next Monday. Until then Marla runs the administration of the office."

"She abandoned you?"

"She was offered a substantial pay raise to stay. I suggested she take it. But she's not a lawyer and has no authority to request a retest, and you're not going to find someone who will."

"Why the hell not?"

"Don't talk to me like that. Don't act like it's my fault. Goddamn, I stayed on as long as I could, sacrificed everything to get as far as I could, including an order to compare my son's DNA with the DNA in your mother's rape test kit."

"You sacrificed nothing."

"I appreciate your situation, Officer Hill. It would be good of you to appreciate mine."

There it is, his fatherhood sacrificing his career compared to my history. To him I have lived a situation. Something to attach a comparative level of appreciation.

"Your son will be wrongly convicted, and Henry Clayton will be the murderer allowed to walk free once again."

"How do you know about my son? How the hell do you know?"

"Look at me. Take a good look at my eyes and tell me what I don't understand. Let's discuss how long you've known about Henry Clayton's counterclockwise swastika. You tell me about his bullshit receipt and Edna Bates Clayton. Talk to me about the crime scene at Auntie Doria's house, and the violence left behind after Clayton murdered Momma and Poppa, and let's review the coincidence of the absence of fingerprints." I reach to his shoulders, hold him there unaware of whether I hurt him. "You tell me what I did and did not see under the table, Mr. Schumacher. You try and erase what that boy saw and never forgot, and you know it can't be done."

I let him go and he nearly stumbles to the floor. "Hill," he says. "You're up against goddamn DNA."

"I want Clayton tested again. I want to be there when the sample's taken."

Schumacher's chest heaves for breath. "Don't you understand? No prosecutor will agree to a second test on the same man already exonerated by a first test. If something different comes up it will toss hundreds, maybe thousands of tests and prosecutions into the shitter. People were set free or convicted by DNA testing. All it takes is one case to prove up a problem and you risk collapsing an entire history of case files. I was the only prosecutor willing to risk it, and only because of Prentiss. Now I'm out of office. It's over."

"I don't give a damn about the system."

Schumacher lists to one side. "The rest of us have to."

He descends toward a catatonic state in an uneven pose. Tears flow even as he watches me. I'm not convinced they are tears for my situation, or for the appreciation of my situation. "I don't want to be the one to tell you this. I suppose I owe it to you." Schumacher swallows at tears reaching his lips. "DNA testing is more than a system of prosecution and exoneration. More than a forensic science of absolutes. It's a means to an end. A governor's pardon."

"Are you telling me Clayton can't be prosecuted no matter what?"

"As forever as a not guilty, protected forever by double jeopardy." Schumacher doesn't move. "We should have paid more attention to the details," he says. "We suffer the consequences of our assumptions."

These are the words Sydney Brey spoke. Are they obvious in hindsight only? For me, though, it goes beyond assumptions, belief in perfection, or whatever clever turn of phrase a person may design. I suffer from an additional flaw. My belief in what I saw, for as much as it sustains me, has also made me oblivious to the plotting of men.

"Who took Clayton's sample in prison?"

Schumacher shakes his head. "I don't know."

"Who would?"

"Marla might." Schumacher corrects himself. "Marla would have access to the file. Definitely. She didn't abandon me because of the pay increase. She abandoned me because of the way I treated you. She won't return my calls. I know she'll talk to you."

As much as I can, I mimic Prentiss. "That's it? What bullshit. You're too late, Dad. You needed to pay attention long ago."

Fred's jaw drops apishly to his chest, hanging for at least as long as it takes me to leave the room.

I sit by Auntie Doria's hospital bed. Mid-afternoon sunlight through half-turned window blinds softens the room's sterile whiteness. She's so peaceful despite the IVs in her arms; a chest drainage tube bubbles like a child blowing air through a straw into a glass of milk. The nurse says she woke up for a few minutes and asked for me. As of now, though, her drugged sleep looks as sound as a person can sleep.

She stirs when I lift the phone at her bedside. Mutters something through her lips. I'm sure something about Denzel. I'm hoping her dreams of him are making her happy.

When Marla Weist answers my call, she's quick with an apology, quick with regret, and quick to ask me whether there's anything she can do.

"Not that," she backtracks.

"Why not?"

"I'm the office administrator, not an attorney. If I'm caught, I'll be questioned about releasing something confidential."

"It can't be confidential if Clayton's exoneration is a public filing, which it was."

"Are you sure?"

"Generally, yes."

"How about specifically?"

"Marla."

"I'll check," she says. "For you." I give her the hospital number and Auntie Doria's room number. She promises she'll call back in less than a half hour.

I sit and wait. Wonder about all the flowers sent to her by her church friends and friends from the neighborhood. I check the names on the cards, try to remember who they are. Auntie Doria will probably tell them all how much the flowers aggravated her. Don't send me flowers, she'll say. They will only remind me of work. And it doesn't help to know they came from somebody else's shop.

An arrangement from Sydney Brey. Simple. Carnations and daisies in a vase arrangement with baby's breath. Thankfully, no daffodils. Auntie Doria must have told people about daffodils, and it's good they remembered.

There's nothing from Leslie, the Miltons, or the face-bender. Auntie will be grateful.

"Richie."

Auntie Doria turns her head toward me, squinting at the sunlight. She lifts her hand to shade her eyes, and I close the blinds then rush to her. I'm afraid to touch her. Afraid of something tender I might break that will send her back into unconsciousness. She grabs my hand firmly, as if she has sent all her strength to her fingertips.

"You're crying, Richie."

"You're in the hospital."

"Am I?"

"Henry Clayton attacked you, Auntie. Don't you remember?"

"Who would attack me? Nobody attacked me."

Her words slough from her mouth, her eyelids flutter and close. With a roll of her head over her pillow, she fights to ask me something urgent before she sleeps. "You been to church, Richie child? You been to church today?"

"Actually, I have."

"Good, child. Go again for me."

"I'm not sure I'm invited back."

The strength of her grip on my hand remains strong even as sleep retakes her. I stand by her, listen to the phone ring six or seven times. A half hour later it rings again six or seven times. But I stay with Auntie Doria, do nothing to end her grip on my hand until she's ready to let go. It takes nearly an hour before she brings her hands to her chest. A comfortable snore, like a clown's laugh on the inhale, an out-of-tune tuba on the exhale.

Outside the hospital, I look at the time on my cell phone. Three minutes after the prosecutor's office closes. I ring Marla's direct line anyway. I'm not surprised to find she's working late.

"The chain of evidence sheet on Clayton's DNA draw is blank, at least the copy I have. I'm sorry."

"Don't be sorry," I say. "It's what I expected."

37

"You decided to show up for shift," Drano says. He takes a seat beside me in roll call's back row, leans into me with his sarcasm. "Are we blessed this morning or what?"

Jack stretches forward on the other side of me, scowls at Drano. "His aunt is in the hospital with a six-inch stab wound in her gut. Excuse enough for you?" Drano's head and body stay as they are, eyes on Jack, shoulder to my shoulder. Blood drains from his face. "You're caught in stupid glue," Jack says. "My three-year-old would say so."

"I'm sorry. I didn't know. Must not have happened during my shift."

"Don't you read the paper?" Jack says.

"Sports and comics, same as you."

I make it a point to stare at Drano's shoulder against mine. "Sorry," he says, straightening. "Sorry about your aunt."

His hands clasp together, rub spastically over sweat throughout morning roll call, warrant sheet handouts, and special assignment detail. He apologizes again.

"You'd like to be anywhere else right now."

"Absolutely true," he says.

Driving our squad away from the station, Jack asks me where I've been staying. I don't answer in the hope he'll move on to something else. At our first stoplight, he asks me again.

"In my car."

"Where?"

"Outside Sydney Brey's house, down the road a bit."

"Night shift got a call on your car from a neighbor."

"I'm not stalking her."

"What would you call it?"

"Making sure she's not next."

The light turns green and Jack eases us forward. "What about me and my family? Why aren't you not stalking us?"

"I'm hoping you can take care of yourself."

We listen to dispatch call in a three-car accident. Two squads respond. It's not in our zone. "You shouldn't go inside your house anymore," Jack says. "I don't see how you ever could."

I brace my elbow against the door, set my chin on my fist. "It's not my house."

"Oy vey." Jack shrugs his shoulders. "My grandmother. Yiddish. It's an expression that fits."

"Last time it was your great grandfather."

"Shee-it. Was it?"

"I promised Auntie Doria I'd pray for her at church today."

Jack calls dispatch, makes the request for me. Our dispatcher asks to repeat the question then says to hold on. The radio imitates the wind, and Drano's message to dispatch asks for more backup on the accident. "You're a man doing the work of half a man," Jack says into the mike. Drano's reply, "I hear hogs farting," spits into the static. Our dispatcher's back with the okay. We get a half hour. We're ordered to check the parking meters, to do something cop-like while we're there.

Drano again. "What hog farters."

The stairs to Auntie Doria's church rise in three tiers, lofting off the earth to an ancient building of tan brick and stone, and a triplet of spires. A cornerstone etched with 1877 seems off by several centuries. St. Rita of Cascia emits an ancient musk made by a mix of eroded wood surfaces and pages inside bibles and prayer books worn thin by the hands of parishioners. Its stained glass true to the Scripture, holds the Ancients themselves. I sense their presence though I deny their meaning. The whole of Auntie's church could easily fit inside the Lord of Light Community Church three times over, but there's something lost, an added sarcasm, when a house of worship sprawls itself and its congregants throughout the length of a stadium.

"You go in," I say to Jack.

He stands a step above me, already large, now Goliath. "I thought you made a promise to Auntie Doria?"

"I said I'd go to church, and here I am. I promised nothing about going inside."

"I'm not sure Auntie Doria would appreciate your technicalities."

I look past him. Catch sight of the back pews, the distant crucifix above the altar. "I'll take my chances out here."

"If you change your mind," Jack says, and heads into the church.

When I first came to live with Auntie Doria, she managed to force me inside this building not by her earnest belief, but by her pull on my arms. As communion lines formed, I'd sneak away and out the doors. I knew Auntie Doria wouldn't leave until the service was over; it wouldn't be right, and a misbehaving boy was no defense to her missing the Eucharist. She wouldn't yell after me either because yelling after a misbehaving boy wouldn't be respectful of the Father's service. So I'd come out here and sit on the top step of the second tier of stairs, or I'd hang my arms over the banister's rail and wait for my lecture when the dress shoes, slacks, and dresses began to saunter down.

"Why'd you run off, Richie child?"

I'd think of all sorts of things to say, none of which satisfied Auntie Doria. Punishment came. She invented time-out chairs and rooms long before anyone thought to make millions off of books and TV shows doing just that. Except Auntie Doria made me sit in my room and ordered me to hold a foot-long bronze crucifix in front of my eyes until I felt the power of Jesus. Sometimes it took an hour or two before Auntie Doria would check in on me, and see how the weight of the cross curved my shoulders but not my will. I never felt the power, and I never lied to her about feeling it either; lying to Auntie Doria to gain my freedom from a Jesus time-out wasn't a choice for me.

"Nothing, Auntie."

"You sure?"

I'd frown and sag my head, shake it side to side. How could I sound respectful even as I rejected her faith? So I failed her twice over. Her sigh came from deep inside her; she would give up and order me to go outside and do my running. It went like this for a long while. Over the years, the Jesus time-outs got shorter and shorter. She gave up on them altogether when I decided to finally tell her the truth. I hung over the banister the Sunday after my eleventh birthday. "It's because of Momma and Poppa," I told her, and my Jesus time-outs came to an end.

I sit on the same top step, feel a rut in the stone perhaps made by my boyhood feet. I pray for Auntie Doria in the way I know how. I long for the sight of her doing battle with her ridiculous glasses, to hear her quote Scripture and lines from Denzel Washington movies in the same breath. I wish to feel her arms around me as if she cannot get enough of a hold, and her body with its size and its lumps a comforter wrapped around my mortality. An atheist's prayer, I suppose. Selfish. An expression of here-on-earth desires even if pure and humble. It's an honest prayer. It doesn't have to explain why we praise Jesus for souls surviving a storm, yet we seal our mouths and minds to His blame for souls perishing in the same storm.

Auntie Doria was able to excuse God for what happened to

Momma and Poppa. I couldn't, and I still can't. It's impossible for me to accept that they did something to push God to destroy them, or cause Him to sit idly by their destruction. It's best, then, less of a sacrilege to Auntie Doria, for me not to believe in God at all. So I pray for her the way I know how.

A boy sits on the top step of the bottom tier of stairs. He looks over his shoulder at me, and I recognize the same rich brown his face shares with his mother's skin. "You're Leslie's boy. From Auntie's barbecue."

He nods at me and smiles, then bites at his lower lip. "Sorry about your auntie," he says.

"I know you are, son. Thank you."

His face brightens. "Momma says she's gonna be all right." He throws me off with "Momma," and I'm forced to catch my breath. "She's gone inside to pray for your auntie."

"Why aren't you with her?"

He rubs at his knees. "Ain't nothing in there for me. I've got Momma but I've got no poppa. Momma says Poppa did the made-me, name-me, and fade-me game. He made me, gave me his name, and faded away before I could walk. She's got no use for him. I'd at least like to see him so I can remember something."

"So you won't go inside the church?"

"Momma tries to make me sometimes, but I run out. It's no use for her to try anymore. I'm not going inside until God gives me my poppa back."

I ask him to stand, and when he does it's as though he instinctively hangs his arms over the rails and gives me a look of a boy expecting a speech he's heard before.

"How old are you, son?"

"Nine next month. Why?"

I blink at a reflection more than a boy. "Just asking."

"I know, I'm small for my age. I don't mean to be. I sure eat everything in sight." He straightens and shows me how lost he is inside his black knit pants and his white dress shirt. "My name's William. William Griffin. Momma's last name, not Poppa's. Some people call me Bill. Momma says if she meant people to call me Bill she would've named me Bill, so you better call me William, at least around Momma."

"William."

He smiles, cocks his head. "What're you doing out here?"

"Honestly?"

He nods.

"Pretty much the same as you."

We watch each other, fascinated with the future and the past within the space between us. He asks, "Do you have problems in the bathroom too?"

"How do you mean?"

"Momma said God is everywhere all the time so I better behave. It's why I have problems in the bathroom sometimes."

"You're serious?"

"Yup."

"You look serious."

"Yup."

"Maybe we should pray for God to keep his eyes and ears shut in the bathroom."

"Nose too."

William Griffin skips up the stairs. When he takes my hands in his, I feel mine reach forward, his reach toward me, as if together we fill a vacuum. "Dear God," he says, pinching his eyes closed. He opens one eye and tells me to close my eyes. "Dear God, please shut your eyes and ears and nose in the bathroom. It would make things a lot easier for me." He opens one eye again. "You didn't close your eyes. This won't work unless we both close our eyes." With my eyes closed, he repeats his prayer.

"William!"

Leslie Griffin stands at the threshold to the church, hands fisted on her hips. She's dressed in a long dark dress, just right for a church prayer, and she's still a hat-wearer, the sort of woman whose oval face and smooth skin make the lacy black chandelier she's under look good. Her hat shades her eyes beneath the sun, brings a deeper brown richness to her skin. "Oh!" she says, relaxing her arms. "Mr. Hill. Officer Hill. I thought my boy was talking to a stranger."

"Does he do that often?"

"No."

He insists, "I'm not doing it now."

"What sort of prayer were you teaching my boy? Bathroom prayers on the steps of this church!" She says this while bringing one fist back to her hip.

"I taught him, Momma. It was my prayer."

She rolls her eyes at us both. "A grown man shouldn't encourage a boy this way."

"No, Ms. Griffin," I say. "You're absolutely right. I'm sorry."

"Why aren't you in church praying for your auntie?"

"I was just discussing it with your son."

William holds my hands, leads me up the stairs. His touch toward the church is not at all like Auntie's. Gentle, encouraging. "Might as well," he says. "Since God is everywhere, I suppose it makes no difference if we go inside. I don't want you to get in trouble with Momma."

We rise toward the entrance, meet Leslie at the door. She tells me she'll be running Auntie's flower shop for the time being. "I'll take three dollars over minimum wage pay and keep track of all the inventory and the money coming in so Doria doesn't have to worry." There are no questions to ask; it's her statement of the way things are going to be until Auntie Doria's on her feet.

She's not much over five feet even in her heels. Though she stares up at me, it's me looking up to her, studying a seriousness I missed at Auntie's barbecue.

"What?" she says, her fist again eased off her hip.

"Thank you, Ms. Griffin. I'm grateful for all you're doing." If it weren't wrong for so many reasons right now, if I were a different kind of man, I would tell her how beautiful she looks even with a chandelier on her head.

"I've worked in an office before. I know what I'm doing. Wish I could afford to do it for free."

"Just the same. I'm grateful."

William tugs me forward. Shadows replace the sun. Steep arches, painted light yellow, replace blue sky. Morning light through stained glass makes the Ancients come alive. Their colors engulf me.

"We'll sit in back," William says. "No need to go too far in if God is everywhere."

Jack sits in the front row. In his uniform, his back looks constructed of masonry. With the turn of his head, it's as though a statue has come alive to witness a miracle. The corners of his lips edge up.

"What kind of prayer should we say for your auntie?"

William is down on the kneeler, palms pressed together. His smile appears refreshed at the sight of me. I lower myself beside him, bring my palms together. "Auntie Doria wouldn't like us to discuss our prayer out loud. She says a personal prayer works best in our minds. Letting it out of our mouths only dilutes it."

"What's dilute?"

"Weaken."

"Momma calls them big-mouth prayers. All mouth, nothing big."

"Your momma is a smart woman."

William closes his eyes, lowers his forehead to his fingertips.

His tongue works the inside of his mouth over and over until his brow furrows and his face tenses.

I turn my attention forward, to the crucifix. Rather than pray, I give silent thanks. To whom, I'm uncertain. I thank this boy beside me, in particular for the energetic way he says "Momma." His voice carries the word, not as a lost echo from my past, but as a soaring aria blazing inside my ears. Its one lyric sings a possibility to me; perhaps I can provide as a parent what I longed for as a son. With my eyes closed, I sense Auntie Doria kneeling beside me. Punching up her glasses, she nods her approval.

38

"Key date this afternoon," Jack says.

"Are you sure?"

He turns our squad onto Main, the courthouse a half mile down. "Do you know what day it is today?"

I think about it. "Thursday."

"Lucky guess."

"No," I say. "There were yellow roses on the altar. St. Rita of Cascia always has yellow roses displayed on Thursdays. From Auntie's shop."

"How?"

"I assume the boy's mother. She's taken over the business while Auntie recovers."

Jack mulls things over until we're parked behind the courthouse. "Nice girl," he says. "Really nice."

He studies my indifference, penetrates its surface, and smiles at what's beneath it. "Your key date cases include one against Sam Botsworth. Should've put on a clean uniform for the occasion."

The headrest, in my condition, feels as comfortable as a down pillow. I don't want to leave it.

"Your criminal damage to property case."

"Did you bring my reports?"

"In the trunk."

Jack makes his simple observation. "You really look like Exhausted's ugly brother."

Sam Botsworth sets me up with my own police report. "You testified under the prosecution's direct examination that you saw my client kick his foot through the basement window."

Botsworth's client looks like he's beside the point, small at counsel table, arms hanging loosely from shoulders barely there. A white boy with a face drawn tight under stringy blond hair. It's hard to tell how old he is, and I can't recall what I wrote in my report.

"Officer Hill?"

Expensive suit, silk tie, pressed white shirt. Gray hair thick on his head and over his eyes. Fifty maybe. His face looks freshly honed through a pencil sharpener. Sam Botsworth. Sam is whom it's all about. His performance is a courtroom advertisement for clients. Flamboyant over misdemeanors like this one, as if life hangs in the balance. I wish to be asleep, to be able to sleep, at Auntie Doria's bedside. I give the only answer I can think of.

"I don't recall."

Botsworth postures for the judge known as Judge Fish for the way he can sleep at his bench with his eyes open. Jack sits in a chair in a row before the bar and shakes his head at me. Behind him, defendants waiting for their cases to be called seem impressed with Botsworth's show at my expense. "You don't recall," Botsworth says with a strut before the witness stand, "what you did not put in your own report? Do you recall what you did put in it?"

"Not verbatim."

"Do you remember whether you put your name, my client's name, and the city where this all happened in your report?"

The prosecutor objects but gives no reason. The judge overrules her objection.

"No," I say. "I didn't write in my report that I saw your client kick out the window."

"A three-year police veteran, trained at the Chicago Police Academy, testifies he saw such a thing but it's not in his report?"

I wish to close my eyes and dream of another place, with Sydney, fallen into her arms once more, reliving an experience imprinted over my skin. "Because I didn't see it happen. The homeowner told me it happened."

"Then it's hearsay, Officer Hill, wouldn't you agree?" Botsworth nods toward the judge, and the judge, usually lost in the redundancy of his court call, turns toward me with a critical eye. "So you say you saw it happen on the prosecution's direct, you say you didn't see it happen on my cross-examination, yet neither version is in your police report."

The prosecutor has turned her attention to another file, her next case. Botsworth stands close to me, elbows on the banister of the witness stand. He smells of yesterday's alcohol and today's mint candy. "Isn't it true you've been under a lot of stress lately, Officer Hill? Personal matters distracting you?"

Jack shifts in his seat and starts to open his mouth. He reconsiders; his hand, I notice, reaches into Botsworth's briefcase.

I'm told by Judge Fish to answer the question.

"I didn't put it in my report."

Botsworth laughs. "Not my question, but I'll take your answer." He turns from me, says with a downward flip of his hands that he's through with the witness. The prosecution has no re-direct, and the judge says there will be no need for closing arguments. I'm excused.

Sitting on a bench outside courtroom 400, I'm hit with Jack's elbow-nudge into my ribs. He tells me my performance in court might get back to command, and I'm even more of a mess. But he's smiling. Says he's got a plan to make things right and it's already in progress. Taking his cell phone, he dials a number, then tucks the phone inside his breast pocket.

"Just a few seconds," Jack says. He rests his hands on his lap, sits especially straight, a sinner composed like an angel.

From within courtroom 400, a sudden jingle. Tchaikovsky's *1812 Overture* as played by a loud band of impish beeps. A commotion erupts. Courthouse security guards spin about quickly on their heels and rush inside.

Sam Botsworth admits the source, denies responsibility. "But I turned my cell phone off! I always turn it off!"

He's led from the courtroom by two guards, one with a light touch to his shoulder while they walk. "When do I get my cell phone back?"

"End of the day," a guard says.

"How can I run my practice without it?"

"You should know better. Especially you."

"But I do know better! I did turn it off!"

Botsworth doesn't notice me. His face red, hair fluttering like a windblown flame.

"Caller ID blocked?" I say softly.

Jack nods. "Go home, get some sleep," he says. "Then gather the rest of your stuff and stay at my house for a while."

Botsworth stands at the elevators with the guards, waiting to head down to courthouse holding for an hour or two, direct contempt, because all judges despise cell phones going off in their courtrooms. Judge Fish in particular. Ruins his sleep. When the elevator doors open, Botsworth glances back and raises a middle finger. Jack waves back.

"I'll take you home," Jack says. "Sleep, visit Auntie Doria, then move in with me." I walk with Jack down the courthouse hall. "Promise you won't stand my family up this time."

"All right."

"All right what?" Jack asks, and waits for my answer.

We stand at the elevators. When the elevator door opens, Jack says, "You're still an ass."

39

Jack waits for me to go inside Momma and Poppa's house before he drives off. He was quiet driving me over. Perhaps he regrets his invitation to move in with him for a while. I enter the house slowly, out of exhaustion, out of expectation. With the wind through the opening door, it's as though this house inhales me and holds its breath to keep me.

If this house truly has Momma and Poppa in its bones, it shouldn't be angry or mystified. My erratic behavior toward it is predictable. This house holds every reason to make it mine, and every reason to run away. Its schizophrenia is mine as well, but it's impossible to know which of us acquired the disease first and infected the other.

I take a drink of cool water from a glass, and splash the rest on my face over the kitchen sink. I watch myself towel off in the reflection of a window. Instinctively now, I check to make sure the window lock is in place. Check all the windows, recheck the front and back doors. A third time. Search under the couch and behind it. Open closet doors in a rush and expect something violent to come flying out. Nothing.

I stand at the dining room table and lean toward the tablecloth. Kneeling, I raise it slowly. A sudden crash in the kitchen and I run to it. The glass I drank from, fallen to the floor; its lime-green color shattered into the pinnacle display of an exploding fireworks rocket.

I check the bathroom, behind the shower curtain, and a closet too narrow for a child to hide in. I check inside anyway. The bedroom I sleep in, always last, should be the first place to check. Under the bed, inside the closet. Nothing.

Sitting on the bed, I feel my shoes and socks slough off by themselves, my uniform slacks and shirt; they pile up together on the floor like shed skin. I stand and look at the bed. How beautiful the sight. Cream-colored spread over white sheets. I can't recall when I last made it, yet it appears fresh as if done this morning.

Off toward a back corner of the bed, a stain of black. Perhaps ink from a pen's explosion. I move to touch it when something dark drips on my fingers.

A curse, a warning, hovers overhead.

411 forwards my call to the Lord of Light Community Church. I ask, then demand, then infuriate, for Henry Clayton. The preacher's secretary stutters, tries to say a word while I shout at her for Clayton, no excuses. She gives the phone to the preacher. His damned voice, his shroud of tonal peace, pleads with me to calm down.

"Clayton's not there, he's here in my house and you know it."

"I beg to differ," the preacher says. "He's never left the Lord of Light since you assaulted him, may the Lord forgive you."

"Then put him on."

I repeat my demand, get silence, and wonder if the preacher has hung up. It doesn't matter. I go on anyway, ordering Clayton to appear. I'm an insistent child piqued in a tantrum. I'll rant until Clayton appears from his hiding place inside this house. The attic. I didn't check the attic, or the basement. It's something any good cop would know to do, but I'm hardly a cop at all. I'm not a son. I've failed as a nephew. I'm not a friend, not really. Not a husband. An uncertain lover. I've tasted the things a man needs to live, and have failed at all of them.

A whisper carries more power than a shout, and the whisperer inevitably draws attention away from the screamer. Made nearly deaf by volume, the human ear aches to know what the quiet has to say. The mystery is first in the location. Overhead in the attic, below me in the basement, moving down the hallway toward the bedroom. This whisperer is so expert, his approach makes no sound. No wonder why Auntie Doria, her gospel music in her ears, was unable to run away.

When the whisperer nears, his words become clear. They cause me to spin about, flail my arms at empty air inside the bedroom. "This is Henry Clayton."

His voice is unmistakable, whether affected by the pretense of religious rebirth, or warped by the symbols he displayed as a youth, I know Henry Clayton. He's not here to touch me; he's not here to be touched. His voice comes through the phone cradled in my hands.

I hang up. Slump to the bed. Beside me, another drop of black falls like blood from a wound, from the swastika freshly painted on my bedroom ceiling. Half as large as this bed, angry, menacing, its arms in the counterclockwise direction.

Only now do I notice the silhouette, an oblong shadow on the other side of a window shade. Raising the shade, I find one of Auntie Doria's empty soda bottles placed upon the inside sill. Clayton's whisper increases its volume inside my head, like a thousand shadows chanting the impossible proof of his innocence. There will be no fingerprints on this bottle, or any inside this house but my own. It's a pattern, at least, that I'm certain about.

40

The doorbell's ring wakes me from a sleep I don't remember. I open my eyes to the counterclockwise swastika on the bedroom ceiling that Clayton both put there and couldn't have put there. Graying light through windows must mean early evening; it somehow adds a depth-dimension to the swastika's form, lowers it from the ceiling's surface and makes it blacker.

A woman calls my name. I put on fresh slacks and a light sweater, unaware of my pace nor caring whether the voice at the door has enough patience to wait for me. I descend the stairs, arrive in the dining room to see Sydney Brey leaning over the railing, staring through the picture window.

Her voice muffles through the glass. "I knew you were in there."

"How?" I call out.

"Because you're not parked outside my apartment."

I try to wipe the evidence of sleep off my face before I open the door. Blink. Flex my jaw. The heaviness remains. On the other side of the screen door, Sydney smiles at me, eyes glistening, too energetic for me to stand. She comes in without asking.

"You have a habit of doing this," I say.

"Doing what?" She kisses me on the cheek. That's become a habit of hers too. "Do you want me to leave?"

I exhale, a release of frustration and expectation both. "There's a counterclockwise swastika painted on the upstairs bedroom ceiling."

"I take it you don't paint."

"No."

"Sorry about your auntie."

"I saw your flowers." She smiles though I don't thank her for them. "Clayton was in church when this artwork was made," I say. "He claims he was in church when Auntie Doria was attacked." I hang my head, notice Sydney do the same. "He has a hundred witnesses. Weekend and weekday church-going witnesses."

"The worst and most effective kind."

"What's your story looking like right about now?"

"Nothing's been typed yet." She touches my arms, turns me gently, and kisses my lips. "You talk as though I don't hold out possibilities."

"What might those be?"

"Clayton has friends outside his church. The aiders and abettors. White supremacists have a habit of displaying the American flag. Most have a habit of going to church. If they can't find an existing church to hide inside, they have a habit of making up their own. God and country. For whites only, you know? And they always hang together in a group because white supremacists are cowards when they're alone, which is why their skin's so pale-white. It's the color of surrender." She grips the door handle. "I arranged the interview you asked for at the Hall. With Dan Hubert, the biggest kid in the tree house. He thinks it's about their party's candidates for next spring's primary."

"When?"

"Now. You'll rile things up a bit with your handsome light brown. It could tweak a better story out of him." She smiles, brushes her hand over my chin.

I look at my shoes, notice how I've dressed, my slacks and my dress shirt. "I'm wearing all black."

Sydney Brey smiles. "Your clothes," she says, "are absolutely perfect."

She drives her old Mustang cautiously. I expected her to be far more reckless. She's the age for it and has the energy and look of someone wanting to be someplace, not on the way there. Below the speed limit. Signaling for every turn and lane change. Perhaps she enjoys making people wait for her.

The radio plays WVOL. How strange to hear her voice in the car while she concentrates on driving, lips closed. A fund-raiser walkathon for a boy stricken with leukemia. Five minutes later she's back with a report about an impending garbage strike.

"How do you do it?"

She looks at me, uncertain of my question.

"Go from a boy's leukemia to a garbage strike."

"It's my job." She grips the steering wheel tighter. "The leukemia deal was recorded three days ago. The garbage strike yesterday. In between I've showered every day."

"Still," I say.

"What?"

I wonder if this is a good time to mention it, the easy way she shifts from one type of person to the next. A passionate lover, soft and generous, to something I could describe as the nemesis within her. Cold, powerful, an I'm-here-to-do-my-job personality. I'm uncertain which side of her I'd be saying this to right now, and whether I'd have to say it to her twice.

"Nothing," I say.

"Must be something."

"I mean it's nothing important."

"Red River Falls at night," she observes. "It looks like every other town and suburb at night. Have you noticed?"

Leaper Street's four-lane road cracks and potholes ahead of us, its patchwork resembling the flow of black through veins.

Bungalows give way to a forest behind a spired wrought iron fence; despite the roll of tires over pavement and the distance of the Red River, the power of the Falls reaches my ears. We pass the cemetery entrance and move on.

"Have you accepted the New York job yet?"

"Not officially."

The yellow center stripes flare at the approach of headlights. "There's a place in town," I say. "It would surprise you."

"Where?"

"Behind us, a mile back. We drove by a cemetery. It's where the Red River cuts through the rock, drops over fifty feet, and churns itself up."

"Never been inside. I'm not a fan of cemeteries." She pulls her car toward the curb. "Is it beautiful?"

"I haven't thought about it that way before."

"What way have you thought about it?"

"Ghosts," I say.

I've silenced her for a few seconds. "Maybe you should start thinking about its beauty."

This far west on Leaper Street, the bungalows and cemetery forest have given way to a mix of one and two-story businesses. They're set back from the street by the narrow width of sidewalks and a few sparse trees doomed never to grow larger than they already are. All of it bathed in light-orange streetlamps.

She parks and motions to the storefront ahead of her car. Single story, slanted roof. Vertical blinds cover the plate glass, aglow from within.

"We're here," Sydney says, her voice flat. It's clear she's got her business skin on.

41

I recognize Dan Hubert, the thick-necked man standing beside Henry Clayton outside Riddy's house the day of Riddy's murder. The diplomas on his office wall show me he's a lawyer. For the third time, Sydney calls him the Grand Dragon of the local Klan, even though he's corrected her twice. "It's not like that anymore," he says. "Those names are long gone."

She apologizes, says it's a force of habit from her days growing up in the south; her daddy was an assistant to a Grand Dragon for several years. Mr. Hubert, a neckless stump of a white man in a gray suit and tie, sets his fingertips together in front of his smile.

"I've learned about you since the last interview," he says. "You were born in Vermont and raised in New York before you moved to Red River Falls."

"South Bronx," Sydney says. "You wouldn't believe how fast white sheets get dirty in the South Bronx."

The office we sit in is at the back of the building. Sparsely furnished: Hubert's desk, a side table with coffee supplies, and our two folding chairs. Its dark-paneled walls are saturated with political campaign posters for local candidates. An unimposing space made imposing by Hubert himself. There's a smell to the brown walls and darker floor tile, more than hinting at what this place may have once been. Molecules of spilled beer, particles of grease from a grill, permanent in the air.

While Sydney asks her questions, I study the posters. White

boys. All of them in business suits. Rather than Hubert's pugilistic form, these posters show milk advertisement models with virtuous last names. Glistening skin, polished whiteness, teeth pushed to the front of their mouths to form impressive smiles. The corners on each poster display American flags caught in a patriotic breeze. Slogans of America First. Family First. Country First. Makes me wonder about the things they want to go last. An American flag, an impressive floor-to-ceiling job, silken and gold-tasseled, serves as a backdrop to Mr. Hubert.

"No more Grand Dragon stuff, burning crosses, lynchings and so on?" Sydney asks.

Hubert smacks his lips. "How many times must I remind you? It's in the past, Ms. Brey. Far in the past."

"How far?"

"I thought this interview was for a story on our primary campaign."

Hubert had clasped my hand in his when I first arrived, a show of warmth—"Coffee? No? Water? No? Please sit here"—a display of generosity. Now his stare increasingly settles on my face, his eyes compelled to study me, the green of my eyes surrounded by light brown. "What, precisely," he asks, "brings you here?"

Sydney interjects. "He's with me."

"How is he with you?"

She smiles. A business smile. Something of an attack. "We're co-workers," she says. "Equal and definitely not separated. Would it bother you to know we've made love a few times?"

I'm witness to her confidence. Strong voice, vertical posture, her left leg bouncing happily over her right knee. She doesn't break her stare or her smile away from Hubert. She enjoys watching his neckless connection between head and body expand within his shirt collar, perhaps anticipating this volcano to pop.

"If he's your choice, Ms. Brey."

Hubert closes his eyes momentarily, opens them and interlaces his fingers. This is his job. He's to deal with the Sydney Breys of the world, run interference so his candidates don't have to. Don't show her any anger, rather state the case so attractive to the kind of white boys and girls he's looking for. "I don't know about equal, Ms. Brey," he says, practiced. "All we want is the separation. Each race allowed to make its own destiny in this country."

Sydney writes in her notepad. "Good answer, Mr. Hubert. Really good. Now tell me about the Jews."

"How do you mean?"

"Separate? Annihilate?"

"They're already taking over."

"You mean they're really smart?"

"I mean they're taking over industry. Entertainment, manufacturing, everything."

"Smart and creative, those Jews. But I recall the last time I interviewed you, you said the black man was lazy, uneducated. Although a few may be exceptions to this rule, as a group, blacks simply were inferior. Am I remembering your words accurately?"

"Close enough."

"Then which is it, Mr. Hubert? The Jews are too smart so they have to go. And the blacks aren't smart enough, so they have to go. Shall I write down that the superiority of the white race is its desire to be average?"

"Here's what we're saying, Ms. Brey. There are pure whites in this country who simply do not wish to mix with nonwhites. We don't want our children to mix with nonwhites. And before you ask more of your sarcastic questions, let me ask you a serious one if I may."

"It's your office."

"I wasn't sure of that anymore." Hubert smiles, broadens his shoulders. "Imagine you're arrested on a serious felony. How would you feel if everyone in the courtroom were black? Your lawyer, the prosecutor, all the staff, and the judge and jury. Especially if the victim is black. Are you telling me that you, as a white defendant, would be as comfortable locked in a courtroom with all those black people passing judgment over you, or would you prefer a courtroom of white people?"

Sydney writes on her pad. "Really good, Mr. Hubert. I haven't thought of it that way."

Mr. Hubert nods. "Don't you see? We want what the blacks want. Blacks want a black judge and jury. And they want black construction crews on job sites. Black businesses running the show. Blacks vote for black candidates because they're black, even if black voters don't know anything else about the candidates. In fact, the more liberal the black man is the more he's likely to agree with me on this very thing."

"What about the Chinese, Japanese, Koreans and other Far-Eastern races?"

"They can get together or divide themselves up, I don't care."

"Tell me, how many different separations should this country expect if your candidates gain office?"

"Just one. The whites. The rest can go wherever else they please."

"Like reservations?"

"The details can be worked out among those people, I'm certain."

"So instead of making ourselves more tolerant, we should give up and separate."

"There's no such thing as tolerance. Not if you're being honest with yourself."

I raise my hand. Hubert nods at me. "How many votes do you expect your candidates to get?"

"You look worried."

"Just asking is all."

"Our expectations are seven percent in Red River Falls. Consider what this means. Over twenty thousand eligible voters and at least fourteen hundred wish to vote exactly as I do. Fourteen hundred adult men and women in Red River Falls, maybe as high as two thousand, walking around the same town you do. Raising their children and grandchildren to believe as I believe."

"I'm grateful for the other eighteen thousand."

"They don't vote in the numbers we do." He clears his throat, widens his smile. "It was less than three percent only four years ago. It's more than doubled since then. Now multiply our numbers by all the cities and towns in the United States and think of the possibilities."

Hubert stands from his desk, pours two cups of coffee, and sets them on saucers in front of Sydney and me. "Sugar or cream?" he asks me.

"No thank you."

"I'll have some now," Sydney says. "Black is fine." She takes a quick sip. I push mine away.

"Another question, sir, if I may. Do you know who I am?"

"I do."

"And I know you're the attorney who helped Henry Clayton get his DNA test approved."

"Shoot. I paid for it myself."

"Why?"

" 'Cause he was innocent." Hubert eyes my coffee cup. Pushes it back toward me. "Don't be rude, Officer Hill."

"I'm not a coffee drinker."

"A cop not a coffee drinker? There's something new. How

about water or some orange juice?"

"No thank you, Mr. Hubert."

"Well then." He watches Sydney take another sip. "Suit yourself."

"Sir, I believe Clayton is guilty. I know he's guilty. I believe you or somebody from your group helped Clayton send someone else's DNA to the forensics lab rather than his. Someone without any criminal history so it wouldn't be on the DNA database."

Sydney gives me a blank look.

"You're hilarious," Hubert says. "Why would you come here to say this out loud?"

"Just getting it out in the open, is all. I'm laying it out there to see what you had to say."

"Did you think because you asked the question I'd simply throw my hands up in the air and confess?"

"No, sir. Just looking for your reaction."

"How am I reacting so far?"

"You're doing fine."

"Tell me. What would my motive be?"

I indicate to the posters on the walls and lean back in my chair. "This place. Who I am. What Clayton represents, one of your own."

Hubert shakes his head. "We don't accept anyone here who prays to a Jewish god or a Jewish savior. Clayton went Jew-loving-Jesus on us the moment he went to prison."

"Bullshit," I say. "You know that's bullshit. Even a white jury couldn't stand what Clayton had done, and was willing to believe a frightened mixed-blood boy. Seems to me Clayton's conviction and death sentence went against everything this little club of yours believes in." Hubert's eyes form twin smiles. He begins to laugh and I note Sydney scrapes her pen covertly over her notepad. Shows me what she's written—*You've blown it—*

underlined three times, three exclamation points.

"Hill," he says. "You're a clown. You're an old joke nobody wants to hear anymore. Prentiss Schumacher murdered your parents, and I believe his DNA will soon prove I'm right. Ask yourself why I would sacrifice a man like Prentiss for a Jesus-lover like Henry Clayton. And while you're at it, why don't you tell me how the hell anybody could sneak Prentiss Schumacher's juice inside your mother's crotch sixteen years ago unless Schumacher was the one who did her."

He enjoys this. Enjoys the heat he sees rising from me. Sydney coughs and extends her arm across my chest.

"I haven't figured that last part out, Mr. Hubert. I admit to it."

"You haven't figured anything out. There's nothing to get figured out."

"Well," Sydney says brightly. "This exchange was interesting, but may I ask another question about your primary campaign?"

"Ms. Brey, I don't mind our chats. I find them helpful. But you've brought this son-of-a-bitch in my office to call me a goddamn liar and criminal."

Sydney turns to me, displeased. "He's about to tell us to get out."

Hubert folds his arms, lips rigid. Sydney's already standing when he tells us to get out.

In the lobby outside Hubert's office, white boys in suits line up near the exit door. Five of them. I recognize three from the posters on Hubert's walls. They raise glasses as we approach and spit into them several times. Hubert calls out from his office door. "Did you enjoy your coffee, Ms. Brey?"

She clutches at her stomach, face stricken. "You knew!" she says to me, and runs out the door.

42

Sydney slams her notepad on the Mustang's roof. "Just what the hell were you doing in there?"

"I asked the man some questions. You certainly didn't try to stop me."

She looks across the street, shakes her hair. "You were as subtle as a clown at a funeral." She scowls at me. "I thought cops know how to peel back the layers, get to answers by inches without letting the target know he's giving himself away."

"You asked Hubert if he thought we were fucking."

"Making love," she says, swings the driver's door open and throws herself in. I tap on the passenger window, tap a few times more before she unlocks the door and lets me in. She repeats, "Making love. I don't fuck with people."

The Mustang pulls from the curb, Sydney gripping at the steering wheel as though capable of ripping it off. "Why didn't you tell me about the coffee?"

"I thought if I let it go," I begin to say, already knowing the pitiful sound of my reasoning. "I thought I was being subtle."

"Do you have any idea how ill I feel? Like butterflies goose-stepping up and down my throat."

"Prentiss Schumacher told me it's a tradition called a plantation cocktail. It's why his DNA is going to come back a match with the DNA from my momma's rape test kit."

"He's convinced you of this?"

"It's why he tried to fight off giving a DNA sample. The rest is what I know."

"You and Prentiss Schumacher know things, and the rest of the world is full of shit."

"That's right."

It's hard for me to understand everything she's angry at. I'm near the top of the list. The way she bites at her lower lip, how her eyes seem to focus both on the road and on something else I cannot see, tell me there's more. Her business skin is still on, tighter than ever. She's a reporter in exclusive possession of certain facts, fantastic speculations, but without a conclusion to the story.

Her eyes flash at me as we pass an intersection. She coughs and excuses herself, pounds her hands on the steering wheel. "Hubert's right, though," she says. "A plantation cocktail wouldn't explain a match between Schumacher's DNA and the sixteen-year-old DNA in your mother's rape test kit."

I grab my knees. Stare at angled light moving across the inside of this car. She glances at me, makes her turn off Leaper onto Wickers Street. "Shit," she says, and swerves hard to the right. Parks at the curb and kills the engine. "A hundred times shit." Head tilted down, her hair fallen forward so I can only see the outline of her face. She presses her fingers over her eyes, palms aside her nose. "It's me," she says. "I should've known better. I should've prepped you."

Lips thinned, melded together, she apologizes.

"Your walk," I say.

"What?"

"I noticed your walk."

"Where?"

"At the restaurant, when you walked away."

"It's nice to know I left a lasting impression on you." She kisses me, her business skin beginning to slip away.

The air in this car smells spent, inhaled hard and released so many times the oxygen barely sustains us. Suffocated by words, we regain our strength through a kiss. "Chances are," she says, reclining back in her seat, "I've passed on some of my gestapo butterflies."

She starts the Mustang and pulls away from the curb.

Wickers Street is a dark, two-lane road, its street markings worn off in spots. It takes us through an industrial area, factories and warehouses mostly, directly toward the hospital where I intend to violate visiting hours all night at Auntie Doria's bedside. It's the excuse I give Sydney to decline her invitation to her apartment. She accepts it, doesn't ask what I might be afraid of.

A sedan in front of us slows, comes to a stop at a railway crossing even though the gates are up and there's no sound of a train. We stop, the sedan in front of us now with its emergency lights flashing.

"Go around," I say.

"Oncoming traffic." Sydney slides her hand to my thigh. "You noticed my walk?"

"That's what I said."

She smiles at the steering wheel. "You mean my ass."

I step from the Mustang and walk toward the sedan. The driver's window, tinted fully black, rolls a quarter way down; I can't see the driver's face. There's dampness in the air, an increase in humidity. Although starry overhead, a flash of lightning ignites low over the western horizon. "Engine problems?"

"No." A young man's voice. Breath laced with pot and alcohol.

"Anything I can do?"

The window lowers the rest of the way. A white boy in his late teens, shirtless, turns to show me his neck. Clockwise swastika tattooed below his right ear. He levels a gun barrel at me, displays a twisted smile. "Get back in the bitch's car."

"No trouble here," I say, easing away from the window. An SUV has arrived behind Sydney's car. A man steps out the driver's side, rifle in his hands. The headlights of a car behind him keep him in silhouette.

I slip back to my seat, close the door, and turn to Sydney. "Who arranged the meeting time with Hubert?"

"Why?"

"Just tell me."

"We both did. I wanted it an hour earlier, but it was agreed."

"Did you tell him you were coming alone or with somebody?"

"I told him you were coming."

"By name?"

"He asked me. I told him."

The SUV behind us rams us forward.

"What the fuck is this about?" Sydney shouts out her window. "Hey! My parents got me this car!"

I grab her hand and tell her to sit tight. "Guns, Sydney."

"What?"

"The car in front, the SUV behind us. Guns. Some men drew them on me. Told me to get back in your car."

On the other side of the tracks, the two-lane road is blocked on both sides, headlights set on high beams. At least two more pairs of headlights behind them. The SUV bumps us again, pushes the Mustang's hood under the crossing gate. Sydney braces herself, arms stiff to the steering wheel, her body as flush against her backrest as her strength will allow.

"Did you bring your gun?"

"No," I say. "I don't carry my gun on a date."

"You thought a trip to a Klan office was a date?"

"If I get off one shot, they'd get off ten."

Laughter, revving of car engines. A stereo plays. Screaming guitars, screaming vocals. Unintelligible words.

"Why don't they shoot us now?" Sydney says.

A figure appears from between the cars across the tracks, approaching, its blackness fluctuating in the glare of headlights. It taps on my window, motions to roll it down.

"Don't," Sydney says.

A fist against the glass. A growling voice. "Do I have to break it?"

I lower the window. See the black mask, like a phantom, extend through. "Get out."

I hesitate. Interpret the anger. "Hello, Henry. Bring your bible?"

An arm extends through, a gloved hand and the blade it holds accelerate down. There's a tearing above my right knee, pain like glass shattering throughout my leg. "No more running for you, nigger."

I'm pulled from the car, two pairs of arms dragging me from the Mustang. Below me, tracks and railroad ties slip away. Sydney, eyes wide behind the steering wheel; her mouth shapes into screams, but I cannot hear. She disappears behind her windshield, soaked over in reflections of headlights.

I struggle to keep alert, and I'm thrown into the back of a car, the dark inside saturated with the mixed odor of acrid sweat and anticipation. Three men, all in dark masks, two of them in front. The one beside me laughs at the mess my blood makes on the floorboard. "Watch," he says.

"Where?"

"Ahead, asshole. Your girlfriend's car."

Someone at the Mustang's passenger door opens it and slips inside; the Mustang pulls forward until it stops centered on the tracks.

"What we have here is your final warning."

"Clayton. I already know."

A hand at my knee, punches the wound, and the pain cuts

through my flesh. "Shut up and watch."

Waiting. Breathing the soured air these men exhale. It makes me wonder what it takes to block off Wickers Street in both directions. No complaints from other drivers. The station a ten-minute drive away; no cops arriving to investigate.

A rumbling shimmies up the car and fades. Drunken shouts from somewhere behind this car. Clayton's voice beside me. He tells me, "Train's coming."

The rumbling returns. This time, it doesn't fade away.

"Your man's in the Mustang."

"Doesn't matter."

The three men focus forward as though they watch a movie unfold. A new light appears and sets the Mustang's driver's side dimly aglow. The rumbling becomes the earthquake, moving along an inevitable fault line of steel.

"Less than a minute."

"Clayton. Let her go."

Chiding laughter beside me. "Oh! Kill me, kill me instead. Let the damsel go! Believe this. I'd kill you both if it was my choice to make." His gloved hand at his own throat raises the mask. Revealed. A white boy with blue eyes. Warped by a familiar hatred, this face shows me before it speaks. "I'm not Clayton." A stranger to me, he returns himself beneath his mask.

Laughter from the men in front, their masks pointed at me for a moment. Not Clayton's laughter, and they show me a glimpse of their anonymous white faces before re-masking themselves and returning to their show.

Gates fall like guillotine blades, surround the Mustang front and back. Sheet metal on the driver's side glows white hot, intensifying. A hopeless scream of metal grinding over metal, repeated blasts from foghorn bellows. Impressive clamor of a freight locomotive struggling in vain to stop before the crossing. Pieces of the Mustang dissolve, regain form only to dissolve again, its outline undefined, moving as if made of sand the wind works to erode.

The Mustang disappears with the rush of the train. Sound of metal screaming over metal suddenly muted, the blare of the train's horn deepening, fading, then gone. Maintained speed, train car after train car so improbably rumbling by unaffected. The lights on the other side of the tracks flickering through dark rectangles make it seem as though the movie is at an end.

"Long one," the voice beside me says with the passing of the last train car. Crossing gates bounce then lift. On the other side of the tracks, the Mustang sits as though reconstructed out of air. Its headlights flash off and on one time. The passenger door opens, and a man exits and walks to the SUV. One by one, the other cars back away, leaving the Mustang alone. Peering hard through the windshield, I make out the distinct taillights on one car; a glint of light off its top. The rack of MARS lights. A squad from the Red River Falls police fleet leaves with the others. The Mustang eases back. U-turns away.

"Looks like she's listening to instructions." The voice beside me turns my way. "And what have we learned here tonight, Officer Hill?" His fist strikes my face once. If he struck me a second time, I don't recall.

I regain consciousness on Main Street. Propped up against the door of a closed credit union office. I'm made aware of my condition by the occasional stares of pedestrians. A look of interest, and a look away. Blood, from my right knee down to my ankle, soaks over my pants and shoe.

Three pleas for a cell phone. The fourth to a white boy willing to drive me to the hospital; he lets me make a call.

"Jack," I slur into the phone. "How long have you been home?"

"Theresa's been scratching my back since I got off shift. You think I'd be anywhere else?"

I suspect you, I wish to say. Something honest I could tell him: After all I've witnessed, Jack, the smallest provocation causes me to suspect you, and it always takes proof to the contrary before I'm able to let my suspicion go. No matter the proof from the day before. Since paranoia requires a false fear, then I cannot truly suffer from paranoia, can I, Jack? It's the impact of so much hate without reason, hate not from one man but from Dan Hubert's seven percent. If Jesus were to resurrect in Red River Falls, if He came back to earth as a brown man, there would be a group of white boys ready to use His cross to burn Him alive. How could it be any safer for a brown boy still hiding under the table? It is something other than paranoia I feel from the streets of Red River Falls. Something very close to the truth.

I don't say these things to Jack, and I don't level accusations against him. I can't. If I did, I'd lose the only real chance I have to prove my fear wrong.

"I'm bleeding outside the credit union on Main."

"I'm leaving now," Jack says.

The white boy takes his cell phone, asks me if I'm all right. He moves away but stays nearby until Jack arrives, watching with concern and discomfort while I laugh. He doesn't ask me again whether I'm all right.

43

A pint of blood, suturing of muscle tissue, nineteen stitches, and a tetanus shot. After two days in the hospital, I refuse the Valium.

Hospital policy bends enough to allow me to stay with Auntie Doria. I had been polite about it but had refused to stay in any other room. It was simply easier for them to give in.

"Halle Berry and Derek Jeter." Jack stands in the dark of Auntie Doria's hospital room. "Halle Berry and Derek Jeter," he says again. "They're proof enough."

I hand Jack the key to Momma and Poppa's house, tell him where my clothes are, shaving supplies, service revolver and police uniforms. Ask him to find something special for Auntie Doria. I also insist he leave the swastika on the ceiling untouched. Unreported. "It's another layer peeled back," I say. He understands I want to be the one to paint it away.

As far as my injury is concerned, I tell Jack to stick to the story. There was no attack. What I have is a badly twisted knee and a bruised face from when I fell to the asphalt playing basketball. Basketball. The white boys in command will nod, mutter "Of course" and not have any doubts.

"You'll be ready for work tomorrow?"

"Desk assignment."

"Shee-it. More days with Drano."

I'm sunk into a cushioned chair, my right leg propped on a pillow atop the foot of Auntie Doria's hospital bed, lost in gauze and tape. A crutch leans against my chair. Jack presses his hand on my shoulder. Together we listen to Auntie Doria's clown-laugh-tuba-thump snore, proof of her profound sleep. We admire her peacefulness and wish we could share a taste of it with her.

"Seems to me," Jack says, "we ought to take all these supremacist white boys"—he says "boys" like I do, with a puff of extra breath over the "b"—"and find them their own place to live. Put them on an island and build a fence around it. In a few generations, their offspring's eyes will drift together into one. Give them their wish; let them interbreed until they stupid themselves off this planet."

"Jack," I say. "Been thinking about this much?"

"Shee-it. Halle Berry and Derek Jeter. They ought to be proof enough. Love between the races brings us closer to perfection."

"These white boys aren't separating. They're infiltrating."

"Are you sure you saw a squad car?" He scratches at his jaw. Tells me he's sorry for asking again. "Shift records and dispatch tapes wouldn't help identify it. Something like this, a cop's breaking protocol. Likely it's someone off duty, but he definitely needed a squad car to block traffic."

"Mileage logs," I say.

"Hardly accurate."

"Not the total miles. The end versus start mileage between shifts. Look for a gap."

A light tap on my cheek, Jack's face the serious gray of this room. "I want you to do it," he says, "so you'll know not to suspect me anymore or again, whichever way you've been suspecting me." His face remains serious, perhaps more so. "You're obvious." He tilts back, brightens with his lean against the wall. "Auntie Doria's snore sounds like a pinwheel-hat-and-tuba parade playing *Flight of the Bumblebee.*"

"You should tell her when she wakes up. She'd like to hear that."

"I'll pick you up before shift, bring you a fresh uniform."

"Jack," I say. A tremor overtakes my voice. "I thought the man in the car was Henry Clayton."

His eyes wide, beaming, Jack tells me to have confidence. He has confidence. "You thought Sydney was going to die. Terror plays tricks on people."

"I was terrified sixteen years ago."

"Of course. But under those circumstances you were also being the best son you could possibly be for your parents. For them you remembered everything and everyone. You know I'm right."

As he turns from me, I thank him. He stalls outside the doorway, silent, and I thank him again, louder. Hallway light throws his shadow into the room. I imagine his face, downcast, wondering why I continue to doubt him. It's likely the seriousness over his face permeates his body, explains the deepening of his shadow before it fades away.

When I wake up in the morning, my bandaged leg is propped up on a pillow on a wooden chair, and my chair has been turned. Auntie Doria lies on her side, her chest drainage tube gone, her lips sealed. Quiet. Her closed eyes, without her glasses, look like grated manhole covers. I move to kiss her, stand without using my crutch. Although there's pressure around the wound, and no bend to my knee, I can tolerate the pain.

Auntie would be embarrassed by all of this. Her hospital gown covers so little in back, her hair a tangled mass. Her smell like disinfectant. When she wakes up for good, she'll hate her helplessness most of all.

Jack walks in with one of my uniforms on a hanger, my shoes more polished than I've ever seen, and my duffel bag. "I cut a slit in the right pant leg," he says. "Wash up and get dressed. You've got work to do."

"Did you bring something for Auntie Doria?"

Jack reaches into my duffel bag.

Auntie will open her eyes to the sight of the Holy Crucifix and Denzel Washington dangling from knobs on her IV drip stand. Groggy and still drugged she'll mistake these things for what's at the end of the post-apocalyptic tunnel of white light. She'll come to, get her bearings, and instead know my selfish prayer has been answered.

I'm released into an overcast morning, a uniform cloud cover dimming the entire sky, but without the strength to rain. On the other side of the parking lot, Leslie Griffin trails William behind her by the hand. He points at me, says something and waves; Leslie keeps moving toward the hospital entrance. Beneath another chandelier hat, she considers me invisible while she adores Auntie Doria.

"I've got one of your suitcases in the trunk for after shift," Jack says from inside his car. "Getting in?"

"Another minute." I rest on my crutch and peer over the roof of Jack's car, watching mother and son until they disappear into the hospital.

Something about Leslie's single-mindedness, to ignore me this way. If I cornered her, demanded an explanation, I know what she'd say. I'm a bad influence, a man to avoid because, above all else, she wants her son to believe in God.

44

When I moved in with Auntie Doria after Momma's and Poppa's murders, I had been away six weeks in a foster home. Back in school, I sat at the same desk in the same classroom with the same students, but it seemed the time away had changed everything. Charlie Watts noticed it too.

He passed a note to me and it read, "What's it like?" I passed a note back, saying, "What's what like?" His stuck-out ears seemed to stick out farther, flap a bit, when he read my note. He worked furiously at his next note, too focused to realize the teacher's hand waited to intercept it. She read it, looked at me just as dazed as Charlie Watts looked, then she sent him to the principal's office and let me be. I never got to read his note; the teacher crushed it in her hands and slipped the wad in her skirt pocket. After school, I met up with Charlie Watts and started to walk with him toward his house. He said he wasn't supposed to talk about the notes, or anything about it, especially not with me. He was nervous because there was more punishment waiting behind the principal's warning.

"Who's gonna tell on you?"

He flinched away from me, stuffed his hands in his back pockets. "I made a promise."

It was the first time, and only time, I put my hands on Charlie Watts in that way. A rough way. My hands at his collar, gripping him with a foreign rage. I had him on the ground, chest-straddled. His fight back was worthless. "Tell me!"

At the time I had begun to suspect something about myself; I've only recently come to understand what it was. In Charlie Watts, in everyone but Auntie Doria, I was seeing Henry Clayton. Voices bent into his hateful voice. The shapes of faces, whatever their shade, became his. It seems to me now that Charlie Watts knew this better than I did. He saw the revenge in my eyes, the way they pictured him as Momma and Poppa's murderer. "No!" he persisted, and I weighed my knees more heavily over his chest.

"Tell me!"

"I'll tell you what I'm thinking now—you're different!" He screamed this over and over, and the people in the neighborhood I once lived in began to pour from their houses. "You don't belong here anymore!"

His words fired at me, shocked me. They were words which couldn't possibly exist. Suddenly weakened, I let him escape. I remained alone, knees on the sidewalk, hands aloft as if I still held Charlie Watts and begged his forgiveness. The adults studied me from their porches through narrowed eyes, lips closed and downturned; they slipped into their homes and slammed their doors shut. It was the same way in school. Children functioned around me to get by but collectively locked me out of their lives. It was as though the time they had spent with me, with Momma and Poppa, playing in the yard or experiencing the Hitchcock movies and wonderful books, had never happened. They had nothing real to say to me anymore and didn't care what I had to say to them. Charlie Watts had nothing to say. He never came by, called, or talked to me again. I went to his house to apologize, and his mother answered the door. With Charlie Watts standing beside her, her eyes focused over my head, she told me he wasn't home.

I chose to stay emotionally inert, physically withdrawn, and deceived myself into believing that isolation was my idea, not theirs. Auntie Doria connected me directly to Poppa, and Momma's writings in the margins of her books connected me directly enough to her. This was all I needed to get by, so I had convinced myself.

I think of these things from behind the front desk window at the police station, assigned to complaint intakes, my injured leg throbbing beneath the countertop while I sit on a tall stool. Officers walk by; like the children at school, like Leslie Griffin, they ignore me or do the minimum to acknowledge I'm alive.

WVOL broadcasts the national news, weather, and sports over the radio on a shelf above the complaints intake window. The local news arrives for the sixth time during the morning hours before my lunch break. Sydney Brey again reports on an arrest for sexual assault and the county board's meeting to discuss upcoming zoning issues. Nothing about a society of hate permeating Red River Falls, or a train almost striking a car at the Wickers Street crossing.

I leave a message on Sydney's voice mail at work. A thank you, words of concern, and the apology I was never able to give to Charlie Watts. I don't expert her to call me back.

More officers pass me without looking, or with a glance of defiance. As with Charlie Watts in my grip all those years ago, I stare back with the face of Henry Clayton filling my vision, each of them suspected.

It's amazing, really. The power of a lost childhood friend.

45

To some officers, squad cars are alive, each with a personality, not always good, and a sense that glass and sheet metal form a willing, breathing bodyguard. Mileage records become a daily physical, an indication of health and maintenance. The numbers measure heartbeats and birthdays, like the lives of children. These officers consider mistreatment of their squad cars as a form of child abuse, which has, in the past, led to confrontations at the station with officers from other shifts. Several officers don't give a damn about the squad cars. They abuse and neglect, overwork the brakes and engines, and can't wait for the next new fleet of cars to arrive. Regardless, mileage checks are mandatory before and after each shift simply because the City of Red River Falls needs to know. The price of gas and fleet maintenance, no longer negligible line items, are numbers subject to public scrutiny by administrative rule.

Twenty-five squad cars comprise the department's fleet, not counting prisoner transport wagons, the Chief's car, and two EMT vehicles. Absent an extraordinary reason, no officer may keep a squad car at his home. Any damage, any unusual sound, and, above all else, the mileage, must be accurately logged.

It's a basic paper trail not maintained on computers, but in a file cabinet within the records department. With one date involved, it's only a matter of time, and not much time. A squad car taken for a covert purpose, unknown to command or dispatch, outside protocol, is likely to have a mileage gap between scheduled shifts. If a gap fails to exist, then corruption extends up the line of command, and to dispatch.

Squad 15, shift one ending at 3:30 p.m. 27,334 miles. Not recorded as used for shift two, ending at 11:30 p.m., began service during shift three at 11:47 p.m. with 27,341 miles. An unrecorded seven mile gap, just about right for a trip to the Wickers Street crossing and back.

Review of the fleet video record in the ramp bay outside booking shows one man removing a squad car key at 6:15 p.m. The video is low quality, a snapped frame every few seconds. It's as though an omnipotent hand comes down to move a toy man's limbs and body, and my brain has to fill in the gaps to imagine motion. Two frames prove the toy man to be unafraid, his face trained on the camera; such arrogance can only thrive in a blatant man with plans rooted in fear. What catches my eye, though, is the blur in his right hand. I can't make out the details before he steps out of view, but the sight of it sends me back to the mileage records. I had ended my search too soon, again overconfident, a dangerous habit I can't seem to lose. Past Squad 15's records, Squad 22's records show a similar seven-mile gap between shifts. The toy man in the video carried two sets of squad keys, not one.

I stand with mileage log records in my hands, hunched over my crutch. All my movements have been far from secret. I walk like injured prey, bang my crutch about, groaning while I strain to angle myself in positions that allow me to do this work. Making another photocopy, returning the original, I realize a message will be passed on: Rich Hill is investigating the event, fear hasn't taught him a damn thing.

Gone fifteen minutes longer than my permitted lunch break, I'm back at the complaints counter. With what I now know, I'll have to wait for Jack Harter to return from patrol.

46

Blond Boy appears as a portrait of the model Hitler Youth, standing guard though first shift has ended, out of loyalty. It's what my eyes tell him. Yellow-blond hair with depth to it like cream. White skin made fresh and vigorous with the flush of energetic blood. Broad shoulders. Blue eyes wide as if vulnerable to any unreasonable suggestion. At the moment, though, Blond Boy stands as though he's mounted on a pole. His eyes angle toward the ceiling, near tears, but instinctively shift to the sight of my approach; he's struck by the wreck of my leg and my hobbling over my crutch.

"Eyes back on the ceiling," Jack barks beside him. Jack's face has gone red. He tugs at his collar, and paces in small steps around Blond Boy. He looks as though he wants to strangle him; Blond Boy looks as though Jack already has.

"Tell him," Jack says.

Blond Boy flinches, shakes his head. "I can't."

We stand outside the active evidence vault. Much more than a vault, it occupies a full quarter of the police station's basement. It's where active evidence is cataloged and maintained in pending cases through final appeals, awaiting court orders requiring evidence destruction. It holds a dozen refrigeration units where bloodstained clothing and other bodily fluid evidence are documented, categorized, and stored. Rape test kits are never destroyed. Even before DNA testing became an accepted science, blood proteins and blood typing required this procedure as part of the police department's state certification.

"Then I'll tell him," Jack says.

Blond Boy trembles, manages to speak up. "You weren't supposed to be in there."

"I've been a Red River Falls police officer for seventeen years," Jack shouts at his ear. "I'll go where I damn well want, and a rookie cop can't tell me no."

"The rules. I'll get fired."

I set my crutch on the floor, limp up to Blond Boy. My eyes make it to his chin, yet, even more than Jack, I'm able to make him tremble just by being here; he squeezes his eyes shut when I ask the question. "What won't you tell me?"

"That's the same question I can't answer."

"Why can't you answer?"

Blond Boy bites at his lips.

Jack stuffs his hands in his pockets, speaks in a low voice. "Your mother's rape test kit. It's gone from the active evidence room."

I think to put my hands on Blond Boy, grab his collar, rush him against the cage door sealing off the active evidence vault. It's not my damaged leg stopping me. It's the way Blond Boy stretches his head and chin to the side, as if begging me to hit him, and I see for the first time, the name on his tag plate. W. Jensen.

We're eye to eye, his size reduced by tears flowing to his chin. "I'm not like them, Officer Hill. I swear I'm not."

"Not like who?"

"Please, sir. Don't make me say. I'm from Ohio, but I have a fiancée in Red River Falls."

"We all have family in town."

Jack coughs, hands me my crutch. "Autopsy records will only show the sample draw from your mother. We need the kit to prove who raped her."

"Henry Clayton," I say.

Jack nods. "That's who I mean." He growls at Blond Boy. "We needed the rape kit for a retest."

I wait for Blond Boy to look at me again. When he does, he goes on muttering and crying over how he's not like them. They assume he is, but he didn't destroy anything or throw anything away.

"But you're not saying who."

Blond Boy shakes his head.

"You insist you're not like them, but they count on you to look the other way. Your silence allows them to thrive. You stand guard over what they've done."

He looks over his shoulder at the cage behind him. "Only when Officer Harter needs a partner to fill in."

"Dranowski assigns you here?" Jack asks.

Blond Boy stiffens. Won't answer.

I say, "I already know."

Exhaling hard, Blond Boy slips a pitiful glance toward me. "Dranowski." He mumbles over the name.

I step to him so our eyes nearly touch. I want him to not only hear what I have to say, but also to smell the scent of my words. He seems to understand, manages to steady himself and close his eyes when I speak the nightmare I want him to breathe. More than listen, he absorbs. Takes in the experience of a boy who witnessed his parents' destruction, and what it means to the boy as well as the man; the impossible suffering I endure knowing their murderer walks freely over the earth.

Hobbling to Jack, I wait for the impact to either come or fail. Jack asks, "What's Drano's connection to Henry Clayton?"

Blond Boy inhales, and his eyes have gone blank as if he's made up his mind. He removes his tie and unbuttons his shirt's top buttons, pulls cloth away to lay bare his neck and collarbone. White skin unspoiled by symbols. "Look for it," he says, and I strain to hear his breaking voice. "Counterclockwise."

Jack grumbles. "Hardly an answer."

"No," I say, watching the deepening slump of Blond Boy's shoulders. "He's told me what I need to know."

Second shift officers have moved on to their assignments, leaving the locker room to first shift officers unwinding from their day. Their voices and echoes are filled with a typical mix of laughter and opinionated disgust. Showers go on, hissing of snakes, and the steam forms a translucent cloud over the whole of the room.

Standing at its threshold, seeing only the backside of the first bank of lockers, I listen for his sound. Nothing. I cannot wait any longer and I hobble in, the beat of my feet and crutch over the concrete floor aping a drunken man's waltz.

These officers gather in the third row of lockers. Standing, sitting, leaning, lost in conversations. Jack, I see, is the quiet one staring into his opened locker. It's as though he has learned to imitate the way I stare into an abyss. I watch him unclip his tie and unfasten his shirt's top two buttons; the easy way he pulls down at his shirt collar and T-shirt to rub at his neck and collarbone.

I approach Jack and sit beside him, my right leg sticking out askew like a kickstand.

"How's the leg?"

"It hurts like hell."

He nods at me, tight-lipped, and rubs at his neck some more. Other men here notice me, quiet down a bit, but continue with their conversations. Jack reaches into his locker and offers me a can of Coca Cola. "Still cold from the vending machine," he says. I take it and thank him.

I sip its sugary carbonation and consider the sparks over my tongue and the roof of my mouth. It's a rest stop for my brain before I move forward.

Jack asks, "Find anything?"

"Something. I don't know what it means."

"It's always this way. A fact gets screwed up by other possibilities." He twists his neck so I can see below his right ear, flesh unspoiled down to his shoulder.

I drink some more, grunt an agreement with him. Watching me swallow, Jack says, "You have that look again."

"I always have that look."

"Then I'm always right about you having it again."

Blond Boy works his way down the row, towel draped around his waist, another around his neck. Water drips from his hair. Veteran officers make little room for the rookie. Whistle at him as he goes by. He knows enough not to look me or Jack in the eye.

"Cold drink?" Jack says, extending a can of cola toward Blond Boy. He refuses it, thanks him in a hollow way as if thanking a stranger.

"Passing out the beer, Harter?" Drano asks. He's still tight inside his uniform. "Nothing for me?"

"Last one," Jack says, extending the cola. "It's yours."

"Poisoned?"

"I suppose we'll find out in a few minutes." There's no hesitation; Drano takes the can and pops it open.

"You know," Jack says. "You never take a shower here. Never in the years I've known you."

Drano drinks from the can, wipes his mouth, lips gone thin. "Sure I have."

"I've never seen it." Jack turns to Blond Boy. "Have you ever seen Drano take a shower?"

"I haven't been here long."

"See, Drano? Even your partner agrees with me."

"You know why. Don't screw with me."

"I don't know why," Jack persists. "Why don't you tell me why."

Blond Boy sits, inanimate, while other men lose interest in their own conversations and draw close behind Drano.

"Because I shower at home with my wife." Drano looks around the locker room in search of laughter. The silence disappoints him.

"I've heard she sleeps through that too."

"Up yours, Harter. It's your partner who never takes a goddamn shower here. Never has."

"I don't sweat," I say. "I don't have a reason to."

Drano guzzles his cola, his fingers denting into the can. "I'm a fat man, boys, in case you haven't noticed."

"Simply plump," Jack says. "Middle-age-man disease. It's not like high school gym class. You're among friends now."

"Right."

Drano finishes his cola, crushes the can, and throws it on the floor at Jack's feet.

Pulling a plastic evidence baggy from his locker, Jack uses it to pick up the cola can, and seals it up.

Drano's eyes widen. "What the hell are you doing?"

"Unbutton your shirt," I say.

"Why?"

" 'Cause I'm asking."

"Go to hell."

"Not the response I'm looking for."

"It's a goddamn good response, Hill."

"Are you refusing to take off your shirt, Officer Dranowski?"

"I am."

Drano looks behind him, asks the other men there whether they can believe this shit. Several move forward, I count only four but try not to be overconfident. Maybe there's less. Two, though, step in front of Drano, facing Jack and me. Blond Boy sits among them, desperately lost, looking like a child who wishes nothing more than to run away.

Jack nods at the men protecting Drano. “Mind if we all loosen our collars a bit?”

“Funny, Harter,” Drano says. “Get your warrant.”

“We need a warrant to get your shirt unbuttoned?”

“Right. Absolutely right.”

Jack raises the evidence bag, dangling the cola can inside. “A warrant may take a couple weeks. Pity.”

Drano’s eyes narrow, his voice unsettling in its sudden show of confidence. “You got your empty soda can. Empty is all you’ve got.”

He turns and motions to the men at his side to leave with him. Other officers remain to dress in their street clothes before they go. No swastikas, but no acknowledgment we’re here, or that anything unusual has happened. Complacency, then departure for home.

Jack and I sit alone with Blond Boy. It’s hard to tell whether it’s the showers hissing, or air escaping through Blond Boy’s pores. “When you’re as white as I am, people make assumptions.” Blond Boy looks at me with noticeable discomfort, whispers, “And not just men like Drano.”

“Are you expecting me to apologize?”

“No, sir. But at least try to understand.” His deflation complete, Blond Boy sags as if the last bone has been removed from his body. “I was expected to stand up and walk away with the others just now.”

“Go home,” I say. “Drop your badge and service revolver. Take your fiancée with you back to Ohio.”

Blond Boy dresses into his street clothes, works to avoid looking at me or Jack. “It’s in Ohio too,” he says. “It’s everywhere.” He manages to raise a weak smile toward Jack, coughs a few times. “You’ll be next.”

"Me?" Jack's eyes narrow. "How do you know?"

Blond Boy stares at the slits in his locker door. "It's so hard to be complacent," I say to him, "when you actually have a conscience. You knew about Auntie Doria and Sydney."

Blond Boy doesn't acknowledge me, makes me invisible for his own sake. He moves mechanically, tying his shoes, gathering his comb and shaving supplies into a gym bag, walking away as if his feet were set on rails; his gun, badge, and uniform, though, remain on the floor.

Showers off, locker room empty of other men, Jack and I wait.

"Caught you checking my neck," he says.

"Who shouldn't I suspect?"

Jack doesn't answer; he understands there is no answer. He has thrown himself into my world, shares my form of invisibility among people he has worked with for seventeen years. As we pass through the police station's rooms and hallways, these people and their conversations wilt away from us. Brick and mortar deny the echoes of our steps.

Inside his car, Jack says, "My house."

Not a question. Not even a sentence. Rather it's an acknowledgment of Blond Boy's warning and my singular option. Born and raised in Red River Falls, I'm kept here by too many things. Auntie Doria most of all. And, I admit, Jack Harter. Also keeping me here are things that would chase a more reasonable man away. River ghosts. How they once frightened me, now beg me in clear voices to find answers, resolution, and justice. I must be with Jack, a ghost myself in his home, if this is to ever end.

47

Theresa Harter apologizes the moment she meets me at the front door. She describes her house as an avalanche, a glacial outcropping, and she cradles the diminutive boy responsible for it all. Tyler's skin appears soft, like hers, and the boy watches me with brown eyes large below black, feathery hair. I attempt to show them my brighter side by thinking of Charlie Watts, the times we played on the swing set with Momma and Poppa; my effort to disguise my face beneath imagery. But the remoteness of this memory causes the opposite result, deepens my hurt. Perhaps the sight of me tilted on my crutch adds to the impact. More likely mother and child take my appearance as a symptom of a more obvious problem.

Theresa's and Tyler's eyes absorb the truth, an overwhelming sadness, really. Together they perceive my sadness, dissect its parts with their innocence, and readily discover the details. Rage. Hopelessness. Pain. Theresa holds her child, her beautiful child, embraced not only to her chest, but also away from me.

Jack senses this, loses his smile. He asks Tyler what he wants to be when he grows up. The boy dutifully announces he wants to be a policeman, but even that fails to rescue Jack's smile.

"Are you the man Daddy says doesn't like Chinese food?" Tyler intones.

My weight now fully over my crutch. "That's me."

I am a man too troubled to sleep well in his own bed, too

troubled to believe his bed is actually his own. Closing my eyes, lying beneath the covers in someone else's guest room, I know the thought of sleep is sheer fantasy. My eyes close in pretend sleep and something new engages my thoughts. Theresa and Tyler embraced in the loving way I once embraced Momma and Poppa. How my innocent childhood shies away from me. Whether this is out of fear or embarrassment, I'm left in the night to think it over.

Opening my eyes, waiting for them to adjust to nighttime's glow, I'm aware of neat bookcases holding classic literature, and bucolic landscapes within frames upon the walls. A cross hangs on the inside of the bedroom door; area rugs pat over the wood floor. This bedroom gives the appearance of being apart from the rest of the house; not a room on the first floor of two-story suburbia, but a space tucked high up within a Victorian bed and breakfast. An adult oasis, I suppose, away from raising a child. It makes me wonder whether Theresa and Jack escape here once in a while, as I now do, to separate from the real world if only for a brief time.

I listen to voices permeate these walls. Theresa's doubts. Jack's insistence that matters have been thoroughly planned. Although their words reach me in whispers, they are urgent whispers that would prefer to be shouted. I doubt there has ever been an argument so divisive inside this home before tonight; I've never been inside this home before tonight. The packing of suitcases, the gathering of a sleeping child. Jack has his way.

At the bedroom door, Jack doesn't pretend I'm asleep. "Listen," he says, leaning inside. "Sorry about all this. She didn't mean it. It's just the situation right now."

"It's all right, Jack. I agree with her."

He stands there mute. Nods his head with a lethargic grin. "We're going now."

He closes the door but the handle doesn't catch and the door moves open an inch. Heavy padding of feet over the floor, dodging toys and books along the way to the back door. A rush to the outside, and the locking pop of the deadbolt. There's no sound of a car engine. They cut through their backyard and the backyard of a neighbor. Meet a taxi at the corner a block down, someone Jack knows. No questions will be asked. I listen, hear no evidence of their departure, and wonder how far along they are in our plans, and how long before he sees them to safety and returns.

My position is inevitable. Wakefulness even within an oasis of peace. Hunger and thirst will be ignored. No trip to the bathroom. Beneath the covers, on my back, covered in the light brown of my skin and black of my clothes, I fold my hands over my service revolver upon my chest. Eyes opened, ears alert. Sleep is not meant to be part of this night.

48

The footfalls of river ghosts.

They don't tread upon the earth. They lack defined surfaces, create no friction, have no mass. Yet their appearance is unmistakable. River ghosts arrive in shafts of cold within warm air, with touches of breath where no person breathes. Their presence comes from within the person sensing them and listening to them, their approach tracked by the rising pores of human skin. How strange to feel them inside someone else's home, in this room I've never occupied before. Does it prove time and place are irrelevant to ghosts? More likely I carry them, sometimes trailing them along, but more often within me.

I force my lips to part, shape them to speak. Momma? Poppa? No sound comes out; the terrified child frozen inside a nightmare, unable to talk although the child's eyes are open and his mouth stretches wide. Still, they hear me and understand. Their touches surround me, urgently lift me from this bed.

Stepping to the floor, I rise as ghosts do. I reach for the crutch leaning against a bedside bureau, but I'm told no. It might interfere, create a sound. I have to float without sound over the floor to the hallway, and it's as though I've passed through the door.

I consider the pain in my leg. Isolate it. Place it outside of me as if it were another ghost following along, encouraging me to step with caution. My gun feels iced in my hand, pressed to my side. Ahead of me, Tyler's toys and books lie translucent in a moonlit night that steals away color. I weave around them, their placement foretold to me as I move. First to Tyler's room at the end of the hallway. A chalkboard displays a clumsy alphabet, some letters turned the wrong way. Stuffed animals and piggy banks on shelves, cabinets full of framed photographs of his history from month to month. Mobiles of rocket ships and flowers tied to ceiling light fixtures. His bed made up with small pillows under the blanket, crudely emulating the presence of a small child.

Everything in place and I turn from the bed. Shafts of cold urge me back, frantic whispers of ghosts at my ears. *Check as Momma and Poppa would check.* I fold the blanket down, push the pillow into the headboard, and run my hands over the top sheet. A touch of frayed thread under my palm. Running my hand over the spot at the edge of the pillow, I feel the length of a cut, slip my fingertips down, and understand the power of the blade. *He's here. Do you understand his anger? He knows you've been made aware.*

Something behind me; nothing there but the warnings of ghosts. I reach for the light switch by the bedroom door and wonder. Drop my hand to my side. I decide to take comfort in my invisibility, and I'm told, *It wouldn't work anyway.*

In the hallway, I step to the farthest wall, inside the deepest shadow. *He could be almost anyplace. Wait him out for a change. Let him know he's lost control this time.*

I'm soundproof. Breaths swallowed, heartbeats negligible, arms at my side, the gun in my right hand held with my finger curled over its trigger. I look down the length of my body inside this hidden space, and I'm gone. I've become the ghost, held silently by the hands of Momma and Poppa. Their touches strengthen me, lift me off the ground. There's no use doubting my ability to withstand the waiting. Let the hours go by, I no longer perceive the passing of time. *Don't cry, boy!* Poppa says.

Momma says, *It's all right. Just be quiet about it is all.*

Overhead, a sound. *He's moving,* Poppa says. Momma warns, *Be still, son.* Through shafts of cold, the texture of my skin, I tell them both I won't hide under the table this time. Momma waits for the shadow within moonlight to appear at the other end of the hallway. *I know,* she says, and I'm lowered to the floor.

I'm amazed by the way his shadow lengthens, as if he, too, floats over the earth. But he is unaware, or perhaps unaccepting, of other, more invisible shadows. Although he faces me, he slips into Tyler's room. Inside he will see. Blanket drawn down, pillow pushed to the wall. His presence and anger found out. He will drift from shadow toward flesh and bone, still something far short of human.

A blade emerges first, then he steps into the hall with one leg. The other steps forward, and he touches the floor, shifts a wooden board. He's made fully visible by sound. I'm witness to his mortality.

Imagine his shock at the power of a gun firing from blackness, a bullet ripping through his flesh, launched by a man who isn't there. He hurries away down the hall, holding his arm, and when he turns, moonlight reflects off the blade still grasped in his hand.

I feel as though I've returned to earth through an infinite passage. There are no longer shadows here, simply flesh and bone, and blood, crimson droplets guiding me along. My breaths and heartbeats nearly overwhelm me as if rebounding from imposed silence. When I turn the corner, he waits for me at the threshold to the kitchen, drives his blade through my ribs and watches my fall.

The gun in my right hand won't rise, the barrel lying worthlessly on the floor. I look for the final attack, but he's gone. Lights in the house flash on at once, like sparks in my eyes. I have to work to see the man returning to stand over me, dripping his blood over mine.

Henry Clayton examines his knife, then lowers himself to scowl at me. "Looks like I won't be doing my arm curls tomorrow. On the other hand, looks like you popped a lung."

He runs his blade above my right knee, digs at the surface of healing flesh. Isolated pain comes rushing back, takes over the length of my body. His smile, so much like the one twisted over Momma, mistakes the tears on my face for agony.

"Yup," he says. "There's air bubbling out your side."

Clayton straightens, kicks away toys on his way to an easy chair. Sits on the edge and watches my struggle for breath. "Damn, mud cop. You got the other lung working, don't you? Not answering? Fine. I don't want to hear what you have to say anyway." He touches at the wound in his arm, licks his blood off his fingertips, then settles back in the chair with his blade over his knees. "Guess you and Jack figured me out. Took you forever, but now I've got to think some."

I gasp at the pain, like a claw tearing my flesh from within. Clayton notices, waves a hand at me to encourage me to speak.

"Where the hell is your bible?"

He cocks his head to the side. "I have no idea. I've never owned a bible in my life."

"Aren't you a preacher?"

"Never!" He pounds his injured arm down on the chair. The pace of bleeding increases yet he seems unaware. "Do you really think I'd bow down to a Jew just 'cause he's hanging on a cross? Do you think I'm out of my mind?"

"Henry, yes. Exactly what I'm thinking."

He turns and laughs at his shoulder, as if someone stands there to laugh along with him. "Here's the thing. I had this all figured out. So many years and now I need to do some new figuring."

I work my left hand toward my ribs, put pressure on my

wound despite the added pain. Waiting for a chance to reach the gun beside my right hand.

"Never appreciated what you did to me, Richie boy. Never did. And I particularly didn't like that jury convicting me when there was no evidence. Nothing."

"I pointed you out."

"That's what I didn't appreciate. All those people believing your lies."

"All those white people, Henry?"

The gesture he made before, the pull of his head toward the scar on his neck, now profound, as if he motions toward a person at his shoulder to come forward. "Look at you. You're a sin of nature. Nobody should care who you point out."

"I need to know before you kill me. Who took your DNA at the prison?"

The blue of his eyes shrink, compressed by thickening white. "This has always been about the joy of intimidation. Killing you would risk making things look so obvious."

"Whose DNA, Henry?"

"I gave my DNA."

"We both know you're lying."

His gesturing stops. "It's a beautiful thing, don't you think? Microscopic swirls and all sorts of mystery. Did you ever look at pictures of DNA strands? You should. I had lots of time to study the way they curve and twist. They join together like no man and woman ever could, connecting in so many places it blew my mind. Fantastic microscopic sex. What life is all about. Microscopic sex."

"I've never looked at it that way."

"It's amazing, though. All those medical doctors and lab technician people, and then the lawyers and government people right up to the governor. Patience is all it takes. It just proves sometimes getting around all those smart guys is so damn simple it makes you want to laugh. Doesn't it make you laugh to think about it?"

"Who came to take your DNA?"

"No, sir. You're not even close to the right question." He leans forward, a twist again toward his neck. "What do I do with you now? There's the right question."

He grabs his knife, presses the tip into my left hand inching toward my gun. "Nuh-uh, Officer Hill. That's not the answer to my question either."

It's too bad for Henry Clayton, how he fails to twitch toward his scar, to look over his shoulder for somebody there. "I'm really annoyed," Jack says. "All this blood on my new carpet."

"See there?" Henry eases back. Closes his eyes. "You guys did some figuring too. It's something I should've known, simple as fishing. The bait and the hook. See what I told you about simple?"

Henry begins to stand. Jack backhand slaps him across the jaw, sends him reeling away from the chair. Before Clayton can reach my gun, Jack kicks him in the same spot, sends him rolling to his back.

"You're a pacifist, Rich," Jack says, pocketing my gun. "You have to aim to kill."

"I think things worked out pretty well."

Jack reaches beneath my left arm to clasp my back, gets me on my feet to the couch. Clayton moans on the floor, curling to his knees. He opens his eyes, stares at the blood on my chest. "You should be laying down," he says.

Jack barks at him to shut his mouth.

"There's no need to talk to me that way."

Though blood pours from his left arm, and the swelling over his jaw is already pronounced, Henry Clayton manages to sit on the floor, surrounded by Tyler's toys and books. A twitch in his neck, smaller than before. "I'm not here," he says. "Praise be."

I shake my head at Jack to leave him alone. "Just put your cuffs on him."

"I don't have my cuffs with me. I thought you were going to kill him."

"What made you think I'd kill him?"

"Just about everything."

"Get the cuffs."

"I left them in my car." Jack paces the length of the couch then stops. "I'm not leaving you alone in this room with Henry Clayton."

"Gentlemen," Clayton says. "I'm here to convince Officer Hill to work this entire misunderstanding out before it's too late."

Jack nods at him. "You go ahead and practice your insanity defense. You're doing great."

"Insanity defense for what?"

"Home invasion," I say. "Attempted murder."

"But you brought me here. It's your fantasy about your parents' murders." Clayton's voice softens, his demeanor opposite his assault. It's as though he has not only disappeared, but been replaced. "You won't let go. Fact is, all I've done is present flowers to your parents' graves, left a note begging to help you find the real killer, come to your auntie's house to show you more proof of my innocence, and beg again and again to let me help you. All you've done is attack me, in my church no less, in front of so many God-fearing people and, can you believe it, most of it caught on closed-circuit TV videotape. How do you think this will play out in court, Officer Hill? Really." He raises his hands before him. "I didn't even bother to wear gloves. You don't need to wear gloves when you're invited into someone's home. How was I to know you would plan to beat a lie out of me?" Clayton rubs at his jaw and nods to Jack. "It's your kitchen knife, not mine."

"You killed my parents."

Clayton twists his head toward the scar on his neck. His mouth shifts into a tortured smile, and he speaks with a growl. "You can't put that on me no more. I've been reborn, made into new flesh. All my past sins belong to Jesus now. I am another man."

Momma's and Poppa's cold touches embrace my face, their lips sweep like a breeze over my ears. *His smile is the sinner's unrepentant pleasure and the vanity of the reborn surfacing together on the face of one man.*

Clayton's eyes lose focus, his voice gone as if stolen.

"What's going on?" Jack says.

I say, "He can hear them."

"Hear who?"

Clayton stands and his stare circles the room. Words boom from his throat without distinction. A preacher upon the pulpit, at his sermon's zenith; or a condemned man with the noose around his neck, able to confess but not atone. "After all," Clayton says, arms spreading outward. "It is far better to be righteous than it is to be right."

Movement of cold over my skin compels me to ask him why. Clayton tilts his head back. Laughs as if he expected the question and long ago plotted his answer. "So many people like me out there, you just don't know. Why?" he throws back at me, laughing anew. "Because I wanted to. Because I could. Because nobody can do a goddamn thing about it on earth or for eternity." He levels his head, beams his stare at me more pointedly than his blade. "I got a goddamn pardon from the governor, and my soul's rebirth from my preacher."

Jack touches at my gun in his pocket, his fingers reaching around the handle, lifting. I call to him, ask him to think about what he's doing. He freezes and the cold rushes away from me, leaves me with an overwhelming sense of emptiness, as if I'm witness to a scene in which I play no part. Jack moves again, his motion with the gun fluid. He aims and fires, and the bullet penetrates above Clayton's left eye. A hole no larger than a dime.

Clayton remains balanced over his feet, his eyes wide open but unaware. Blood flows down his face; he tilts, then collapses to the floor.

Jack lowers my gun, returns it to his pocket so calmly it's as though he were handling a wallet. He steps to Clayton's head, watches blood pour toward his shoes. "Now we don't need a court order for a new DNA sample," he says. "Plenty of DNA available right here."

He winces at the way I'm backed up on the couch, my mouth gaping, gasping out words. "What did you do, Jack?"

"Isn't it obvious?" He looks down at Clayton. "The son-of-a-bitch was right." Unemotional, eyes clear, Jack says, "He got to live after murdering two saints and a goofy old man. I can live after killing one devil."

He stands there watching blood flow, a quiet born-again Christian. Murderer. Willing martyr. Husband and father. A mortal friend. He's all these things inside his large frame. He knows my discomfort and my indecision. "I'll make this easy for you," he says, tossing his cell phone to me. "I'm willing to confess. I'll play this any way you want, but you've got to make the call."

There's no regret in him; he holds himself stoic, arms straight at his sides. I run my fingers over his cell phone's numbers, feel their give beneath my skin. Check a digital clock on a side table and see it blink 12:00 at me. It takes to the seventh ring, and instead of hello, I hear only breathing.

"Sydney?"

Her words tremble at the sound of my voice. "This isn't a good idea."

"Clayton's dead." Silence. "Did you hear me?"

"I'm not so sure it makes a difference."

I consider Hubert's percentages, Clayton's final words. "Listen, Sydney. I need you to turn on your police scanner no later than two minutes from now."

"Red River Falls?"

"No," I say, glancing at Jack. "County sheriff. Don't bother with Red River Falls. And Sydney, you don't have to hold back anymore. No more waiting. You'll understand from the sheriff's dispatch what's going on. Everything we've talked about is on the record now."

"Anything in particular?"

I hear her noises, her rush out of bed, knocking over something and swearing at it. "Everything in particular. Just listen to the sheriff's dispatcher on your scanner."

She's gone without a good-bye. I hang up and start dialing the County Sheriff's office. Listening to the ring, a voice putting me on hold, I again look at Jack and notice a subtle change. A shift away from stoicism toward pain. Not a loss of confidence. It seems as though he has passed from this moment to his future, and shows a doubt perhaps even he cannot withstand.

"We won't be able to work together," he says. "Command won't allow it while the investigation remains pending." He inhales, more of an exasperation. "Besides, I won't be able to look at you."

Even now his eyes focus somewhere beyond this room. There's a practical reason for our separation when trying to get away with murder. What I know about Jack, though, teaches me better. The problem is the way I'll look at him with a gratitude approaching worship. Certainly he will see it in my eyes; I doubt I could ever stop myself. And the trouble with my worship is that Jack Harter is not Henry Clayton. Jack is a man whose religious faith shows rather than tells. He could neither use his faith as a disguise nor try to run from it.

County Sheriff dispatch answers. I cry into the phone. Cry for Momma and for Poppa. It's just as well. My crying goes down on tape when I tell county dispatch that Jack Harter is a goddamn hero, and to send an ambulance as fast as is humanly possible.

The touch of river ghosts returns, spreads a cooling chill over my wounds, softens my pain, and eases my breathing. I'm lifted by their sense of sadness, now soothed by relief. Jack holds a picture at his side. I didn't see him move to find it, and possess it, but it's there clutched in his hands. A portrait photo of his son. He says only, "I feel the cold."

If a man like me believes in river ghosts, if Momma and Poppa touch me like angels, as they do right now, then how can I deny the existence of God? The irony of my new faith, though, is that it gives me the power to witness the depths of Jack's despair. He is lost over the scene of his own violence. And it is God he fears most.

49

If Sydney Brey had any doubt New York would want her, it has to be gone by now. At first she refused to relent the airwaves to sports scores or traffic reports or news occurring halfway around the world. She went on, telling my story the way she saw fit. She held on to the microphone and let the story rip as though she had been practicing it for weeks just waiting for Clayton to make a wrong move. Since then, for two days now, it plays over WVOL, and other media have grasped for the story far too late.

Sydney has seen fit to finish her broadcasts with Momma's and Poppa's names, in full. Cherished mother and father, may they now rest in peace.

"What's this girl really like?" Auntie Doria says at my hospital bedside. She's tried to put on makeup but has overdone it, red over black cheeks, and her hair has trouble cracking the dent lying on a pillow for six days straight has put in it. With one hand she clutches at the cross Jack brought to her from the house, the other punches at her glasses twice waiting for my answer.

"She's an Irish girl."

"Don't matter to me. Does she make you happy?"

"She's moving to New York any day now," I say. "It's for her own good."

"Oh?" Auntie Doria lifts her glasses off her head, puts her big face so close to mine it's like talking to her nose.

"I'm staying in Red River Falls, Auntie. I'm not going anyplace else."

"Wouldn't bother me if you left, Richie child. I want to see you happy."

"It would bother you."

"Just the same, I wouldn't stand in your way."

Auntie Doria settles back in her chair, looks over her shoulder at the sheriff's deputy at my door. "He should be protecting you rather than guarding you from running away."

"Just a precaution after something like this."

"How long?"

"Until the results come back."

"You sound certain."

"I am."

She pushes at her glasses but holds her hand at the bridge a while. "That preacher man had me fooled a little bit even if he had the Scripture numbers wrong."

I ease myself up, pillow pressed to my side. Auntie grimaces along with me. "Can I help you with anything, child?"

"Got to pee."

"Ain't nothing I haven't seen on you before."

"It's been a few years."

"Still."

She helps me stand, hobbles along with me, keeps her hand on my back until I reach the bathroom door. The guard in the hall watches me with a frown on his face. "It's not like I'm about to do a wind sprint, Deputy," I say. He ignores my laugh. Considers me a job to do, a possible suspect, a possible victim, in the matter involving Henry Clayton currently described by the Sheriff's office as The Incident.

I believe Jack would enjoy knowing I'm thinking of him while I take my pee. He'd tell me of the newly discovered benefits of an uncircumcised penis. "What makes you think black men aren't circumcised?" I say into the toilet bowl.

Through the closed door: "Who you talkin' to?"

"Nobody, Auntie."

"Sounds like somebody."

My heart falls away when I think about Jack Harter. Perhaps when we're both older, decades older, I'll be able to tell him how much I love him, and thank him far too late for the way he's shown how much he loves me.

Auntie Doria sleeps in the reclining chair beside my bed. Her position modifies her snore, sharpens the tubas into trombones, which slide into whistles on the exhales. Her breathing fills my hospital room with the smell of the dinner she bummed off me. I'm too sore inside to eat much anyway.

The flowers Sydney Brey sent me came with a note to listen, absolutely, to her 6:08 p.m. broadcast. Her voice fills this hospital room, combines both her professional tenacity with her passion. Rather than her recorded report, which has been playing since Clayton's death, she reports a new story, live. It's about a lawyer's motion already on file in a Texas civil court. The motion anticipates the results of Henry Clayton's new DNA retest, comparisons to his original DNA submission, as well as a review of the original DNA results supposedly taken from Momma's rape test kit before it disappeared. A submitted cola can is also of interest. Filed on behalf of victims' families, and despite the finality of official pardons, the lawyer's motion seeks to reopen the cases of three people convicted of murder who were later exonerated by DNA evidence. In the meantime, a lawyer in Michigan has filed a similar motion but on behalf of four defendants convicted of murder based primarily on DNA evidence.

"Looks like the unsinkable Titanic has struck the iceberg again," Sydney says. She shuffles at some papers, announces that her tears don't translate well over the radio. "The last thing I have to say before I sign off is thank you to the WVOL listeners for putting up with my voice. This is my final broadcast from this chair. It is my hope a certain man follows me to New York when he's able. My guess is you won't for some special reasons. I'll understand. But please don't forget about me."

My head sinks deep into my pillow, my hand around a short note tucked under my dinner plate. It's in Jack's handwriting, that's clear, although I don't know how he manages this while he's under house arrest. I read it again to be sure, to enjoy it, I suppose, and to remind myself to pass the information on to Sydney in New York. There's no mistaking how it helps Jack's situation. The fact that Officer Phillip Dranowski has failed to show up for shift since the Clayton incident, his wife both unknowing of his current whereabouts, and pleased about his departure as she possibly can be.

50

Being under house arrest for a month has its advantages. Even if it's inside a house like Momma and Poppa's. I have time not just to paint over Henry Clayton's counterclockwise swastika, but to sand it away, apply spackle, and then paint over it. It's something I had to do before putting the house up for sale. I hear nothing from Momma or Poppa, no touch of objection by ghosts flowing over my skin.

I've regained most of my strength, although with the last coat of paint, I'm ready to sit for the rest of the evening. From my chair, I watch scripted lives play on the television screen for a half hour, then turn the set off out of boredom. I think about running again as soon as house arrest ends.

Looking out the picture window, I wonder why I've merited two deputies. Wonder how many Jack has to suffer. I can only imagine the questions Tyler has, and in private, the questions Theresa has for Jack. She will have to learn to accept his incomplete answers about the death of Henry Clayton. More importantly, Jack will never speak what he sacrificed for my pitiful friendship, or what I continue to sacrifice for his.

Revenge has its price. Although it's something we're not supposed to admit to out loud, the truth is that revenge also has its rewards. Henry Clayton's death allows me to peacefully sleep, even in this house. Of course the memories are there, just as strong: the hurt, the loss, and the what-might-have-beens. Now, though, I feel I've been able to do something tangible in response. At first I thought keeping the truth about the way Henry Clayton died a secret would be difficult. I would collapse, inevitably, under the burden caused by maintaining this lie, and the truth would come pouring out of my mouth.

Not only do I withstand the truth, I find myself enjoying the lie. The lie keeps Clayton's death fresh, a perverse satisfaction, but satisfaction nevertheless, to balance against the sixteen years I spent thinking about the way Momma and Poppa died. In this way, I've come to believe in a form of closure which actually works. It's not the sort of thing I expect to hear discussed on television talk shows.

I search for Momma's favorite book, *The Odyssey.* She claimed it was the birth of the modern story. All novels have their roots tapping there, she said, good fiction as well as bad. I never grasped her rapture for its words, yet I grasped the joy she had for the tale. I think about Odysseus lashing himself to the mast while keeping his men below with their ears made deaf by wax so they could steer their ship clear of the rocks. Only he, among mortals, heard the temptation of perfect beauty no man was meant to resist or survive.

Could a reasonable person compare my history to the story of Odysseus? I survived by tying myself to the mast of truth of what I saw as a boy, unswayed by the so-called perfect science of men. Also like Odysseus, I'm aware other dangers remain. It's unavoidable when the only motive involved is hate. Hate hides the details. It is the ultimate rationalizer. Hate motivated Henry Clayton and Phillip Dranowski. It motivated other men to protect them through complacency even if not directly guilty of a crime themselves.

As Henry Clayton said, it's simple to defeat man's technology. I suppose human nature, especially hate, will forever make the defeat of proclaimed perfection a simple matter.

My palms caress the cover of *The Odyssey,* sense the countless times Momma held her hands there. My touch over hers is only fitting. Below me, on the bottom shelf, I think to close the space made by Clayton's theft of *A Tale of Two Cities*. That, too, is fitting.

The doorbell rings in the morning. Fred Schumacher stands on my front porch in a pressed suit and shirt, polished shoes, and silk tie. "Official business," he says. I note the depth of his voice and the strength of his posture have only partially recovered.

I peer out the door. "Where're the guards?"

"They've been called off. You and Jack are off command's shit list and back on duty."

"And you?"

"I gave my *mea culpa*. The disciplinary board members, thankfully, all have adult children. They voted to give me a three month suspension effective two weeks ago, but I keep my law license."

"Then how can this be official business?"

Fred touches at the doorjamb. "It's not."

He hands me a sealed envelope addressed to Officer Richard Hill, returnable to the prosecutor's Victim's Assistance Division. Fred tilts his head back and tries to smile. Like his voice, his smile only partially succeeds. "The new DNA lab tests came back on Clayton's blood and Drano's saliva on the cola can. And the truth shall set you free. You and Jack. Maybe my son. We'll see."

I smile at him, at what he doesn't know about the truth.

"The lab also retested the original swab we thought was from your mother's rape test kit. Seems somebody managed to get my son's sperm on a buccal swab."

"Riddy," I say. "Then Clayton killed him."

"Perhaps, or Clayton had Riddy killed. The thing is, that's all there was. The new testing reconfirmed the swab lacked vaginal fluid."

"Reconfirmed?"

Schumacher fights to keep his eyes on me. "The flaw was also in the first test on the swab. DNA labs report what they're asked to identify, and population percentages. They don't draw other conclusions unless someone asks." He extends the envelope enclosing the lab test results. "That, I'm sad to say, was my job."

I don't take the envelope. "There never was a rape test kit used on Momma."

"How'd you know?"

"Because she dared to live happily with a black man."

Caught in the evenness of my stare, Schumacher lowers his arm, the envelope loose in his fingers. "No," he says finally. "Or it never made it out of the morgue."

We stand at the threshold to Momma and Poppa's house, silent for a time. He wipes his brow, sets the envelope at my feet. "Do with it what you want. I needed an excuse to see you and apologize. If it means anything to you, Richard, I'm sorry. For myself and this town."

He begins to leave, but I pull at his sleeve. "The counterclockwise swastika," I say. He seems pleased I've engaged him in conversation. My words grab his attention. "It was originally used as a symbol of peace. Long ago, in a different culture." I extend my hand. "I know you're sorry, Mr. Schumacher."

"Henry Clayton," he says methodically, as if the name supplies its own definition. He shakes my hand then spins about, walks away, and gives me a half-lifted wave from his car. It's striking, really, how much older he looks.

With his visit, I accept that it's time.

The old logs in the fireplace burn hot, throw flames aloft through the flue. Charred ashes rise in the heat, the remains of

Schumacher's Department of Justice report. The A-disk liquefies, turns into blue smoke, and Clayton's receipt puffs away as if it never existed. Only Riddy's photograph takes time to burn, permits me to watch blackness overtake these white boys, their eyes unaware of its approach. An unknown youth is the last to vanish.

My hand extends the DNA lab test envelope, unopened, before the flame.

51

This walk is perhaps the longest walk I've ever taken. It's not about distance, for the walk itself is fifteen steps long from my car. It's a walk motivated by a decision I've made. Twice before I've come here, twice before I wasn't sure, and decided I needed to wait until the next day. This third time, I'm about ninety-five percent sure, the threshold I needed to reach.

I knock on the door, feel the racing of my heart, and fight off the urge to flee. When she opens the door, my fear eases.

Pink roses, Auntie Doria advised. Roses to show interest, pink rather than red so as not to scare her away. I extend the bouquet forward. William Griffin intercepts them. "They're for your momma," I say.

"I know that. I know that." He looks to his mother shaded below her green chandelier hat. "You tell him I know, Momma. It's just you weren't raising your arms fast enough. Officer Hill kind of looked silly holding them."

"Were you going someplace, Ms. Griffin?"

"I was," she says.

"First could you remove your hat? Just for a minute is all."

She squeezes her lips together but doesn't say no. She lofts her arm over the brim and takes her hat off in a smooth motion.

"Now," I say. "That's better. That's what I wanted to confirm ever since we met at Auntie's barbecue."

"What did you want to confirm?"

"You're beautiful, Ms. Griffin. Which is what I've been meaning to tell you for a while now."

"He called you beautiful, Momma." William smiles up at her. "It's a fact, though. Anybody can see."

There's no smile to her, not yet. Perhaps not ever with me in her sight. "At least take these, Ms. Griffin. They'll die soon without water. It would definitely be a shame."

She takes the pink roses from me, her hands brushing against mine. "More than flesh makes a man or a woman beautiful, Officer Hill."

"I know, Ms. Griffin. You're beautiful; any man can see it's true. But I see the way you are, how you took care of my auntie and her shop. How you watch over your boy. It makes me wish we'd start calling each other something else besides Ms. Griffin and Officer Hill."

For a moment I think her look softens. I'm mistaken. She remains firm, wishes me a good day, "Officer Hill."

"Momma!" William howls.

She begins to close the door on me. I step forward, knock one last time.

"What is it?" she says. Her impatience with me sends William staring at his shoes.

"Ms. Griffin. Leslie. I'm calling you Leslie. I can't help the way I am. I can't help what I saw as a boy. Those things happened and I can't change them. Sometimes I've gotten so angry I got to believe this whole world was a sham. But I have to tell you, I talk to my momma and my poppa. Sometimes they hold me, not in any crazy way. In a spiritual way."

"What are you meaning to say, Officer Hill?"

I cough and I straighten myself at her door. "If I feel Momma and Poppa are with me, well," and I look at her the best I can. Eye to eye, the best way a man can look at a woman. "I believe in God, Ms. Griffin. I definitely believe in God. I just don't want to be told how."

She steps to me, studies my eyes. Reaching to my cheek, she wipes away a tear I didn't know was there. "I suppose I don't have to go anywhere for a while."

Leslie Griffin smiles, leads me into her home. It's more than a step off the walk. It's an embrace of Momma and Poppa, an acceptance of their faith, a faith I denied myself because of the evil of one man.

There's a rush in my soul—how wonderful to think these words—my soul! Its power draws my imagination back to Leaper Street Cemetery, where the sound of the Red River Falls rushes over Momma's and Poppa's headstones like God's whisper. Between their headstones, an unopened envelope lies on the grass. When I had placed it there, it felt as though I had delivered their murderer to them, as well as one of the men who helped set him free.

William Griffin grabs my hand, asks me if I'd like to play catch with him in back. I shiver, sense a breeze blowing between Momma's and Poppa's headstones. The breeze lofts the envelope into the air, touched by cold mist, drawn toward the river where the waterfall captures it and swallows it in an eternal back-eddy. Held there until dissolved.

I know all this, can see it though I'm miles away. It's the strength I've gained. Given to me by the gentle touch of a boy.

ABOUT THE AUTHOR

Bruce Steinberg writes under B. R. Robb, a long-ago moniker predicted by his parents. A graduate of the Loyola School of Law in Chicago, he has worked as a lawyer for over twenty-one years, as a prosecutor, public defender, guardian ad litem for abused and neglected children, as well as in private practice. His previous novel, *The Widow's Son,* won Grand Prize at First-NovelFest2000. Along the way he has written as a freelance reporter for area newspapers and currently is the *Footloose* columnist for *Silent Sports,* a magazine covering non-motorized sports in the Midwest. He lives with his wife and son in the far reaches of the Chicago suburbs.